The Fall of America

Book 1 – Premonition of Death

WR Benton

LOOSE CANNON ENTERPRISES
Paradise, CA

No part of this book may be reproduced, stored in a retrieval system, or transmitted by any means, electronic, mechanical, photocopying, recording, or otherwise, without the written permission of the author and/or the publisher. This is the work of fiction. Names, characters, places, and incidents are the product of the author's imagination or are used fictitiously and any resemblance to actual persons living or dead, events or locales, is entirely coincidental.

2nd Edition
ISBN 978-1-944476-36-6

© Copyright 2013 W.R. Benton
All Rights Reserved

Edited by: Bobby La Cour

Author images, © 2012 Melanie C. Benton
Cover design and layout © 2013 by DancingFoxPublishing.com
all rights reserved.
Cover Image: Oziris. www.sxc.hu
Bullet Hole Brushes by: http://obsidiandawn.com
Logo fonts [*Shortcut, Dirty Ego*] by Eduardo Recife, misprintedtype.com

www.loose-cannon.com

Books by W.R. Benton

War Paint

Fur Seekers (Co-authored with Grady Clark)

Red Runs the Plain

The Fall of America, Book 1, Premonition of Death

Jake Masters, Bounty Hunter

Nate Grisham, Black Mountain Man (Co-authored with Grady Clark)

Nate Grisham, Renegade Trapper (Co-authored with Grady Clark)

The Youngest Mountain Man

Missouri in Flames

War Paint

James McKay, U. S. Army Scout

Blood Money

Hell Comes To Dixie

Alive and Alone (Young Adult)

Simple Survival, a Family Outdoors Guide (Non-Fiction)

Impending Disasters (Non-Fiction)

Bubba's Dawg Might be a Redneck (Southern Humor)

Adrift (A Story of Survival at Sea)

W.R. Benton
The Best in Post-Apocalyptic

Dedication

To Vickie Burrows, an intelligent, tough, and yet gentle woman.

To Alisa McDonald Butler, hard working neighbor and wonderful woman!

To Tatanka Ska, may the Great Creator bless and guide your warrior spirit.

And, finally, to my friend and fellow veteran, Stanley Holewa, Hooaahh!

Table of Contents

CHAPTER 1

The sound of my shotgun was loud in the small storage shed and earsplitting scream pierced the night. I grimaced as I popped the breech open and immediately inserted two fresh shells. While I'd only seen one man, that didn't mean others weren't near, so I waited unmoving.

I remained motionless, listening to everything but the dying man, because to move might mean my death. I heard nothing, but I remained in the darkness.

Above the moaning and whimpering of the injured man, I heard a slight whispering sound, only I couldn't determine exactly where the sound was located. The noise reminded me of material rubbing against material, but I'd been wrong before and it had cost my first wife her life. *Come on, move you sonofabitch!*

I waited with my senses on edge and my trigger finger ready to respond.

Long minutes passed and then I heard the night sounds return outside the shed. The crickets were making noise and my dogs had finally stopped barking, so if anyone else had been around they were gone now. I knew it was safe to check the man I'd shot.

Pulling a small flashlight from my pocket, I turned it on and moved the narrow beam of light toward my victim. The man lay on his back, his eyes open but unfocused, so I moved the light to the center of his chest. My shotgun blast had taken him in the center of the upper body and I found it strange he'd lived at all. The shot should have killed him instantly, or so I thought.

A small caliber pistol, a .38 caliber snub-nose, was beside the body. I picked the pistol up, opened the cylinder and found four bullets. I snapped it shut and placed it in the waistband of my trousers.

I'll drag him off in a bit. I need to get back to the house so Sandra doesn't worry, I thought as I turned and made my way out of the shed. I glanced at the sky overhead and noticed it was clear, with millions of stars sparkling radiantly, as I called Dolly, my biggest dog. Once she was at my side we moved toward the house. Dolly was a German shepherd that was trained for security work.

After I entered the kitchen, Sandra asked, "Trouble? I heard gunfire."

"I killed a man in the shed."

"What was he looking for?"

"Most likely anything of value. Right now generators, batteries, and gas are big trade items around here." I met her eyes and slowly shook my head over the senselessness of the killing.

"Have something hot to drink and unwind a bit, because I know you're all worked up over shooting that man."

I sat the at the table and watched my wife as she poured me a cup of coffee. Sandra wasn't a beautiful woman, but she was attractive, and we'd hit it off the first time we'd met, only I'd been married then. She was the athletic type, always walking, running, or going to the gym, only those days were finished as far as I was concerned. She stood a foot shorter than my 6 feet 6 inches and was usually around a hundred and twenty pounds, but she'd lost weight over the last few months. I had a good hundred pounds on her, except I'd lost a lot of weight as well. Just staying alive was an effort these days.

She placed a coffee cup in front of me and said, "I think a drink will help you relax a little. It's a shame we have to defend our home like they did back in the 1800's."

As I raised the cup my hands were trembling. I'd been like this after combat in Iraq, too. I'd spent three tours in Iraq and two in Afghanistan, all combat tours, and I'd returned home from the sandbox a hard man. I got out of the army as soon as my extension expired and attended college using the G.I. Bill, which paid me a little extra to live on while I attended classes full time. It was in college where I'd first met Sandra.

"Are you okay?" Sandra asked as she moved to my side and pulled my head to her hip. She gently stroked my hair.

"I'm. . . no, I'm not okay at all. I just blew a man apart in my shed and he's dead. This isn't a war zone, but what was I suppose to do? I *have* to protect what is ours, or we'll lose everything we own and if we do that we die."

"Honey, you did the right thing and we both know it. Since the police don't exist any longer, we have to enforce our own laws. Baby, you're not a mean or bad person that's what you're thinking, let it go. We have to survive."

I placed my elbows on the table and lowered my head to my hands. I remembered two years ago as if it had happened yesterday.

First the stock market crashed, followed by a large number of banks folding, but most Americans didn't panic, because it'd happened before. Then the President had been impeached over some affair he'd had with a male cabinet member and his wife had made statements that suggested corruption and illegal activities within his administration. An investigation condemned the man. It had gone out of control from that point on. Jobs just weren't there, families were forced from their homes due to nonpayment of mortgages, and third and fourth generation farmers started losing their land. Food and gas prices had climbed steadily, to the point the average family had to decide between food, gas, or heat. The country that was once thought of around the world as the land of luxury was suddenly a vagabond.

At the beginning, large sums of money, trillions of dollars, were borrowed from China and Russia in an effort to stimulate the economy, except it didn't work. Our credit rating as a nation fell so low, we were unable to borrow money or even pay the interest on our loans. Without a demand for our goods, jobs weren't created and our products were grossly overpriced, or so most of the world thought. Shelves of American goods lay in foreign stores. I realized we were in serious trouble when all Spanish speaking Americans started moving to Mexico. Other Americans followed, illegally of course. With no demand for our products, the job market died. Then, the suicides started.

Our elderly, unable to get proper medical treatment or even basic medications from pharmacies, began to kill themselves. Hospitals closed, doctors and nurses went home, and patients were left in their rooms waiting for family or death. The permanently disabled and mothers with large numbers of children were next, because public assistance stopped. Mental institutions and prisons emptied, because our police and counselors were no longer paid, which only added more chaos to the whole damned country. Of course, the murder rate doubled, then tripled and suicides skyrocketed, as folks were unable to find jobs or food. Then, the bean-counters lost their jobs and no one knew what the statistics were after that point.

I'd run my own security business for years after college, only to lose it toward the end of our collapse as a nation. We'd bought a home years before in the country and then finally, one day, I no longer had a job to go to each morning. Without funds, fire departments, police departments, our military, and other public service agencies soon folded and then our society reverted back a thousand years, with killings being so normal no one even discussed them.

My first wife, Mary, was killed one morning when I was in town trying to find food and gasoline. I'd returned to find her battered and raped body in the living room and it'd almost killed me as well. I'd buried her out back and from what I can remember, it was raining that day. My memory is unclear about long periods of my life after that, and for months to come I was confused and indecisive about many things. I often thought I'd lost my mind, but now I can see I blamed myself for her death. I'd made a serious mistake and it'd cost my wife her life, so now I never left the farm without Sandra at my side.

I'd into Sandra over at a friend's house one afternoon while trading gasoline for bullets for my deer rifle. I remembered her from college, we talked a while that day and things just moved forward from then onward. A year later we were married by a Baptist preacher, that accepted half a hog as payment.

"John!" I heard a voice.

"Huh?"

"Are you okay? You were moaning and rocking from side to side."

I gave a dry chuckle and replied, "I'm fine, just tired is all, and killing that man didn't make my day any better."

Sandra gave me a weak smile and replied, "Would you have preferred for him to kill you?"

I gave a deep laugh and said, "You know I wouldn't! It's just that I saw so much killing in the war and now the whole country has gone insane. People are killing each other over a gallon of gas, a few heads of cabbage, or even a pig."

"People are hungry, and not all of them had the sense to stock up on supplies like you did with Mary. Heck, we started storing things as soon as we were married, too, and things were already pretty bad then."

I took a sip of my coffee, thought for a moment and then asked, "How would you feel if I asked Tom and his wife to move in with us?"

"Well, it might be a good thing, but we're both pretty private people."

"Baby," I said, and then pulling her closer to me I continued, "I worry that one night Dolly won't warn us or I'll not hear someone breaking in. I honestly need another set of eyes and ears to help us survive. Even with the dogs outside, there are ways to silence them. I've discussed it with Tom and he thinks it's a good idea, only he's not discussed it with Sue yet."

"I've thought about that and it has me concerned as well. You seem to think you can stay awake all hours of the day and night forever, and you just can't do that. I don't see a problem with it, as long as they take the downstairs and we stay upstairs."

I gave a low chuckle.

"What?"

I smiled and said, "For a moment I thought about calling him and telling him the news, but then I remembered the phones no longer work."

We shared a brief laugh and then I said, "I've a man in the shed to drag away. Come and we'll saddle the horses."

Sandra didn't argue, because she knew what had happened to my first wife. I picked up my shotgun and we moved toward the door with Dolly following.

We quickly placed blankets and bridles on the horses and I made small talk with Sandra as we saddled. Dolly sat by the barn door and kept an eye outside.

Once at the shed I went inside and tied a rope to the dead man's feet, unraveled the rope and then mounted. I looped the rope around my saddle horn a few times and then asked, "You ready?"

"Of course, let's get this over with."

"Keep my shotgun ready at all times and don't shoot unless you don't see any other option. I doubt we'll see anyone, but you can never tell." I handed her my shotgun and started my horse at a slow walk.

We didn't see anyone and the trip to the spot I had in mind was uneventful. I was untying the man's legs when Sandra approached and shined the light of her flashlight on the dead man's face. I heard her gasp.

"Do you know this man?" I asked.

"I . . . I know him."

"Well, who was he?" I suspected she either knew more but didn't want to tell me, or she was truly shocked.

"I went to college with him, and his name was Larry Patton. His father owned the local beer brewery and was filthy rich. I dated him a few times off and on, but never really got to know him well. He had a holier than thou attitude I didn't like."

"Well, let's hope he made his peace with the Lord before this visit. When rich people turn to stealing, you know things are turning rough, huh?" I said, and then scanned the surrounding countryside.

"I think money is useless right now, and folks want food or things they can trade with so they can stay alive."

"Well, in that case we're rich, because we've enough food to keep an army alive and for a long time. Do you want me to bury this guy?"

Silence followed for a long time, but finally she replied, "No, we need to get back before the whole house is stolen."

"You bet," I said as I thought, smart woman I've married because she learns quickly.

As soon as we entered the barnyard, Dolly began her warning growl and I slipped from my saddle. I moved the safety switch on the shotgun to off and turned to Sandra. "You stay in the shadows while I check things out. Keep your shotgun ready," I said just above a whisper.

I called Dolly in a low voice, pulled a leash from my pocket and attached it to her collar. I then moved forward, my senses on edge. I remembered I still had the pistol from the dead man in my waistband and a 44 magnum in a holster on my belt, so I knew I had a backup. In the darkness I saw nothing, but knew Dolly would alert me to anyone near. I'd been a dog handler early in my army days and Dolly was well trained. Abruptly my dog stopped moving and gave a low warning growl, but no matter how hard I tried, I could see nothing.

Suddenly, someone or something moved in the darkness and I brought my gun up to my shoulder, and sighted down the barrel. I took a deep breath, held it in, and as I slowly let it out, I started squeezing the trigger.

I heard a voice say, "Your dog doesn't like me much, does she, John?"

My heart was beating hard, except it got louder when I realized I'd almost killed my best friend. I took another deep breath and blew it out hard before I said, "Tom, what in the hell are you doing here this time of the night. I almost killed your nasty ass."

"What? You mean you didn't know it was me?"

"How am I to know who it was in the dark? I killed a man earlier tonight and I thought you might be one of his friends returning." I spoke, pushed the safety on, and then added brusquely, "Don't ever do that again or we might not be so lucky. Good Lord, you're smarter than that!"

"I . . . I had . . . no idea, honestly. I just thought Sue and I would come over and discuss the move, if you don't mind." I could hear fear in his voice and think the seriousness of the situation finally registered in his mind.

Tom was a prior service member too and had been with the 82nd airborne at Fort Bragg, North Carolina for years. Of course, he'd done a few tours in the sandbox, and I had a hard time accepting he'd been so dumb tonight. He'd been trained as an army ranger and it irked me that while the whole world was turning to hell, he'd turn stupid. So, I said as much to him.

"Look, I admit, what I did wasn't very smart, except I thought you knew I was here. Our bicycles are on your front porch and we agreed earlier today for me to bring Sue over as soon as the two of us discussed your idea."

Let it go, I thought and slapped Tom on the back as I replied, "Look, I didn't shoot you, so let's learn from it. We didn't come by the front of the house; we were down the logging road behind the barn a bit dumping the body of the man I killed earlier tonight, so we never saw the bikes."

"Is Sandra with you? We knocked, but no one answered."

"She's always with me." I said and then turned to called out, "Sandra, come on in, it's only Tom and Sue!"

"What about the horses?" She yelled back.

"Tom and I'll put them up."

As Tom and I walked toward the barn, Sandra approached and said, "Hi ya, Tom."

"Hi, Sandra, you'll find Sue on the front porch waiting for you."

In my barn, after we'd pulled the saddles and bridles from the horses, I asked, "Was Sue receptive to the idea of us living together?"

Chuckling, Tom replied, "She wasn't crazy about the idea, but she's smart enough to realize we can't stay awake forever and guard our place. She didn't give me a yes or no, but she knows we can't continue to live as we once did. Times have changed and today a man's life is worth very little."

"The man I killed tonight was the son of a wealthy man and he was in my shed looking for something to steal. Money is worth very little these days, unless you have gold. Paper bills don't even make good toilet paper."

As I rubbed my mare down, I thought of the changes that had come to our nation and how difficult it had been for many American's to adjust. As a nation, we'd grown soft before the fall, and we'd forgotten how to do simple things our parents had done as a matter of everyday living. Most of the people I'd known bought frozen dinners or ate junk food, instead of cooking from scratch at home. Easy things like butchering an animal or milking a cow were no longer practiced by most people, so when the end came, they had no idea what to do or how to do it. Store shelves had emptied within hours and there were no more deliveries, because we had no gas. In the first month alone, over 400,000 had died in Ohio, with New York losing over a million people, most by starvation. By the second month, the poor had gone looking for those that had what they needed and the death rate had jumped out of sight. Looting for food was a common problem at first, but soon the food was gone and so were the people. The people had either died or moved to where food was easier to find the countryside. I'd hear rumors of cannibalism and suspected it to be true, but with the power out and communications no longer working, I have no way of knowing for sure.

"What you thinking on so hard over there?" Tom asked.

I placed the brush on a bale of hay and said, "Remember how before the end came all the liberals were screaming about saving whales, abortions, political correctness, and gay rights?"

"Yea, so? They were always screaming about shit."

"Where are all of those folks now? We knew years ago we were heading the wrong way and our elected officials did nothing for us. Don't get me wrong, whales need saving and I have no issues with gay folks, but instead of binding our nation into a stronger cohesive group, had different agendas. Then, the democrats and republicans splintered into small parties, each with a different ideology."

"Well," Tom gave a light chuckle and then continued, "most of the liberals I know are dead. Most couldn't cook a pancake without a microwave and right now, I think most Americans would be more inclined to eat a whale than try to save it."

Sandra and Sue suddenly ran into the barn and after catching her breath my wife said, "Riders coming and I make out about a half dozen of them."

"Turn the dogs out of their kennels, get into the house, and then cover us from the windows with the shotguns," I ordered and turning to Tom I asked, "You hot?"

"Now, what do you think? I have a .45 Commander in a shoulder holster, a 9mm on my right hip, and a pump shotgun on your front porch. I suggest we move that way so we can welcome your guests properly."

CHAPTER 2

As Tom and I stood on my front porch, a group of five men on horseback rode up with guns and compound bows in their hands. They were a dirty and mean looking group and I scanned them to see which I would kill first, if it turned to shooting. I immediately spotted a man near my age, holding an M-16 like he knew how to use it. Must be prior military or police, I thought as I slipped the safety off on my shotgun. I was holding my weapon with the barrel up, but fully aware I might have a fight on my hands. *You'll be one of the first to die, my friend*, I thought as I asked, "Who are you and what in the hell do you want?"

My dogs, all four of them, were sitting in the grass off to my left. I knew none would move without an order from me, or a movement from one of the men toward me, so I felt comfortable with the situation. Of course, having Sue and Sandra in the upstairs windows reinforced my confidence.

A fat man riding in the middle said, "I'm D'Wayne Patton, and I've come for the body of my boy."

"Is that all?" I asked, knowing the man had other motives.

Giving a dry chuckle he replied, "Well, we do intend to kill the man who murdered him."

"Ride north, about a half a mile, and you'll find the body of your boy, unless the coyotes have been feeding on his nasty ass, I ain't real sure what you'll find. As for the man who killed your thieving no account son, that'd be me." I stepped from the porch and lowered the barrel of my shotgun until it was pointed in the general direction of Patton.

"Easy with the scattergun," Patton said in a nervous voice, "because it can do a lot of damage."

"Oh, I know well the damage this gun can cause, which is why I have it pointed at you. Your son was a thief and got what he had coming. Times are rough, Patton, and I need what little I have to survive. Also, you just threatened me and I take all threats seriously. So, if any of your boys get the urge to start shooting, you'll be the first to die, Mr. Patton. You'll be talking to the devil before you realize I've pulled the trigger."

Looking around at his small group, Patton ordered, "Don't none of y'all start anything. Let's just get Larry's body and get the hell out of here."

"But pa, he killed Larry! He just admitted it!" rail thin man of about forty said in anger.

"James, you heard what I said! This ain't the time or the place to start anything. Our time will come, but later when we're ready for a fight."

If I'd been thinking properly I would have killed Patton right then, except I was trying to avoid a fight. I watched the small group closely until James replied, "I hear ya, pa."

"Now, I suggest very strongly, Patton, that you and your men get off my property. My patience with you and your kind is growing thin."

"Let's go get Larry and then go home." Patton ordered and pulled his horse to the left.

As the rest started to turn, I noticed James swing his right hand up and out, pointing a pistol at me. Before I could react, I heard one, two, and finally three pistols shots from beside me. Glancing at Tom, he was holding his .45 Commander and was in a shooters stance.

My dogs were barking and wanting in on the action so I yelled a command, "Stay!"

As James was knocked off his horse, I heard Patton yell, "No fighting! I want no shooting! I ordered no shooting from the start!"

James lay in the grass unmoving as the small group brought their prancing horses under control. As soon as the group was facing me once more, I heard Sandra call out, "Patton, I want you to dismount, easy like, and check your son. More than likely he's dead, but it might be his lucky day."

The group glanced upward, and for the first time saw the two armed women in the windows. Patton placed his pistol in the holster on his belt, unforked his horse and made his way slowly to his son. Kneeling, he turned the man over onto his back and using his right hand felt his neck for a pulse. He shook his head and stood.

"Frank, I want you and Bill to place James' body over his horse. Tie him on well because we've a fair distance to cover."

The two men looked up as Sandra called out, "Leave the guns on your horses and do as the man said. One false move and both of our shotguns will start throwing lead, so I suggest you both move at a snail's pace."

It only took the two men a couple of minutes to tie the dead man to his horse, and during the whole time Patton stood and glared at me. While it was fairly dark, the oil lanterns on my porch didn't throw much light , but I could feel his hate.

Glowering at me, Patton said, "Do you have a name, mister? You've killed two of my boys and a man doesn't forget something like this."

Giving the man an ill-felt smile I replied, "My name is John, and you remember it, Patton. I want you to also remember that we protect our lives and property here. Now, move to your horse and get out of here. Do it now!"

"I'll be back and when I do it'll be an eye for an eye, so don't think I'm riding out of here and forgetting what you've done to me and mine."

"I said get off my property and I mean now!"

Turning their horses, the small group started down my long driveway toward the macadam road out front. None of us moved until they were all out of sight.

"I think you just made the mistake of your life," Tom said as he moved to my side. "We should have killed all of them."

I was worried about repercussions too and replied, "I think you're right, but maybe he'll change his mind once he has time to think about it a while."

"I want you to remember he was once a successful business man and as such, he knows how to handle men. Any thriving businessman is likely ruthless and hard. We'll have to keep twenty-four hour watch on the place now, because I'm sure he'll return and this time with many more men."

"Tom, I just couldn't start shooting people and you know it."

"I know, but to just let them ride off was a big mistake. Mark my words, there will come a day when you'll regret letting him live."

I turned and headed for the house as I said, "Maybe, but I sure hope not."

Over the next four days we moved all of Tom's belongings to our house, and I was pleased with the gear and supplies he had. Like me, Tom had seen the end coming and was prepared, while others, especially those who'd live on government assistance and progressives didn't. Did those people honestly expect the well to never run dry? Then again, many of them were third or fourth generation free-loaders and it'd paid well in the past, so in a way it was a profession. Others listened as our government, which always downplayed the seriousness of situations to avoid panic, had promised our setback was only temporary. It wasn't until welfare, military retirement, Medicare, social security, and other government plans were eliminated that the general population fully understood the gravity of the situation. Panic struck the masses.

Most, like my brother Bill, never planned ahead and actually lived from paycheck to paycheck, barely surviving. Bill wasn't a dumb man by any stretch of the imagination, but he used to laugh while I worked in my storeroom moving foods around and adding water containers. He'd called me a fool at the time and I'd suspected I might have been, but now I know I saw it coming. All a person had to do was read the paper, go online and check the news, or simply speak with folks. Many had not thought past the current day either, except all of them, including Bill, were dead now. I've heard over fifty percent of the population died during the first year, but I have no real way of knowing. As I explained earlier, all the bean counters were gone.

"Now," Tom said as he sat at my kitchen table, we'll make some traps to help protect this place and I'll feel a lot safer."

I leaned forward, suddenly interested and asked, "What do you have in mind?"

"Wire up a little homemade shake and bake, some foot poppers and some nail pits. You know what I'm talking about."

Of the three, the homemade shake and bake would take some effort, so I asked, "What do you have as a source for detonation?"

"Some blasting caps I got about five years ago. I told the feller that sold them to me I had some stumps to clear and he believed me, but I had this in mind from the start."

Sue and Sandra, both confused, gave me questioning looks, so I explained, "Shake and bake is an old soldier's term for napalm. Since we don't have a squadron of fighter jets, we'll make the containers and store them high in the trees."

"I still don't understand." Sue said, and then took a drink of her coffee.

"It's simple to make, but hard on your enemies. We'll take five gallons of gasoline, mix about four bottles of liquid soap with it, and let it set a while. We really need more soap, but we're limited and can't spare any more than that. Once it's sat for a while we'll secure the container, oh maybe twenty feet up in a tree, attach a blasting cap and run the wire down to the ground. From there we'll run the wire to a source of power, and I have some old tractor batteries that should work fine. Then, when your target is under the tree, you attach the wires to the terminals on the batteries."

"Why use soap?" Sue asked looking over the rim of her coffee cup.

"Liquid soap causes the burning gas to stick to whatever it lands on, so it's a pretty deadly affair once popped," I answered.

"Sounds like some nasty crap to me." She stated, and met Sandra's eyes.

Tom laughed and said, "The army taught us how to do it, but we're jury-rigging these things so they might not work at all. I guarantee you, if they do blow, we'll have some surprised folks under the tree."

"And the toe popper thingies?"

"Shotgun shells with the primers resting on nails. We'll simply drill out some holes the same diameter of the shells in some two by fours, then in the center of each hole we carefully lower a shell. With the shell resting on the nail, all it takes little weight to push the shell down onto the nail, the primer fires and the shell discharges."

"I don't understand. Where will you put them?"

Tom laughed and took over for me, "We place them on trails. First, we dig a hole and then place the trap in the hole, with the top of the shell almost flush with the walking surface. Someone will walk down the trail, step on a shell, and *bam*, you have a man down with a serious injury to his foot and maybe the groin area. We can also place them along the sides of the trail, near where we have a main trap. When the first man steps on a shell, the others will move to the side of the trail for protection and maybe we'll injure some more. They're nasty as all get out, but they work and are cheap to make."

"Won't they see them?"

"Not if we camouflage them and sprinkle a little loose dirt on top of the shells."

"Which reminds me," I said, and gave each woman a warning look before I continued, " we have the traps all out, do not go walking in the woods or anyplace away from the house without one of us with you. These traps will hurt anyone that steps on them."

"Sandra, how are we sitting on medical supplies?" Tom asked.

Sandra had worked at the Mississippi Veterans Hospital for over four years as a registered nurse, and she'd been placed in charge of our medical supplies. Smiling, she replied, "We've all we need, unless one of you comes down with yellow fever. I've got painkillers, antibiotics, and all sorts of medication stocked, but don't laugh when you see the labels."

I saw confusion on Tom's face so I added, "The meds and supplies were ordered online before things turned rough and Sandra got them from pet supply stores. In those days you could get any medication you needed and in large quantities. The bottle caps, however, came with little dogs and cats printed on them.

"We're fine in the medical department, so don't worry about it for the time being."

Sue, who'd been quiet during our discussion asked, "What are those nail pits you were talking about?"

I took a gulp of my now cold coffee and said, "The longest nails we have will be driven through wood and placed in a hole on the trail with the points up. Using a piece of cloth, you can then cover the hole and sprinkle dirt over the thing to hide it. It's better to use a mat made of natural materials, but that can be hard to do because, with time, it changes color as it dries out or rots away. There are a lot of different kinds of nail traps we can make, so stick around and learn."

"So," Tom said as he stood, "Let's get busy, we've a lot of work to do. While we're making the booby traps, I'd like you ladies to do a complete inventory of what we have on hand, down to the last bean."

Sandra smiled and said, "I have it already completed. I thought while you two were working, Sue and I would make four grab and run bags. That way if we have to leave the house in the middle of the night or some other time, we'll not leave without something with us."

I smiled, proud of my wife, but added, "Be sure each bag has a complete medical kit, with pain killers, antibiotics, and the works. Also, consider our needs for a fire, sleeping, food, extra socks, and water containers. From this moment on, I want each of us to always carry a sheath knife, disposable lighter, and a pocketknife. If we have to leave, it'll be a rush and what we don't have on us or take, we'll have to do without. Let's get to work, people."

Tom and I soon had six five-gallon cans high in the trees and detonators attached to each. All the wires ran to a heavy duty, fully charged tractor battery about fifty meters from the trees. Tom had labeled each set of wires and separated them for quick use. We'd ended up using less soap than I wanted, but we couldn't use all we had in stock.

As we walked back to my house I asked, "Shouldn't we have let the soap mix a few days before placing them?"

"Maybe, but to be honest with you, I don't think we have a couple of days. Patton will be back or if not him, someone will visit and we'll need the napalm then. Of course, the longer we wait the more mixing the soap will do, so time will actually help us."

"Now, I've been thinking of stringing wire around the yard. Do you think it will help?"

"Well, it can't hurt, so let's do it."

We walked in silence a few minutes, and then Tom asked, "Have you ever seen those spikes that police officers used to throw on the road to puncture a car tire? I think they're called ninja stars or something like that."

I chuckled and replied, "Not really, except in the movies. Why?"

"I want the women to make us a few hundred so we can scatter 'em around the house."

"They'd only work at night." I stopped walking, and gazed into his eyes.

"Not if someone attacked us on horseback. While I don't like the idea of hurting an animal, I suspect those things could do real damage to a horses foot."

"Isn't there a soft area toward the rear of the hoof?"

"Yep, but doing this bothers me."

I placed my hand on his shoulder and said, "Tom, I don't like the idea any better than you do. I love animals much more than people, because they're innocent and loving, but we've got to do whatever we can to stay alive."

Over the next few days the women spent long hours turning out our little ninja stars, and I was satisfied with the quality. No matter how I tossed them, they always landed with one sharp barb up, so I knew they'd work.

While they worked on the stars, Tom and I filled hundreds of sandbags and placed them almost waist high around the lower level of the house. I knew they'd stop most rounds and we had them in a double row, around every room on the ground floor.

Finally, Tom said, "Get the backhoe and dig me about four or five pits in the front and back yard. Make them about five feet deep, four wide, and close to six feet in length."

I knew a lot of different things could be made in holes like that, so I had to ask, "What's on your mind with the pits?"

"Some we'll fill with snakes, some will have sharpened barbs sticking up, and in others we'll place maybe five or six rows of toe poppers, farthest from the house I might place some napalm, so when they go off at night we'll have nice dark silhouettes to shoot at."

I had a silent laugh, because a pit with any kind of snake in it would scare most people to death, while the toe poppers, depending on how you landed, could really mess a man up. I had an idea that Tom intended to fill the snake pits will copperheads or rattlesnakes, which were common to the area.

"If we dip the sharpened barbs in human waste before we place them, it's a guarantee of someone getting a serious infection."

"Where'd you learn that?"

"My dad was an airborne trooper in Vietnam and he said the V.C. did it all the time. If a soldier stepped in a punji pit in Vietnam, he was always airlifted out and put on an I.V. with antibiotics."

"Well, that sounds like a good job for you, my man, because I'm not into human waste. But, on a more serious side, I think the napalm pits will have some broken glass, nuts and bolts, rocks or other junk thrown on top of them."

"I think that would give us maximum casualties for the buck and while fire scares, stuff flying through the air cripples, and kills. I've some commercial grade fertilizer in the barn, add a bit of it to each napalm pit, say five pounds or so. It'll cause a huge explosion, and it's better than flour for burning properties." I chuckled to myself, because most civilians never realized common household and garden items could be turned into deadly explosives.

Within ten days we had the place as fixed up as we could make it with what we had on hand. We'd also made a slight change to our usual guard duty. Now we'd place one person out in the dark, near the road, with a portable two way radio so we could be informed before anyone attacked us, maybe. While I had a generator and could charge the radio batteries repeatedly, I had to use it sparingly, so it would last as long as possible. I wasn't worried about gas, but a mechanical breakdown. Like most farmers, I had a large 500 gallon gasoline storage tank behind the barn that I'd used in peaceful times to fill my tractors and pickup truck. In the evenings, I now chained my meanest dog, a huge Doberman with a nasty attitude, to the tank and knew Skillet would warn us if anyone came looking to steal gas.

It was a little after midnight, as I sat in the living room monitoring the two-way radio, when I heard Sandra report from near the road, "I'm coming back in. I hear many people moving down the road from the east. Copy?"

"Copy. Return to base."

A few minutes later she stood in front of me and reported, "Sounded like well over fifty men from what I could tell. I didn't count them or see them well, but they were noisy, and I heard a couple talking and one fool laughed."

"Wake Tom and Sue and be sure to let them know we have visitors coming. Tell Tom I said to lock and load."

As she disappeared into the darkness, I said a silent prayer for God's guidance. While not an overly religious man, I've always been a believer, and think I survived my combat tours in the service because of God. Once again, I'd turned to my Father.

CHAPTER 3

Sandra returned a few minutes later and said, "They're both up and moving. Tom said they'd cover the front and rear of the house from the upstairs."

"What's the weather like outside now?"

"It's around 65 degrees, overcast, with a light mist falling. Why?"

"Well, if your mist turns to rain, they may call the attack off until daylight."

"I have a feeling they're pretty sure they can take this place, and I'm not so sure they can't."

With my right hand, I gently stroked my wife's face. I felt her fear, but there was a side of me that she'd never seen, and I could protect her. Her eyes could barely be seen from the small candle burning on the coffee table and I said, "Baby, Tom and I have this place ringed with traps, and I think we have a better than good chance of surviving this. Many of the men tonight will be lightly armed, most will have bows and arrows, and few will only have clubs and knives. Stay strong and we'll survive this."

Lowering her head she replied, "There are so many of them and there are only four of us."

I gave a weak chuckle and said, "Keep in mind, Tom and I are both combat veterans and we're way up on them in experience. But, just to be safe, I want you to put the packs you made up for us over here, right beside me."

"Base, two, over." I heard Tom on the radio.

"Go, two, this is base."

"I have spotted movement all around the front of us and four reports the same behind us. Are you in position, yet?"

"Negative on position, two, give me two minutes."

His radio clicked twice, so I knew he'd understood. Turning to Sandra I said, "You need to get to the back of the house. No matter what you hear out front, stay in position. Do you understand?"

She nodded, stood, and as she walked into the dark hallway, I worried about her. Some people aren't able to kill another human being, or so my drill instructor had yelled one morning during basic training at Fort Leonard Wood, Missouri. Would Sandra be able to kill if need be? Or would she freeze and die? I knew the answer—only time would tell.

I picked up my radio and spoke, "Two, this is one."

"Go, one."

"In position."

"Copy you are in position. I think they're holding off just outside of the yard and planning something. Over."

I heard one, then two shotguns go off, but they were off to the side where we'd placed the toe poppers and I suspected they'd tried to move in on the side of us. Screaming came from the general area, and then I heard a man distinctly crying for help.

Unmoving, I scanned the area in front of me, because I knew Tom would be doing the same. We would die if we became distracted. After a long period of maybe ten minutes, another shotgun shell exploded and a second man added his cries for help.

Most likely, I thought, *the second man went to help the first and stepped on a toe popper.*

My thoughts were disrupted by a huge explosion of fire right in front of me, followed by screams of pain. Tom had ignited one of the napalm traps. A man ran from the fireball, completely engulfed in flame, right toward me. I pulled the trigger on my shotgun and watched him knocked back to the dirt hard, as a full load of 00 buckshot struck him in the chest. He lay unmoving, but still burning. I quickly changed positions to another window.

It was at that point a small band of about six on horseback raced for my porch, only to encounter our ninja stars. Horses reared, riders fell, and I could hear Tom's old deer rifle, a 30.06 with a mounted scope, firing slowly from the window above me. I added shotgun blasts to the night air. The men on the ground were easily seen, as Tom had predicted, by the burning gasoline behind them. I, like Tom, continued to fire until the last man fell.

Silence followed, with light from the burning gas casting eerie shadows that danced on the walls inside my house. Occasionally a moan or cry for help was heard, which instantly brought a single shot from Tom. I spotted movement less than 70 feet from the porch, but smiled and let the man continue to crawl toward me.

Forward he crawled. I watched closely as he'd move an inch or two, then stop. He was good, and I almost felt sorry for the man. He'd been well trained, obviously prior military, police, or security, because he knew what he was doing. As I watched, he moved to less than 50 feet from the house. He pulled something from his pocket, a flame was instantly seen, and I knew he had a Molotov cocktail in his hand. Still, I didn't move.

The man was instantly on his feet and running right for me, when he disappeared. A loud scream sounded and the man stood from one of our pits. From the light of the burning rag in his Molotov cocktail, as well as the flames of the napalm fire, I could see the snakes hanging from his body. He twisted and turned in all directions, as his screaming grew louder.

Tom fired a single shot and the incendiary device exploded, which covered the man in flames. I immediately grew frightened the man might run to the house in his panic driven pain and pulled the trigger on my shotgun. I had the satisfaction of seeing him go down and stay down.

I heard a whistle blow three times and then silence. Waiting a few minutes, I looked the area over carefully with my binoculars, only there was no movement. Fire from the pit, as well as the man, had died down, but the smell of burnt flesh was heavy in the air. Off in the distance I heard Skillet barking. Two horses that were severely injured lay in my front yard and I felt my heart break each time they'd blow or cry in pain.

Picking up the radio I said, "Everyone stay in position. The whistle blasts might mean anything. Tom, take out the horses."

Two shots sounded and the horses grew silent. I lowered my head for a second and asked God's forgiveness for killing the horses. To ask Him to forgive me for killing the men or women never entered my mind. They'd come looking for a fight, and we'd given them a good one.

After more than an hour, Tom said, "One, two, I think they've gone, because I haven't seen anything move since the whistle."

"Roger. I suspect they're gone, but we'll stay in position until first light."

"One, this is Sandra, I mean three, can you do something about the smell?"

"Not until daylight, three. We all stay where we are." I replied and knew she'd either thrown up or was fighting not to do so. I'd smelled it many times during my wars, only I'd grown used to it, and it no longer nauseated me as much as it once did.

I felt a hard gust of wind come through the open window and watched as the curtains danced wildly along the wall. The wind was followed seconds later by a spattering of raindrops. The rain gradually increased until a full-blown storm was beating a loud tattoo on my roof. Long fingers of lightning flashed across the sky and then exploded in all directions. Thunder cracked and boomed all around me, and I knew then the attack was over.

I picked up the radio and said, "Everyone come to my location. Repeat, come to my location now."

I closed the windows on the bottom floor and by the time I returned, everyone was in my living room.

Tom spoke before I could, "This storm looks serious."

"It's times like this I wish we had a weather station or some way of knowing what's happening." I replied and then turned to Sandra, "Are you still ill?"

"N...no, but I was sick back about an hour ago."

The wind was howling now, and I could only hope we weren't getting part of a hurricane or tornado. Since we lived in Mississippi, a little over 200 miles from New Orleans, either one was possible. Something blew across my porch and it banged continuously as it traveled.

It was then I remembered Skillet. "I've a dog by the gas storage tank and have to bring him in."

Tom nodded, but Sue asked, "Are you sure you want to go out in weather like this for *just a dog?*"

Her comment angered me, but I held my temper as I replied, "Sue, our dogs are family in this house. We love them, and Skillet is scared and wet right now."

I grabbed a raincoat from the hook on the wall, put it on and said, "I want all of you to move to the basement. I'm not sure what this is, but if we get a tornado, you'll be glad you're down there. Sandra, take the other dogs down with you. I'll be right back."

Outside the wind was terrible and I estimated it at around 40 miles an hour, with gusts that had to be in excess of 60. I held my flashlight in my left hand and my shotgun in the other as I approached the storage tank. The rain was falling so hard it actually hurt as it struck my face.

Skillet was under the tank, but the poor guy was soaked, and he stood wagging his tail as I approached. I knelt, pulled his wet head to me and said, "Sorry, big guy, but I've been busy and forgot about you."

I pulled the leash from my pocket and attached it to his collar, which is hard to do in darkness with rain pounding me. I picked up my flashlight and shotgun and then stood. Skillet was happy to see me, and wagging his tail as we moved toward the house.

Nearing the house, Skillet began to growl a warning, and I stopped. Someone, I was sure, was out there. I switched the flashlight off and squinted, hoping to see better. With the weather like it was, it was impossible to hear or see anything, so I reached down and released Skillet's leash. The dog left me at a hard run slightly off my left.

I flipped the safety off my shotgun and followed my dog.

About fifty feet away I came upon man fighting with Skillet, only he wasn't doing well. My big dog was chewing on the man's left forearm like a t-bone steak and jerking his head from side to side viciously. I approached and screamed into the wind to be heard, "Skillet, come!"

As soon as my dog was at my side, I saw the man smile at me in a flash of lightning, I have no idea what he was thinking, however I know what I was thinking. I raised my shotgun and waited patiently for the next flash of lightning. With the next flash, I pulled the trigger and saw the man knocked backward, his smile gone forever.

I patted Skillet on the head and a few times and then moved for the house. I'd taken a prisoner in Iraq once, and he'd been struck in the upper shoulder by a bullet. I'd kept him covered while Frank, our medic, worked on him, except I ducked and turned my head when we'd come under enemy fire again. When I glanced back at my prisoner, Frank was on his back with a knife buried in his chest and a pool of blood under him. I emptied my entire clip into the rag-heads body. That was the first and last time in my life I ever took a prisoner. Maybe I'm cold and heartless, but I'm still alive.

Skillet and I entered the house and made our way down to the basement. It was quiet down there and as I neared the group, Tom asked, "Did I hear a shotgun?"

I started to lie to him, but said, "Yep, one of the men that probably stepped on a toe popper was hiding in the dark."

"Look at all the blood on Skillet! Is he okay?" Sandra asked.

"Skillet let me know about the man quick enough and I turned the big boy loose."

Tom, looking confused asked, "Then why the shot?"

"I thought the man might have a pistol. But, just so you all know, I don't take prisoners and never have."

Sandra gave me a surprised look, blinked a few times and then asked, "Never?"

I explained what had happened in Iraq and it was quiet for a long time. I think one of them may have thought I was a killer, another a man without any mercy at all, or that the war had made me a man suffering from severe PTSD. Only one person's thoughts really mattered, and that was Sandra's. I didn't gave a rat's ass what the other two thought.

"I wish you hadn't killed him, but we don't have a place to keep prisoners. Where could we lock them up and really feel safe?" Sandra said.

Sue gave a weak smile and said, "I thought about that and the amount of food we'd have to give them as well. I don't agree with murder, only we have no idea how badly the man was wounded either, so you may have ended his agony. We could have used up a lot of our medical supplies trying to keep him alive, only to have him die anyway."

Tom simply said, "From now on, we'll take no prisoners. But, understand me when I say this, we will kill cleanly and with no torture. I can justify killing in my mind by what's been said here tonight, torture I cannot accept. If any of you have a problem with this, speak up now."

No one spoke up, so I pulled a towel from a shelf near me and started drying Skillet off. He was soaked, but his tail wagged and he was grinning when I finished the job. I squatted in front of the big boy and gave him a hug. As soon as we broke apart, he licked my face from chin to forehead and I broke out laughing.

When I looked around, only Sandra had a smile on her face and that worried me, I didn't say anything. After all, we'd just survive a vicious attack and some folks react differently following combat. I know, because I used to drop to my knees and puke.

"How's the weather out there?" Tom asked, all business once more.

"Winds from the south, I'd guess 40 miles an hour, with gusts over 60. It's raining like a cow peeing on a flat rock, except horizontal, and dark as all get out. I noticed hundreds of lightning flashes and if the television still worked, I'm sure some weather channel would have shown a radar image with hundreds of strikes around us."

"I find it hard to believe after all the effort we made to prepare for this day; we forgot to get anything to help us with the weather. We could have installed a battery operated weather station for less than a hundred dollars."

"All I have is an old thermometer nailed to the barn door and that's it. We either have what we need now or steal it."

"What I'd like to have is a barometer so I could see what the barometric pressure is doing."

There sounded a loud bang upstairs and suddenly the wind could be heard clearly. A number of other loud sounds followed the bang immediately and I knew we had a twister. I could hear things crashing, breaking, and creaking. At one point, I actually heard my home moan.

"Everyone, get under my work bench and do it now!" I screamed as I grabbed Sandra's hand and started moving.

We had to crawl to get under my bench, but once there I said, "We'll stay under this thing until the storm dies down. The frame is solid steel, so even if the house falls on us we'll be safe, maybe."

Tom, always joking said, "With my luck it'll catch fire."

The small window above my bench shattered into thousands of small pieces, which, with the help of the wind, turned as deadly as any bullet. Sue screamed, and I could feel Sandra trembling. Suddenly, my world faded into gray, followed by black.

CHAPTER 4

When I next opened my eyes, the sun was shining and I was on a blanket. I raised my aching head and looked around my basement. I spotted Sue looking out a window, weapon in hand and ready. Sandra was sitting near me with her lowered head on her drawn up knees. While she looked to be sleeping, I needed a drink of water badly.

"W...water?" I asked, and then closed my eyes as I lowered my hammering head.

"Here's a sip, but take just a little at first." I heard Sandra say. "You were injured by flying debris, and I was worried about you."

I felt the cool water on my parched throat and enjoyed it more than any cold beer or soft drink I'd ever tasted. After a moment or two I asked, "Do you have anything for pain? My head is killing me."

I sat up for the medication and felt like my head was split wide-open. She handed me two white pills, which I washed down with another sip of water. I felt a bout of dizziness, but fought it off.

"You'll be okay in a day or two, but the headaches could last a while. I have no way of telling if you suffered a concussion or not, but I don't think you did."

"How's the house? I remember us being under the table during the storm and then nothing."

"We lost the roof on the house and about half of the structure. Tom is upstairs now attempting to save what he can."

"What about the bodies from the fight?"

"He pulled them off about a half a mile this morning, right after the storm stopped, and left them there. He's a good man and took charge when he saw you were out of it."

"We were trained by the army to do just that, take over if one of us fell. Any idea if the storm took our storeroom?" I asked as I eased myself down onto the blanket.

"Storeroom is okay, but our bedroom, the guest room and bathroom are pretty much gone."

I gave a light chuckle, which immediately brought pain to my head, and said, "The bathroom hasn't worked in over two years and as for guests, lately we've shot more than we've put up for the night. We'll sleep down here or in the living room."

"I think we should sleep here and let them have the living room. I'm not sure the house is structurally sound enough for anyone to use the upstairs bedroom any longer."

I shrugged my shoulders, felt the pain pill starting to work and drifted off to sleep while Sandra was talking about the barn.

When I next awoke, Tom was sitting beside me cleaning his deer rifle. It was dark and a small candle was burning on a box in the middle of the room. I raised my head and I could see what appeared to be both women sleeping up against the far wall. My head felt better, but I needed another pill.

Tom, who must have seen my movements, asked, "Are you doing better this evening?"

"Some, but I need another pain pill."

Reaching in to his shirt pocket, he pulled out a pill and handed it to me along with a partially filled cup of water.

"Sandra gave me the pill and water before she went to sleep. She gave me instructions to give the pill to you if you came around on my shift."

I swallowed, nodded in understanding, and then asked, "Did the storm hurt us much?"

"The house is a mess, and things are scattered for a quarter mile or better all around us. We didn't lose any food or water, but the big gas storage tank you had is history. When I checked it out, all that remained was a concrete slab."

"There is still some gas in my shed and about 30 gallons in the barn, but that's it. That storage tank was there well over ten years and now it's gone in one night."

"The power of a storm like we had is awesome and most people are not aware of the force or the destruction they can cause a place. Not that it matters, but you've trees down in the yard, telephone poles down out along the road, and I didn't find a single shingle from your roof. Right now I have tarps covering the open side of your house until we can board it up."

"Has anyone been snooping around?"

"Not since the storm, or I would have seen the prints in the mud. I think everyone in the area is recovering from the storm, but I know who attacked us."

"Patton?"

"No doubt at all it was him. Do you remember a skinny guy riding with them that looked pretty sharp and knew how to handle his rifle?"

"I saw the man and if shooting started, he'd have been the first one I'd have killed ?"

"He was one of the dead I pulled out of the yard — he'd stepped on a toe popper. The buckshot blew most of his foot off, but some of the pellets must have severed a main artery in his leg, because he'd bled to death. He'd placed his belt on the leg as a tourniquet, right above his ankle, so I don't think he knew he was bleeding higher up."

"We've both seen it before. I treated a man once that had a bullet wound to his right arm, high near the shoulder, and I looked for an exit hole as well. Of all places, I found it on his lower back, near the spine. The round had hit the bone of his shoulder and then moved down his back to exit there."

"Did he live?"

"He lived, but lost the use of his left arm, or had when I saw him last. I learned later he was sent to Walter Reed, so they could get him into rehab to try to save the use of his arm. I lost touch with him after that."

The pounding in my head lessened, so I tried to stand. I wobbled and my legs felt weak as I stood and then walked to the window and looked out. The night was dark, the moon not out yet, and stars twinkled high overhead. It looked like the same sky I used to view as a child and it was, except we'd changed on earth. I saw no movement, returned to Tom, and sat in a chair.

"What now?"

Tom chuckled and said, "I have no idea, but let's get through this night and see how you are in the morning. I think we should clear your yard of debris first, because I like to keep a clean view, if possible."

"I've a chainsaw in the shed, so clearing the yard won't be that hard. I think while we're doing that we need to place some range markers out."

"It'd help a great deal. We can place some rocks out and paint them different colors for the range. I figure most of our fighting will be within 200 yards, so I'd suggest that be our last marker."

"Forty yard spacing?"

"That'd work for me."

I thought for a few moments and then asked, "How did you get those dead horses pulled away?"

"I used your tractor and the smell was terrible."

"I'd imagine it was. Did you take them to where you'd placed the bodies?"

"Yep, and then I rode by and looked for Patton's body, only it was gone."

"His old man must have come for it." I replied, and then added, "If you're tired, I can stand guard for a while."

"I'm tired, except you'll not stand guard for at least two more days. You know as well as I do that head injuries can be tricky, so we'll wait to see how you do. I'd imagine you've had some dizzy spells since the injury, or vision problems."

"A bit of both, to be honest."

"We'll wait then. I don't want to have to sleep with one eye open, wondering if you're doing the job or not."

I didn't like it, but nodded my understanding.

My stomach gave a loud rumble and Tom asked, "Are you well enough to eat something?"

"Depends on what you have."

"I've some vegetable soup, peanut butter, and dehydrated milk."

"Sounds good," I replied, "and a lot more appetizing than a MRE, huh?"

MRE was a military acronym for *Meals Ready to Eat* and while they looked horrible, the taste was surprisingly good if heated. A single meal packed a lot of calories, too, close to 1200, which a fighting man needed, and while individual meals varied in taste, most were acceptable hot. The problem many of us had with MRE's was when we had to eat them cold, because they gave most soldiers indigestion. A lion's share of the meals I'd eaten were old, really old. I'd gotten out before the chemical heaters were added to the newer meals, so I ate more than just a few meals cold.

Tom left and put my meal together, and returning, he placed it on the table near me. As I started eating, he said, "I didn't mind MRE's much, except they stop me up like a cork. I could eat two or three and not have a bowel movement for four or five days."

I glanced at him and said, "That's because they're low in fiber. From what I understood, which may be wrong, the military designed them that way to keep soldiers from having to run to the bushes every day."

"Well, they worked on me for sure. I guess it would be hard to fight a war if the soldiers and Marines were running to the bushes all the time, huh?"

I smiled, "Now that you mention it, I don't remember ever feeling the need for a bush in the sandbox. I only found out about the fiber from Sandra, who was a nurse in the reserve. I always assumed it was because I was uptight or scared most of the time."

"I think it was a mixture of both, poor fiber and fear that kept me from going regular. There I was, all decked out in desert camouflage, and do you honestly think I'm going to squat and show my big shiny ass out in the open? I'd have had every sniper within five miles aiming at my rump."

I laughed and it felt good, so I said, "Can't show off a purple heart to the butt my friend."

Then, at my own words, I grew serious and thought, *most of our armed forces have left and hopefully most made it home to family and friends. I wouldn't put it passed the Chinese or Russians to invade now that most of us are starving or dead. Lord, it'd be the perfect time to do the job too, because we've crumbled as a nation. Who knows, they may have been invaded and we just don't know it yet.*

"Why so serious all of a sudden?" Tom asked.

"I was wondering why the Chinese or Russians haven't invaded us yet. You couldn't ask for a better time, and we'd only be able to make a token resistance."

"They may have, but if so, they're not around central Mississippi yet. I think they'd hit the large cities like New York, Washington, San Francisco, and then take their time moving against the rest of the country."

"Well, we may be fighting among ourselves these days, but it might take an invasion to bring us all back together again as a nation."

Shaking his head, Tom replied, "I haven't seen anything in the air in over two years except birds. Except, that means very little, as you know. What worries me is our usual grapevine of communications has stopped."

"Too many deaths to keep it open, I guess. You have to remember, we're rich when compared to most folks, many of which are living on dogs, cats, and rats. I thank God everyday that I had enough sense to prepare our supplies."

Tom moved back to the window and then said, "You finish that food and then get some more sleep. Hopefully you'll soon be back on your feet."

I raised the bowl of soup and finished it off. After I stood, I said, "I'm done. When you get a chance let Sandra know I'm fine and remind her that I love her, okay?"

"Will do, buddy, now get some sleep."

Two days later, I was up moving around just after sun up and as I looked at the devastation of my home, it tore my heart out. One whole side looked as if a giant hand had reached down and ripped it apart. While I had some plywood in the barn, I didn't have enough to cover even half of the missing roof. After meandering around the place for a while, I went into the basement and called a group meeting.

I decided to tell them exactly what I had in mind, "I don't think this place is structurally sound, and we need to move to the barn. I think one big gust of wind and we'll spend days digging out."

"It's due to turn cold in less than a month, so do you think we can survive in the barn?" Sue asked.

Sandra laughed and said, "Sue, our horses live in there, so we'll be warm enough. It won't be as warm as this place, because it's not insulated as well, but we'll not freeze to death."

Tom said, "We can move the wood stove into the barn, except we'll have to be extra careful of fire. With all the hay stored in there, it'd go up like a match."

"We can clear an area around the stove, so that won't be much of a real problem. Do we take or leave the food in the house?" Sandra asked.

"We take everything. Now, I'm thinking we can place our forward listening post in here and it'll be warm enough."

"The only problem I see," Tom spoke, and I could tell he was picking his words carefully, "our line of fire to the road will be blocked by the house. Do you have any idea how many feet it is to the house from the barn?"

"I'd guess about 200 feet, why?

"I'm thinking, and I may be wrong, but it seems if anyone attacked us from the road, they'd naturally use this place as cover, right?"

"Sure, they'd move in close and likely place some men inside too. Come on, spit out what you have in mind," I said, growing frustrated.

"I'll remove one of the napalm bombs this afternoon and place it in the center of this place. Once attackers are crawling all over the ruins, we set it off and we'll clear 'em out fast enough. This place is far enough from the barn that we won't burn up when we torch it."

"That's pretty devious, so let's do it, except we'll use some of the gas from the barn. We'll run out of gas soon enough, so using some to protect us is a good investment. "

"While you two rig the house, we'll start moving the supplies. I'll get the wheelbarrow from the barn, and the job won't take us long."

Tom and I spent most of the day removing downed trees in my yard, to clear a field of fire, and placed a new napalm bomb in the exact center of my home. I had mixed emotions placing the explosive, with half of me understanding the need and, the other half still determined to save what was mine. I finally allowed commons sense to rule and the bomb was placed.

We'd just ran the wires outside the structure when I heard a scream and then a shot. It sounded like a large caliber pistol, but I was unsure.

"The barn, but let's not rush into this, because we don't know what's happened." Tom said, "You cover me until I get to the door, then go around to the back door. You enter; let's say in five minutes, okay?"

I looked at my watch and nodded.

"I'm going now," Tom said and took off running for the corner of the barn.

I pulled the pistol I'd taken from Patton, because I could shoot more accurately with it than my shotgun and didn't want to hit a woman. The shotgun I slung over my shoulder on the sling and as soon as Tom was in position, I took off running for the back door.

It only took a minute or so to get into position, so I stood by the door attempting to get my breath. My head was starting to ache, and I knew when this was all said and done I'd need a pain pill. I kept glancing at my watch and the seconds took minutes to tick off. Finally, exactly at five minutes, I opened the door and entered my tack room. I heard both Sue and Sandra talking, so I listened. I stayed in the darkness of the barn, but slowly moved forward. A big man was standing over both women and held a pistol in his right hand. Sandra and Sue were on the floor.

Finally, a male voice I didn't know said, "You two shut your mouths. Mister Patton told me to bring him a prisoner or two and guess what? You're my—"

Before he could finish, the front door slung open and in stepped Tom as if he owned the place. He held his .45 in his extended arms and was in a combat stance.

It was my chance, while the man was concentrating on Tom, to get a shot off. I raised my pistol in both hands, sighted the man in and took a deep breath. As I released my breath, I slowly began to squeeze the trigger. Suddenly the gun jumped in my hand. My target fell hard against a wall and then collapsed on the floor screaming. Suddenly his screaming ceased.

Tom motioned me forward and we both approached the man cautiously with weapons ready. I knew if the man moved, I'd shoot and so would Tom, without a doubt. I stopped beside the man and saw his hands were clean, so I knelt on his back with my right knee and reached for a pulse on his neck.

"He alive?"

"Strong pulse, so he's not going to die anytime soon. I caught him a bit high in the shoulder, but I'm sure his collar bone is jacked up."

"What pistol are you using?"

"The only one I had on me, the one I took off of Patton's son."

Bending over, Tom picked up the man's pistol, which was a 44 magnum, and threw it to me. As I caught it, he said, "Keep this, I'm sure it shoots straighter than what you have."

"Over on my work bench you'll find some rope, Tom. Bring it to me."

As soon as the man was tied securely, I turned to the women, stood and asked, "Are you two okay?"

"We're both fine, but Sandra took a round through her left arm when the man rushed the barn."

I moved to her side and she gave me a faint smile as she said, "It's nothing, just a flesh wound, and it only grazed my arm."

"Doctor it up now." I ordered and then continued, "Once you're taken care of, take a look at the 'Hulk' over there."

Tom had pulled his knife and cut the man's shirt off, which allowed me to see pieces of bone and shirt near the exit wound. Most folks don't realize that when a bullet passes through a person, dirt, cloth, and bone are pushed through the trail of the bullet. This dirt and other debris is what cause most infections. He tossed me three loaded cylinders for the man's pistol, which I pocketed quickly. I had some .44 magnum ammo in storage, but not a great quantity.

"My boy is bleeding pretty badly. Do we have a compress bandage?"

"There are some large sanitary pads in the medical supplies."

"Uh, it's his shoulder that's passing blood, not the other end," Tom said, and I could see his face was red.

Laughing, Sandra replied, "They'll work as well if not better, because they're designed for blood. They're a lot cheaper, so we have a few cases of 'em."

"Our medic in the army carried dozens of them for compress bandages. He said they were easier to use," I said and grinned, because I loved to teach new things to my buddy.

"Well," Tom said smiling, "I don't think our victim cares much what we use."

Sue, who'd been fairly quiet asked, "Did you change your mind about taking prisoners?"

"Nope, not at all."

Tom stopped and turned. Once he met my eyes he said, "I won't stop the bleeding if we're just going to kill him later."

"No, doctor him up for now, because I have some questions to ask him. If he gives me honest answers he'll live, if not he'll die."

"I want nothing to do with torture, and I said that from the start."

"I'll do the job, but we need to know where Patton is living, how many men he has, and what his plans are. I think it may be time to pay a visit to him and put an end to this shit. If this man answers my questions, there won't be any torture."

As he opened a package of sanitary napkins, Tom said, "I watched an Iraqi killed by torture once, and I can still hear his screams some nights. I want nothin' to do with this, understood?"

"Understood, but we all live with ghosts from our wars, huh?"

Tom grunted in reply.

Then, walking toward the downed man, he replied, "Well, it beats the other options."

Sandra walked to my side and said, "I cleaned my wound, but I'll be down with a fever by tonight. I've taken something for pain, infection, and fever only gunshot wounds always produce febricity."

"Speak English."

"I did," and she gave me the smile I love so much. "Febricity means feverishness, fever, or pyrexia."

Meeting her eyes, so she could feel the love I have for her, I said, "Well, I learned two new words today, febricity and pyrexia. Not that I'll ever use them again in this lifetime."

"Stick with me, baby, and I'll teach you a bunch of new things. Now, let me look at our new patient and see what needs to be done."

Less than an hour later the big man's injury was clean, bandaged and had a solid wrapping on it. I refused to allow him antibiotics, because I wanted to save them for our use only.

"When do you think he'll come around?"

Sandra said, "Hard to say. He hit the wall pretty hard and some wounds shut the body down a while, but I'd guess in less than an hour. His collar bone has been shattered and there is a lot of trauma to the tissue in his shoulder."

"Let me know immediately when he comes around, okay?"

Sandra nodded, but didn't reply.

I moved away from the group, sat on a bale of hay and pulled out my sheath knife. I didn't carry a huge knife, just a normal hunting knife with a good 440C stainless blade. I'd found a 440C blade took an edge quickly and didn't dull as fast as some other blades. Pulling a whetstone from the small pouch on the sheath, I began to touch up the edge. For what I had in mind, I would need my knife as sharp as a razor. A few minutes later, when I glanced up, the other three were watching me. For some reason, I suddenly felt like a convicted killer. *To hell with them, I need answers and this sonofabitch has them, I thought.*

CHAPTER 5

A little less than an hour later I was alone in the barn and the "Hulk" was wide awake and complaining of pain. As soon as the man started coming around, the others suddenly had things to do. Now, I didn't like what I was going to do, but I knew doing it wouldn't cost me a second of missed sleep. We live in rough times, and I figured to do what was needed to stay alive. *If we don't put a stop to this, we'll never have any peace around here*, I thought as I pulled my knife and knelt beside the man.

Grabbing his long greasy hair, I pulled his head back and asked, "Do you want to live or die?"

"Hurt me, ya bastard, and Patton will skin all of ya alive. He's got power and gold."

I laughed and replied, "He may just end up doing that, but you'll be long dead before that happens. What's your name?"

"Hanks, William Hanks, and Patton is my uncle. Don't underestimate the man, he's a killer."

I gave an insane laugh and replied, "Well, it's not your day at all, because so am I. See, I get anxious when I've not killed anyone in a week or so. Let me see, not good, because I ain't killed nobody in almost two weeks."

Looking right into my eyes Hanks said, "Ya won't hurt me, because ya know what'll happen to ya if ya do."

I need to show him I'm serious, I thought and then brought my knife up close to his eyes. He must have figured I was going to cut his throat, but with a flash I brought the sharp blade down, severing his left ear. He screamed and his feet kicked violently at the floor.

Blood poured from his injury and now that I had his attention, I said, "I have some questions and you'll answer em."

"Go to—" He started to say.

But, my blade moved rapidly once more and his other ear fell to the concrete floor of my barn. Again he screamed and after a few minutes he began to whimper like an injured animal.

I raised my knife again, but he was stubborn and spit in my face. I made no effort to wipe it off, but remove his nose with another swift sweep of my sharp blade. He screamed once again.

The strange thing is, I wasn't angry with the man at all. I felt no emotions, except a little respect for his grit and determination to stay silent. He was an unwavering man, I'll give him that much, only not too smart. *He knows information I need desperately and I'll have it, one way or the other.*

"Now, we can keep this up for hours, if you like. I'll take your fingers off one at a time, then your toes, and at that point, I'll remove your pants and we'll get real personal."

"N...no, m...more, please.", the man finally managed to get out though his pain.

With his ears and nose missing, the man presented a hideous appearance. Blood flowed freely down his face and neck, but I made no effort to stop the bleeding.

I placed the tip of my knife against his crotch and said, "I'll ask the questions and you'll answer me. You lie to me or hesitate, and you'll have to squat to pee from then on. Do you fully understand me?"

"Yes, I understand. B... but please, no more cuttin'."

A puddle of urine began to form under the man and I knew he was one scared puppy, and now he'd tell me all I needed to know.

"Tell me everything you know about Patton, you sonofabitch! I want to know exactly where he's at, how many men he has, what kinds of arms they have, and his routine for the guards. You answer me truthfully and I'll let you live, I give you my word. You lie to me and I'll kill you—eventually." I pushed my knife blade forward just a bit and knew he could feel the tip of the knife against his genitals.

In less than 10 minutes I had all I needed to know about Patton and his men. The problem now was, Hanks just wouldn't shut up. I let him ramble as I moved to our medical supplies and returned with what I needed to treat his injuries. I gave him no pain medication, but did wrap his ears and nose with gauze.

Finally, I raised his right foot and removed the boot. His once white sock was brown from constant wear. Removing the sock, I placed it in his lap and pulled my knife once again. Holding the foot tightly in my left hand, I severed his Achilles tendon, knowing he'd not be able to move fast ever again. He screamed and after a few minutes I picked up the gauze and wrapped his new injury as well as I could.

I rolled him over and cut the rope binding his wrists together. I then said, "Hanks, I'm going to help you about a 100 yards from this barn. Only before I do that, there is something I want you to fully understand. You attacked our *women* and by rights I should kill you for that, except I'm a man of my word. If I ever see you again, I'll kill you on sight. Do you understand me?"

"With my tendon cut like this how do you expect me to move?"

I pulled the pistol he'd once owned, pulled the hammer back with a loud click, and said, "Oh, you'll move, or I'll kill you where you lay. Now, which is it?"

Lowering his head he mumbled, "Help me up."

It took me a long time to escort the man a 100 yards, but I wanted him out of our hair and yet not able to warn Patton we were coming for him. The gauze on his head, shoulder and tendon was blood soaked, only I didn't honestly care if the man lived or died. I only promised him I'd not kill him. If he bled to death, well, that wasn't my problem was it?

When I returned, everyone was in the barn and Sue was mopping blood up from the floor. While no one said anything, I could feel a tenseness hanging heavy in the air.

"Did you dump the body?" Sandra asked.

"There wasn't a body, because I didn't kill the man."

"But, we heard him screaming."

"I cut him up a bit, but he'll live."

Sue gazed into my eyes and said, "Cut him up a bit? I found his nose and ears on the floor. You're a damned animal, do you know that? A real coldblooded sonofabitch."

"I *never* said he was pretty. Look, he was tough, so I had to turn mean to get what I needed from him, alright? As for being an animal, I'll do whatever it takes to make sure we all survive!"

"You scarred that man for life!" Sue shot back.

Feeling my anger growing, I said bluntly, "He's an animal and to be honest, I should have just killed the bastard, because that's what he'd do after raping you or Sandra! The only reason I didn't was he provided me the information I wanted."

Tom raised his hand with the palm open toward his wife and while she was about to speak, she didn't say anything.

"What'd you learn?" Tom asked.

"We can take the place, but it won't be easy." I felt my blood pressure drop knowing Tom had his wife's big progressive mouth under control.

Tom shrugged his shoulders and replied, "I didn't expect it to be easy."

I paused a few seconds to gather my thoughts and then said, "Gather around, my children, and I will tell you a tale of the wicked man named Patton."

It was late, near two in the morning, as we watched the house that Patton used for his headquarters. He ran a large group of men, well over a hundred, but most were always out on missions foraging for food, fuel, or women, leaving fewer than ten men at the house on most any given night. I hoped this night the majority of his men were gone, or we'd end up as dead as the Christmas goose.

I glanced at Dolly and Skillet, but both were stretched out beside me and unmoving.

The house wasn't anything fancy, just an old farm house with a stretched barbed wire fence around it. I noticed a bunkhouse out back, but no light was seen. Only one light burned and it appeared to be in the living room of the main house. Since no one had electrical power these days, it was either an oil lamp or a lantern.

Tom, who'd led a lot of ranger recon patrols in Iraq, would move in, check the place out and then return to brief us on what he found. We'd agreed that only one of us should go, so we'd not leave the women without an experienced fighter if things turned to shit. It brought back memories when I looked over at Tom and his face and hands were all camouflaged with burnt cork. We had a few bottles of wine left, so we'd shared a bottle for lunch, and Tom saved the cork to blacken his skin. Once he'd finished, all three of us applied blotches of black on all exposed skin.

From the light of the moon, Tom held his right hand up, with all fingers extended, then opened and closed the hand three times. He then pointed to his eyes with his index and middle finger. His meaning was clear, he wanted fifteen minutes to check the place out and then return. I looked at my watch and patted him on the back. Slowly he moved forward and in a matter of seconds he'd disappeared into the darkness.

As I waited, I didn't really expect gunfire, but if things turned rough, he'd find us willing to back him up as much as possible. The second hand of my watch seemed to move slower than usual, but it'd done that many times when on combat patrols.

Less than ten minutes later, Tom materialized from the darkness and knelt beside me, catching his breath. He nodded a few times and then motioned for us to follow him. Instead of moving toward Patton, he moved away.

Finally, after about a half mile, he stopped.

Giving me a goofy grin, he said, "I counted only ten men, but I have no idea if others are in some of the rooms of the main house."

"Should we go tonight?"

Nodding, he replied, "He can't know we are on to him, so surprise will work in our favor. I figure if there are more men sleeping in the place, we'll be inside and shooting before most of them clear their heads."

Sue asked, "You'll kill sleeping men?"

Tom chuckled and said, "Yes, when we're outnumbered by more than two to one, I surely will."

A silence followed, then finally Sue said, "It doesn't seem... right. Isn't there some other way?"

I knew she had started to say fair, but knew better, because she wanted to survive as much as the rest of us. While I didn't care to kill sleeping men, I'd do anything to protect us, and I started to state that, except my interrogation of Hanks proved it already.

Tom asked as he turned to me, "How do you want to do this?" Completely ignoring his wife's question. I figured he thought like I did, we'd tried talk before and it'd not worked. Now it was time to kick some serious ass.

"I think the best way would be for Sandra and Sue to cover us outside while you and I go right through the front door. Did you see a guard?"

"Actually, there are two. One walking around, while another was sitting on the steps to the front door.

"You take out the walker, then I'll take the man on the steps." I said and then turning to the women I added, "you two will remain outside the fence for fifteen minutes after we leave and then enter the barnyard. If anyone approaches from the road or the bunkhouse, shoot to kill."

Sandra said, "That's the only way I can shoot at night holding a 12 gauge shotgun."

Tom asked, "And, where will the dogs be?"

"They'll stay with me, until I enter the place, then I'll let them loose."

"You know something?" Sandra asked.

"What's that?"

"I almost feel sorry for those men."

Tom and I made our way safely to the fence and while I knew we'd not been seen, my heart was pounding in my chest. All it took was a small noise or something to go wrong and the shit would hit the stump. I pulled the bottom of the fence up so Tom could slide under it and he held it up for me, and finally the dogs. Once on the inside, we both pulled our knives, and I motioned for the dogs to come with me. As I moved toward the front steps, I remained in the shadows as much as possible, because I had no clear location of the walking guard. I moved slowly along the dark side of the house, and when I peeked around the corner my guard had his chin resting on his chest. I motioned for the dogs to stay and both sat in the darkness.

He's asleep, I thought and moved toward him cautiously, expecting his head to come up any second. *Don't wake up now, or I'll have to pull my pistol.*

Once up close, I threw my left hand over his mouth and pushed my knife into his back near his kidneys as hard as I could. His eyes flew open, he gave a loud grunt, and then started thrashing. I struggled hard to keep him in position. Three more times I drove my blade deep into his back, until finally he grew limp. I then cut his throat.

I placed the man beside the steps and called the dogs with a soft blow of my lips. When they neared the blood, it caused both to give low warning growls.

From the darkness a black form moved toward the steps, but I recognized the walk way before I saw it was Tom. He nodded, which answered my unspoken question; the walking guard was no longer a threat. We'd agreed earlier to just walk into the place like we owned it, figuring it would not raise any suspicions and we'd be taken for guards.

We entered and I was surprised no one was in the living room. I'd half expected to find a man sitting at a desk doing paperwork and drinking coffee. An old kerosene lamp was burning in the middle of a kitchen table. Once the room was checked, I released both dogs and they sat at my feet.

Tom pulled two Molotov Cocktails from his backpack. He handed one to me and since I wore my old military battle dress uniform, I slipped my bottle into the left cargo pocket on the trousers. *I hope the women have entered the barnyard because it's about to turn real hot in this place,* I thought as I moved toward the hallway.

Skillet followed slightly in front of me, but Dolly remained at my side as I moved toward the door on the right. I opened the first door and Dolly entered the room, only to come back out. It was empty.

Dolly suddenly growled and a door down the hall opened. I placed my left hand on Dolly's head. In the moonlight from the curtain-less windows I could see a rail thin man and he scratching his crotch as he approached. I moved into the shadows and prayed the dogs wouldn't growl or make a noise, but Tom walked up to the thin man and asked, "Who's to take my shift now?"

Raising his head for the first time, the man looked as if he was going to say something, only before he could speak, Tom cracked him alongside of his head with the barrel of his shotgun. He fell with a loud *thud.*

"Joe?" A voiced called from the room the man had just left, "Ya okay out there? I thought I heard ya fall or somethin'. Joe?"

We moved quickly to the door and just as I was about enter, the loud report of a shotgun was heard outside. It was immediately followed by two more loud blasts. Tom blocked my way with his arm and then I saw his lighter spark and the resulting flame. I watched as he lit the Molotov Cocktail and waited a second to make sure it was burning well.

From inside the room, I heard a voice say, "It's likely it's a couple of the guys comin' back in. They're about half drunk most of the time."

"Get up and get dressed! We have no idea what's going on. I heard gunshots." A different voice replied.

At that point I kicked the door open and Tom threw the fire bomb into the center of the floor. There was a sudden flash of light, followed by yells and screams, and then we started shooting.

Our targets were outlined clearly by the burning gas and in less than two minutes, it was all over.

Skillet gave a growl and then a bark. When I turned to look at him, he and Dolly were running full speed down the hallway. I heard a shot, a scream, and finally after a couple of long seconds another shot.

Tom and I followed and when we entered the living room, the dogs were not to be seen.

"Upstairs!" Tom yelled.

I could now hear a struggle taking place, but I didn't run up those steps. I love my animals, but to rush into the unknown would just get me killed and not help them in the end. Tom and I took the steps two-at-a-time and nearing the top, I peeked over to see a large man rolling on the floor with both dogs nipping at him. A candle glowed on the night table and a woman lay in the bed watching, her fear obvious. She was naked.

"Call the dogs off, it's Patton." Tom said, but held his shotgun at the ready.

"Dolly! Skillet! Come!" I called and they rushed to my side.

Patton sat up, his face covered in blood, his left arm mangled and his recognition of us was immediate, "You, is it? I'll have you skinned alive for this!"

Tom started to lower his weapon, but I said, "Wait, Tom. Patton, you sent a man after us and he attacked our women."

"Women? You attacked me over women? A man who wants a woman just has to find one, take her and keep her. Women, hell, they're all sluts." He shook his bloody head.

The sound of my shotgun was deafening in the small farmhouse. My shot took him in the middle of his chest and the force knocked him back hard. I walked to his still quivering body and said, "Some men, Patton, love their women and don't like them messed with at all."

"What about you?" I heard Tom say, and when I turned he was talking to the woman in bed.

"I... I don't want anything to do with this." She lowered her head and added, "I was taken from a small camp about six months ago, and he made me his mistress. I had no love for him. I hated him!"

Tom ordered, "Then get dressed, you'll come with us until we can figure out what to do with you. Now, move!"

Dense smoke was filling the hallway, so I broke the bedroom window out with the butt of my shotgun and instructed Tom and the woman to go out that way. The window was right over the porch, so all they'd have to do is go out and then jump to the ground. In the mean time, I called my dogs and started down the stairs, not sure what I'd find at the bottom. Nonetheless, I refused to leave my dogs.

CHAPTER 6

I could see fire and flickering light from the top of the steps and hoped the living room was not in flames. Over the cracking and popping of the fire, I heard four or five shotgun blasts outside and one or two of what sounded like pistol shots from near the road. At the bottom of the stairs the flames were just starting to eat at the furniture, so we moved through the smoke, out the door and onto the porch. I inhaled deeply the second I smelled the fresh air, but glancing around I saw no one.

Two men rounded the corner of the house, so I raised my shotgun and jerked the trigger. I felt the gun jump in my hands, saw both men collapse on the ground. I pumped another round into the chamber and moved forward, ignoring one man I'd just shot who was screaming in pain.

"John, we're at your two o'clock!" I heard Tom yell and angled slightly to my right.

As I neared, I noticed Tom first and asked, "How'd it go?"

"We need to move and do it quickly. There was a truckload of those jokers that returned just a few seconds ago, and once they figure out where we're at, we're history." Then, turning to Sue, he asked, "Can you walk?"

"I hurt, but I'll walk. I don't... have a choice, now do I?"

"She took a pistol round through her thigh. I've got a bandage and tourniquet on it, and that'll have to do until we get home," Sandra spoke from the darkness.

"Enough, let's move!" Tom ordered as he pushed me forward.

I was the point man, so I moved forward about twenty yards in front and my pace was fast. While I worried about Sue keeping up I thought, *I'll not risk the lives of four people to save one. I just can't. She either keeps up or we leave her.*

Just as a false dawn began to change the dark shadows into gray, we neared my place. Sue had kept up, mainly because Sandra had held her up as they walked, but at each break we'd tightened the tourniquet. *Loss of blood may kill her now, or she'll go into shock,* I thought, and pulled my small hunting binoculars from my pocket. I glassed my house, except I saw nothing unusual, my place was still a mess from the storm. My other dogs were loose and running around, and I knew if anyone were near they'd be barking.

Tom moved to my side and asked, "Quiet down there?"

"Yep, ole Newt and the rest have the place under control." I put my binoculars back in my pocket and gazed into my friend's tired eyes as I asked, "Is Sue okay?"

"She's close to going into shock, and if that happens we'll lose her," as he spoke, his eyes watered and he turned his head away.

I knew Tom loved her dearly, but I never understood how a big conservative like him could end up married to a big-time liberal. When I'd asked him about it, soon after he'd first met her, he'd replied, "Opposites attract, haven't you heard? She's a good woman, only we argue over some pretty silly things, like politics, gay rights, abortion, and gun control."

I slapped him on the back and said, "Come on, let's get home and have a cup of coffee and something to eat. Sandra will have Sue up pestering you in a week!" I gave an ill-felt laugh and then moved toward my house.

Dolly and Skillet were still at my side when we entered the barnyard and the other dogs came running. Newt was jumping on Dolly and the others were all over Skillet, each of them welcoming us home.

From behind me I heard a yell, "She's fainted! Guys! I need some help here!"

Sue was down and Tom and I ran to her side.

"Pick her up and move her to the barn, gently." Sandra said as she quickly turned all nurse.

Tom kept mumbling over and over, "Don't you die on me, baby. You hear me? Don't die! You hang tough, Sue!"

I didn't say anything because I'd heard it often enough in the war. I'd heard the same sort of language from medic's as they worked to keep our wounded alive and after a few minutes I no longer heard it, because I'd stopped listening to it completely. I glanced down at Sue's face. I had her arms and Tom her legs, and she gave me a slight smile.

"Keep talking to her, Tom." I said and noticed he was moving faster now that we were near the barn door.

"Take her in and place her flat on the floor, where the blankets are," Sandra ordered as she opened the door for us.

Sue was no sooner on the floor than Sandra was kneeling at her side. After a minute or two she turned to Tom, gave him a mean glare, and with narrow eyes said, "Enough with the don't die on me bullshit! I need you to help, so boil some water, pull our medical supplies, and fix the rest of us something to eat. Then, leave me the hell alone so I can save your wife."

Over the next hour we did as instructed and even gathered up enough wood to keep the wood-stove burning for a week. Tom was anxious and I knew it, so I made small talk to keep his mind off Sue, "What made you walk up to that man in the hallway and ask him about shift changes?"

Glancing at Sandra's back, then turning to me, Tom replied, "I figure a lot of the men still alive are prior military, you know, because we're about all that survived the first year. Have you ever seen a military man come looking for his relief on a shift?"

"No, not in any army I was ever in. You stayed at your assigned post until properly relieved, or something like that. I remember it from a general order in basic training. Let's move to the table and have some coffee."

"Yep, that's exactly what general order five says, The man knew I had no reason to be looking for my relief, but I honestly couldn't think of anything else to ask him."

"Any problems with the walking guard?"

"Not once he stopped and lighted his pipe. I saw the flare of the match and knew where he was."

Sandra stood and made her way to us. Giving Tom a slight trace of a smile she said, "She's stable, but lost a lot of blood. If we can give her a couple of days of rest we'll know more."

"Thank God," Tom said, and gave a big grin.

"Who is the woman?" She asked as she pointed to the woman from Patton's bedroom.

"We found her in Patton's bedroom, and according to her she wasn't there by choice," I replied and motioned for the woman to come to us. She'd sat on the floor by the door unmoving since we'd arrived.

She was thin, but most folks were these days with obesity now unheard of among survivors. Her hair was auburn and as she neared I noticed she had blue eyes. Once at the table, I handed her a cup of coffee.

I took a sip of mine and then asked, "What's your name?"

"Martha, but my friends call me Marty."

Tom, looking over the rim of his cup asked, "Marty, do you know how to shoot?"

She nodded and said with a flat voice, "My husband, before he was killed by Patton, taught me, only it's been a while."

Smiling, I replied, "It's like riding a bicycle, once you learn you know how to do it the rest of your life."

Reaching behind him, Tom pulled out a double barreled shotgun that had been sawed off right in front the fore-stock and said, "Pack this, and I mean every single minute of the day and night. You need to always have it within reach."

He turned once more and placed a dozen shotgun shells on the table. Meeting her eyes he asked, "Do you honestly think you could kill a man?"

She gazed back hard and replied, "In a heartbeat. I'll never go back to being what I was yesterday."

This is not the frightened woman I saw in Patton's bed. She'll do, I thought as I took a long pull of my coffee. *I need to get some sleep, but should determine the guard first. The dogs could do the job.*

"Look, we can all talk much more later, but right now we all need some rest. I'm sure we can all sleep, with the dogs running free outside, except to make sure, I'll call Dolly into the barn," I said, and then made my way to the door. I called her and a couple of minutes later Dolly was at my side.

As I moved toward my blankets, I heard Marty say, "Thank both of you for what you did for me."

I simply waved to her and heard Tom reply, "No one should be kept where they don't want to be. If you ever decide to leave us, just give me back the gun and go. I won't try to keep you, but guns and ammo are hard to come by."

I sat on my blanket, glanced in Marty's direction only to find her smiling. I leaned back on my blanket and it felt good to stretch out. *I wonder what she is smiling about?* I thought, and within seconds I was asleep.

I awoke hours later and immediately heard rain hitting the tin roof of the barn. I loved that sound when I was a kid. I raised my head and looked around. All were asleep, except Tom and he stood guard by the door. Dolly was beside me and when I moved, she looked at me. I smiled, patted her gently on the head a whispered, "Stay." A small candle was the only light and it was on the table.

I stood, stretched, and then made my way to my friend, "What time is it?"

He glanced at his old windup watch and replied, "0300, so it's still a bit before first light."

I thought of the old watch and how Tom had replaced his expensive battery powered watch years ago, claiming there would come a day when the batteries would not be found. He was right.

"How's Sue?"

"No change that I can see, but Sandra swears she'd mending well and not to worry."

"To change the subject a bit, do you trust Marty?"

Tom met my eyes and said, "No, not yet. She's got to prove herself to me before I fully trust her, but that would be the same for anyone new. Why?"

"I was wondering if we were thinking the same thing, and we are." I replied and then added, "let me out of here so I can run to the bushes, I have to pee."

Tom laughed and opened the door.

The rain was steady, but not hard and the night air was brisk. I did my morning toilet and as I moved toward the barn, Skillet ran to my side, which startled me a little.

"How are you, big guy?" I asked as I stopped to scratch his ears.

He moved in close to me and placed his head against my thigh. *Lawdy, I wish I didn't have to leave him out in the rain like this. He has to stay out, he's our first line of defense,* I thought as I started for the door.

Once at the door, I turned, but Skillet had disappeared.

"Quiet?" Tom asked.

"Yep, but the dogs are out in the rain and I don't like it much."

"We ain't got much of a choice really. I figure it's just a matter of time before some of Patton's men figure out who attacked them."

"Maybe, but maybe not, too. I don't think his death meant anything to them at all. He was a paycheck, only he paid with women, booze and drugs. Hell, I suspect they're all fighting over who's the new leader this morning."

"Maybe they are." He replied with a flat tone. *He's tired,* I thought.

"I'm going to put on a pot of coffee," I said and moved to the table.

Tom was still looking out the door and I was facing a wall filling an old coffee pot with water, when the sound of two pistol shots filled the air. I spun around, brought my shotgun up, to see Sandra holding her pistol like she was on a shooting range. She had both hands on her pistol, and wore a look of complete anger.

"What are you shooting at?" Tom asked from the door.

"Martha, or Marty! She just went out the back door!"

"Tom, stay where you are, I'll look for her!" I yelled as I began to run.

I'd just opened the back door when I heard the dogs barking and then the loud *boom* of a shotgun. I heard a dog or two yelping in pain, so I moved toward the sound. The rain was harder now, with an occasional flash of lightning, which meant I had to be cautious. At the next flash of light, I saw Marty running toward the woods and I let her go, because I saw I had three dogs down. My dogs meant more to me than catching her, even though I knew she was running to Patton's old farm.

I moved forward and squatted by my dogs. Newt and Benji were both dead, and Skillet was in pain. *Maybe Sandra can help him,* I thought, as I picked him and moved for the barn.

I'm glad it's raining, because no one will see my tears, I thought and then slipped in the mud and fell to my right knee. I stood and moved toward the barn again.

Staggering like a drunk under the weight of Skillet, I prayed, "Lord, I don't usually ask you for much, but this time I need your help. Let this dog live, Lord. He's a good dog, and I don't ask for me so much as for him. He deserves to live. But, no matter what happens, Thy will be done. This I ask in the name of Jesus, amen."

I entered the barn and was met by Sandra. "Skillet?"

"Marty killed Newt and Benji, and Skillet was hit hard. I couldn't see the injury in the dark and brought him in so you could look at him."

"Put him on my blanket and I'll get the medical supplies."

I lowered him to the blanket and gazed into his big brown eyes. I could see his pain and fear, so I rubbed his head and spoke to him, "You're a good dog, Skillet. Good boy."

He whimpered and I heard Sandra say, "You go to Tom and brief him on what happened."

I met Skillet's eyes once more, stood and then walked to the door.

I explained to Tom what had happened and how Marty escaped. He shook his head and said, "I shouldn't have given her that gun yet."

"Well, don't blame yourself, because she was a good liar. I believed her."

Sandra stood and made her way to us. Unconsciously she ran her bloodstained hands through her hair and said, "He's not going to make it, John. He's been hit in the lungs and I can't stop the bleeding. Do you want me to put him down with painkiller?"

I rubbed my tired eyes, fought the urge to scream my anger, and after a few long minutes finally said, "No, we've a limited supply of pain medications."

"You're not going to let him bleed to death, are you?" She asked.

I pulled the .38 snub nosed pistol I'd taken from Larry Patton when I'd killed him, opened the cylinder and checked the loads. As I snapped the cylinder closed I said, "No, I'll do this. He's my dog and responsibility."

"Baby, I know how much—"Sandra started saying, but I ignored her and moved to Skillet.

Once at his side, I squatted. I gave him a smile, stroked his wet head, and gazed into his big beautiful brown eyes. He whimpered again and I felt my heart breaking. Lord, give me strength, I prayed as I stood and extended my hand. My arm was shaking so hard I worried about my aim. I didn't want him to suffer any longer.

My shot was loud and my aim true. Skillet's death was instantaneous. I wanted to collapse and cry, but times were hard, and I knew the others were watching me. I had to set an example. I placed the pistol in my pocket, covered Skillet with a blanket, and went to finish the coffee.

Near dawn, Tom approached me and said, "I'm going out to track Marty. I suspect she's heading back to Patton's, but I need to be sure."

Staring into my cold coffee cup and without looking up I replied, "Don't bring the bitch back here. Get the gun if you can, along with the ammo, but if you bring her back, I'll kill her."

CHAPTER 7

Tom had been gone for a little over an hour, when Dolly gave a low growl and moved toward the main door to the barn. I slipped the safety to off on my shotgun and peeked outside, seeing nothing but rain. Someone or something was out there, or the dog wouldn't have warned me.

Sandra quickly moved to my side. "What is it?"

"I don't see anything, but they might be using the house for cover. You move over to the window and if you see anything, let me know. Dolly wouldn't have growled if it had been Tom, and he's not been gone long enough to return yet." I pushed my old cowboy hat back from my face so I could take a better look.

Sandra moved to the window, and I noticed she switched her gun safety off as well.

Long minutes passed with no further growls from Dolly, and I was starting to think it had been a small animal or something. *She's a good girl, but I don't see anything,* I thought, as I turned and gave Sandra weak smile.

While I was smiling, Dolly suddenly started barking and I saw the gun in Sandra's hands come up. I turned, looked out the door and spotted four men moving toward us. Then it dawned on me, "Sandra, you cover the front! I'm moving to the back! Dolly, stay!"

I was just about to the back door when it suddenly flew open and in stepped a man with a deer rifle in his hands. I noticed rain dripping from him as I brought the shotgun up waist high, fired and saw him knocked to the ground, where he lay unmoving. I knelt beside some empty 55 gallon drums I had stored and waited, but it wasn't much of a wait. Less than a minute later, two men entered, both fired their shotguns blindly, and as they pump in fresh shells, I raised and fired, taking them both with one shot. The one on the left must have died instantly, but the other fell to the ground screaming, his shotgun landing a good six feet from him. I moved to the door, glanced out, saw nothing, and closed it. I then moved to men I'd shot, with the injured man being first. He'd taken most of the blast in his side, but more than few pellets had struck him in the arm, and he was bleeding profusely. A quick search found an old 1911 .45 Colt Commander pistol in his coat pocket and little else, except a small knife on his belt. I heard a shotgun blast from the front of the barn and finished my search quickly. By the time I'd finished searching him, he was dead.

The other two were dead as well, so I move to the front of the barn. Sandra was still at the window, but her shotgun was held in a relaxed manner.

"Do you know where they are?" I asked, suspecting they were in the house.

"In the house, or that's where the last man I saw moved to get away from my buckshot."

I moved to the battery on the floor near the table and picked up the wires to the napalm bomb we still had in my old home. I attached one wire and then said, "Move below the window, because I'm going to set this thing off. As soon as the blast is complete, get up quickly and cover the window again. Ready?"

"Ready!"

I attached the second wire, but heard no explosion. I unhooked the wires and move to the second battery, only again there was no blast. *They've cut the wires,* I thought and moved to the door.

"What happened?" Sandra asked, still kneeling below the window.

"They've either cut the wires or the batteries are dead."

"What now?"

At that exact moment, I heard an engine start and it didn't sound good. I recognized it almost immediately."They have a tractor or bulldozer!"

"Good God, a bulldozer would be like a tank, right?"

"If the blade is raised, we'll not hit the driver and you can be sure they'll have men moving in close behind it." I attempted to sound calm, but I felt fear deep in my gut.

"What can we do?"

I didn't answer, but stood deep in thought, until finally, "Get Sue ready to move. First I want you to saddle the horses and that includes one for Tom. We'll wait until we know for sure what we're facing, but if it's a dozer, we'll have to go out the back."

"She can't be moved!"

"By damn, she will be! I'll not leave her here to be used and then killed by these animals. Now, do as I said!"

It was rare I lost my temper, but I had nothing to stop a dozer, and if Sue died as we moved, then it was out of my control. Only I'd not leave her, because I knew even unconscious they'd rape her. Less than fifteen minutes later, I glanced and saw the horses were ready to go. Looking out the door again, I saw an exhaust pipe exhaling a thin column of black smoke as a dozer rounded the corner of my house, heading right for us. My gut tightened, and I fired a shot just to let them know we were still here.

I yelled, "It's a dozer! Go to the back door and if you have to make room, move the empty drums. They're not heavy and I only had them there so I could hear if someone tried to enter. I'll tie Sue to a horse!"

Looking back at the dozer, I saw the blade was up, and nothing could be seen behind it. I squeezed off another round, and then moved to our backpacks. I quickly put mine on and then moved to Sue. She was either unconscious or asleep, but I waited for Sandra, knowing Dolly would warn me before anyone entered the barn.

Just as I finished tying Sue to the horse and securing the three backpacks to saddle horns, I heard two shots strike the barn and saw Sandra running toward me. As she neared she said, "Raining harder now and the sky is almost black! How do you want to do this?"

"Take Dolly with you, but go out the back and move south into the trees. I want you to travel about a quarter mile, to the fence line and wait for me there."

"What about you?"

"Move! I'll explain later!"

As Sandra led the horses out the back door, I moved to the loft, where I could see much better. Even with the hard rain I counted over twenty men behind the dozer, and smiled as I pulled the last two Molotov cocktails from a shabby table. I might not be able to stop them from taking my place, but there'd be fewer of them to enjoy what I've worked hard to keep. It was then I heard two loud shots behind the barn and began to worry about Sandra. *She's on her own, because I've got my hands full right now.*

When the dozer got to within twenty feet of the barn, I ignited the rags in both bottles and kicked the loft door open. I threw the fire bomb from my right hand, hard, and saw it explode into flames on the dozer, about a foot in front of the driver, who was immediately covered in the inferno. I think my move surprised them, because no one seemed to realize where the danger lay. I switched the remaining bomb to my right hand and threw it at the rear of the dozer, where most of the men were gathered.

I then moved down stairs, picked up a small one gallon can of gasoline, poured it on the floor of my barn and into the hay. Pulling a match from my pocket, I ran it across the handrail on the stairs and dropped it into the gas. I smiled as it burst into flames. *They'll not get my gear or supplies,* I thought while running for the rear door.

Just before I reached the door, I was suddenly jerked from my feet and landed near the men I'd killed earlier. I could hear the sound of bullets striking the building and figured I'd taken a stray round. I felt no pain, but knew I'd been hit. I had to move because I'd either burn to death or be shot again if I remained. Standing on weak legs I noticed blood near my left elbow, but the arm worked and there was no pain, so I moved out the door, holding my shotgun at the ready.

One man ran from the left side of the barn, but I knocked him on his ass with just one shot. I moved in the tracks of my horses, which the pouring rain was quickly washing away. I saw no one else, until I was about a hundred feet from the barn. Glancing to my right, I saw one man down with most of his head missing. I began to run, wanting to put some distance between the bad guys and me, but my arm was starting to ache. *The shock is wearing off,* I thought as I jogged forward, knowing I had pain killers in my backpack but also knowing the risk of stopping, I continued.

I was tired and weak by the time I reached the trees and the fence line. I slowed to a walk as I neared, not wanting Sandra to shoot me in the pouring rain, but I saw no one. Scanning the ground, I saw no tracks of the horses, but with the rain they'd been washed away. I moved to a large oak and sat under it in the mud unmoving for a few minutes. I was out of breath and tired. Finally, I pulled my backpack around and removed my first aid kit, opening it slowly to avoid spilling the smaller contents.

With the open first aid kit in my lap, I rolled my sleeve up to find a long track of a small caliber bullet, likely a .22 or .38, burned into the flesh. While it had bled and hurt like all get out, it wasn't a bad injury. I was lucky, because if it had hit an inch lower I would have taken the round into the arm, so I placed some triple antibiotic ointment on it and wrapped it with some gauze I had in the kit.

"Are you okay?" I heard Sandra yell from the rain.

"Where are you?" I couldn't see her because the rain was coming down hard.

"I'm coming. I wasn't sure if it was you or not, so I stayed hidden until I recognized your walk."

"I had a bullet burn me near the elbow, but I'll live. It didn't do much damage at all." I could now see her nearing and in a matter of a few short seconds she squatted beside me. Water ran from her hair and she looked tired.

"As long as you treated it well, you should be okay. So, what happened back at the barn?"

"I took a few out with a couple of fire bombs, but in the end I started a fire to burn the place down. I didn't want them to get all of our supplies or ammo."

She gave me a weak smile and said, "They didn't get all of our stuff. Don't you remember where you and Tom hid some things?"

Lawdy, what a pretty woman I married, I thought, but said, "I remember, but didn't until you said something just now. I'm tired, hungry and—oh, how is Sue?"

"She started bleeding and I had to wrap her injury again. I don't think this moving is good for her, except we don't have much choice if we want to survive."

I raised my hand to her face, gave her a warm smile and replied, "I wish it was like the old times. We had a good life when we first got married, remember?"

"I remember, only those days are gone forever. For some reason God is making us live like animals now, fighting for every single thing in life."

I let my hand fall, gazed into her eyes and replied, "Don't blame God for what is happening, when you and I both know it was due to the collapse of our economy and a government the whole world lost confidence in. You don't know, but most soldiers do, that America was once one of the few countries in the world that constant war and hunger was missing. Well, those days are over."

"I'm not really blaming God." She then stood before continuing, "But, why did it have to happen now? Why not before or later?"

I stood, turned to her and replied, "Because I think by America taking God out of our lives and government, we lost our favored status with Him. If you think back, years before things fell apart, God wasn't in most homes. We'd turned our full attention to cell phones, computers, and other things, and no longer had an urge to do anything productive. By then, God and prayer was gone from public schools, meetings and even from our money. As a country founded on a strong belief in God, we'd turned our backs on our creator."

"Well, thank you, Pastor John, for the sermon." She shook her head slowly and then said, "Nonetheless, you're absolute right, maybe. You know I believe in God, but all of this confuses me. Now, follow me back to where I have the horses, because we need to put some distance behind us."

We rode close to fifteen miles before stopping for the night in a group of pines. While the rain had stopped, water continued to drip from trees as I made camp. Sue was bleeding again, only it could not be helped, not with us being followed. Once the old tarp was strung between two trees, I gently placed Sue under the shelter and moved out of the way as Sandra treated her injury.

Moving to the trees in the surrounding area I broke off squaw wood near the lower limbs and discovered most of it was fairly dry. I also found a pine tree, and with a few scrapes of my knife I gathered a few lumps of pine pitch, which burned hot even in wet weather. I moved back to camp and soon had a small fire burning in front of our shelter. As it burned, I gathered enough wood to last the night and placed it near the fire to partially dry out from the heat.

Looking over my shoulder as I placed a coffee pot on the flames, I asked, "How's she doin'?"

"Bleeding, but no sign of infection."

Sue moved up onto her elbows and said in a weak voice, "I'll be. . . fine. I'm worried about. . . Tom. What if he goes back. . . to the farm?"

I chuckled, more to comfort her than with humor and replied, "Tom's an old war dog. He'll check the place over closely and right off he'll see the barn is gone. He'll then move to the meeting place we arranged in case of emergencies."

Dolly moved under the shelter and sat beside Sandra, who looked at me and asked, "And where might that be?"

"About a mile up the trail. There is an old abandoned home, or it was still standing a year ago, beside a dirt road." I replied brusquely and was a bit mad, because I'd explained it to all to them before, but they'd not listened to a single word.

"I remember now. It was owned by someone named. . . Wilson, right?"

"No, it was Wilkerson, and they died the first year."

As Sue lowered her head to the horse blanket, Sandra asked, "Do you know what happened to them?"

"No, not really. All I know is the old man was killed one night and then the rest came down with fever of some sort about a month later." I glanced up at the sky and could see more rain clouds gathering off to the west.

"So many have died."

"More will die before this is over. Right now, as far as I know, we've all turned into a bunch of animals with no control anywhere."

"How will it end?"

"At some point, I suspect, someone will gather up enough men behind him and start cleaning house. Those that resist will be killed, and those that remain alive will be loyal to the man. The problem is, no one is strong enough yet to attempt a takeover. Or, if someone is, we've not heard about him."

Sandra nodded in understanding and then asked, "What's for supper?"

"Beans, unless you have other ideas."

"No, beans are good and we need the protein. I have some crackers in my pack, so it'll have to take the place of bread."

"I'm not worried about food much and we've plenty of water, but I need to know if those men are following us or not."

"What does that mean?"

"It means as soon as I eat, I'm moving down our back trail to see if we're being followed. I think if they're following us, they'll be within ten miles or so."

"It'll be dark and late, so how will you find them?"

"I'll move on foot, with Dolly. She'll be able to smell them, if the wind is right, and I should be able to see their fire. Fires at night show up a long way from any camp, sometimes well over a mile. That's why Tom and I put our fires out after supper and do without until daylight."

"They could do that, I mean, put their fire out."

"Yep, they could, but a large group usually has a fire and they don't worry about attacks because their numbers give them false confidence." I said, and then pulled a bag of dried beans from my pack. As I added them to a pot and poured in water, I continued, "Relax. All I want to do is check our back trail and I have no intentions of starting a fight."

"That's what General Custer said, too."

I laughed, and it felt good. "If it'll make you feel better, I'll take horse and not walk. Besides, I'm not sure I can cover twenty miles on foot before sunup, and I want to be gone by then." I placed the pot on some hot coals of the fire, knowing it would be hours before they were tender.

Midnight found me moving slowly over the ground I'd covered earlier. Dolly loped beside me, her head turning in different directions as she meandered around the trail. My mare was a good horse and in excellent condition, so I knew she'd have no problems covering the ground. As I rode, I wondered if Tom had found Marty or had our recent attack been the result of her maybe meeting some of Patton's men on the return to the farm house. Either was possible, but a large group with a dozer takes time to organize, and I found it hard to believe they'd done the job on short notice. More than likely, she'd not met anyone or even reached the farm before Tom had started after her. The man I tortured entered my mind, but I honestly think he bled to death.

It was near two in the morning before I spotted a flickering light off to the left and moved in that direction. I soon found a small sapling and tied my mare, knowing she'd not wander off far if left untied, but I felt better securing her. If I needed her quickly, I wouldn't have time to look for her. Then calling Dolly, I pulled out the leash and attached it to her collar. Together we moved toward the light, and I slipped the safety to the off position on my shotgun.

CHAPTER 8

I was rather surprised when I neared the flickering flames of the fire, because instead of seeing Patton's men, I saw what looked to be four women sleeping on the ground. Sitting on a log, away from the fire, I saw the form a man, or so it looked to be, and he held a long gun. He knew how to guard and was back in the shadows. The only reason I'd seen him, was he'd move his leg slightly and the movement caught my eye.

I leaned near Dolly's ear and whispered, "Stay."

Slipping the sling on my shotgun over my shoulder, I pulled my knife and moved toward the man in darkness. I knew if I got into something I couldn't handle, Dolly would come with just a yell.

I was thankful for the recent rain, as most of the leaves were wet and wouldn't make much noise as I neared the man. I moved to within ten feet of the guard, straight behind him, and watched him for a few moments. Unlike other guards I'd seen in the past, his head didn't nod or lower, so I knew he was fully awake and watchful. Very slowly he moved his head from side to side, scanning for movement. I moved toward him, moving just inches at a time, and all the while hoping he'd not resist me, so I'd not have to kill him.

When I was right behind him, he must have smelled or felt my presence, because his body began to turn. I threw my left arm around his neck and placed the tip of my knife against his back. Then, in a voice just above a whisper I ordered, "Throw the gun about six feet out. I don't want to kill you, but I will if you don't do as I say."

The gun landed further than six feet and I released the pressure on his throat. It was then he spoke, "John? It's me, Tom."

I immediately recognized his voice, so I released him and asked, "What in the world are you doing traveling with four other people?"

"It's a long story, but Marty didn't run to Patton as we thought. It took me a while, but once the rain stopped I picked up her trail pretty fast, and it led me to an old cabin in the woods."

"So?" I felt my anger returning, because Marty had killed my dogs.

"She'd gone to get her mother and two sisters. Actually, she'd thought her father was still alive, but he'd died while Patton had her at his place. John, would you have seriously preferred I'd killed her?" He turned to face me and in the moonlight I could see he was serious.

"Damn it, my dogs are like family to me and you know it. She had no reason to kill them!"

"I asked her about that, and she said she'd decided the second I'd given her the shotgun to fetch her family. She also said she'd not wanted to kill the dogs, but they were threatening her and she saw no other way to do the job. I believe her."

I knew Newt and Benji were good guard dogs, so she may have been forced to kill them, except that still didn't make it right in my mind. I'd talk to her once we got to a better camp, because this was not the time. Placing my knife back in the sheath I said, "Let's go wake your women and get moving. I've a camp a few miles down the trail."

Tom asked with a concerned tone, "How's Sue?"

I grinned and replied, "I spoke with her before I left camp. I think she's on the mend."

At the fire, I called Dolly to my side and placed a leash back on her. Tom woke the women and when Marty saw me, she lowered her eyes. I didn't feel this was the time or place to bring up my dogs, so I kept my mouth closed, and fought the urge to shoot her ass. I was very angry.

Tom said, "Let's get moving, we've a safer place to go to for a while."

"I've a horse just outside of your camp, so the women can tie their supplies on her. We'll all walk, but it'll be easier since no one will be carrying a load."

Once moving toward my camp, I took point, as Tom brought up the rear. I wanted to know if he'd seen anyone trailing us, but suspected if he had, then he'd not have had a fire. Our conversation would have to wait.

We arrived at camp about an hour after daylight and Tom immediately ran to check on Sue. I noticed Sandra give Marty a look that would kill a normal person. As the women moved to the fire, I walked to my wife and said, "We'll talk about it later, but I'm not happy she's here."

"Why *is* the bitch here, then!" She snapped at me.

"I *said*, we'll talk about it later." I was tired and not in the mood to argue or even talk much. I'd been up all night and now we had a day of travel. I didn't look forward to it at all. I moved to the fire, pulled the coffee pot and filled a cup I'd picked up from the ground. I sat the pot down, but didn't say anything to the women, and made my way to the horse. I pulled the few supplies and placed them on the ground, removed the saddle and blanket. Pulling an old rag from a cargo pocket, I began to wipe my mare down.

Once finished, I walked to our fire, sipped my coffee, and said, "We'll leave in two hours. If you want to eat or rest, do it now. We'll not stop until we get to our next camp."

Tom asked, "At the old Wilkerson place?"

I had started to take a drink from my cup, so I looked over the rim and said, "Yep, and while it's not far, we'll need to establish a hidden camp once there. I want us to move deep into the woods, say four or five miles, and then stop for the night."

Tom didn't reply, because he knew the area I had in mind. It was part of a wide forest and few people lived in the area before the collapse. We'd be as safe there as anyplace else I could think of in the surrounding area.

Two hours later, I stood and stretched, but I was still deep bone tired. I pulled off my cowboy hat, ran my fingers through my hair, and noticed my scalp tingled with fatigue. I moved to the fire, squatted on my heels, and downed a cup of warm coffee.

A few minutes later I stood and said, "Time to move."

Tom, who'd been standing guard, walked to the fire and said, "Let's go, ladies, we have to move. Don't take all day getting ready, either."

The women stood and I said, "We only have four horses, and Sue needs one alone because she's injured. Sandra, you'll have a horse of your own, while the rest, except Marty, can ride off and on. That means one of you will ride double, but at every rest we take I want the new rider move to another horse. Marty will not ride at all today."

I was waiting for Marty to say something, but wisely she kept her mouth shut while giving me a mean look. As I moved toward my horse I felt her glare on my back, only I honestly didn't give a damn.

I'd just pulled my poncho from behind the cantle when Tom neared and asked in a whisper, "What about Marty's shotgun?"

"Who has it?"

"I do."

"Keep it until I decide what to do with her."

Tom shrugged his shoulders and said, "Sounds good to me."

Turning to the group I said, "Let's move, we're wasting time."

Sue, who'd been sitting on a blanket under the shelter said, "I'm well enough to ride today and if I get to feeling faint, I'll let you know, Sandra."

I watched Sandra as she thought for a few minutes and then replied, "I don't guess you can do any more damage riding than we'd do tying you over a horse's back. Only you get to feeling poorly, you let me know and we'll stop."

"As we walk, Tom, we have to talk," I said.

He nodded.

Minutes later, as we moved as a group, Tom and I stepped to the front. I spoke over my shoulder to Sandra, "Move back about a hundred yards and cover our back trail for a bit. Tom and I need to talk a bit."

I waited until the group settled in well with the pace of our walk then asked, "Did you see my place?"

"Yep, went there right after I collected the women. I left them about a half mile from the farm and scouted the place out. Nothing was left of the barn and I counted three bodies in the debris, but they were burned beyond recognition. Then, of all things I saw a dozer in front of the barn and counted ten more bodies. What in the world happened back there?"

I quickly explained and once I'd finished he shook his head before he said, "You're a lucky man. If the leader of that group had been smart, he'd placed men all around the barn and ran the dozer into the windowless side of the barn."

"Yep, then picked us off one at time as we ran from the building, but he didn't."

"Well, I didn't see anyone on the way here and that's good, but the rain might have washed any tracks away."

"I was hoping for as much, but they'll keep looking for us."

Tom stopped walking, gazed into my eyes and asked, "Why?"

"Because we've embarrassed the leader of the group and he has to show them he's able to do what he promises to do, or he'll lose control. No, they'll come, but I'm not sure what we can do the next time."

"Give us a few days at the next camp to organize, and then we'll go to our cache and dig up our supplies."

"Oh, I plan to do that, but right now I'm tired and hungry. Enough talk. I want you to fall back and take Sandra's place on drag and tell her to keep a close eye on our friend Marty as we move."

Tom started to say something, but must have changed his mind. He nodded and stood to the side of the trail to wait for Sandra to meet him. I increased the pace.

A week later we were living in the woods about 200 yards west of the old Wilkerson place. Sue wanted to stay in the house, but it was too well known for me to use. However, we'd taken bits and pieces of wood from the old structure and made us a few shanties, which would do for the time being. Sue was able to walk fairly well, but had a slight limp and occasionally needed medication for pain. Sandra, always the nurse, made sure the leg was exercised each day as they gathered firewood for the night. We'd decided at the last minute not to move further into the woods, mainly because we could take parts of the old house if we needed anything for a shelter.

Over time I'd learned about the others with Marty. Carol, the mother of the women, was a widow and just slightly over fifty. Her black hair was streaked with white and she was fairly quiet when compared to her daughters, but I knew little about her. Of all of us, she was by far the best cook.

Alisa was quiet as well, but a very beautiful woman with deep intelligence, who listened much more than she spoke. I would often catch her deep in thought as someone spoke, so I knew she was attentive. I guessed her age to be in her late thirties.

Of the three, Vickie was outspoken, the youngest, and just slightly plump, if anyone could be called that these days. Actually, she may have been big boned, but she had a cocky attitude that I liked. She never avoided any task given her and she was for sure a team player, but at times she didn't know when to keep her mouth shut. I'd discovered her bubbly personality was even rough for her siblings to accept at times, and I'd ended more than one argument.

I had no problem with an outspoken person, except at times they could cause problems in a camp our size. When people are living in close quarters, it doesn't take much to make tempers flare. In less than a month we'd doubled in population and while that sounds good, it's much harder to hide eight people and feed them than four.

Tom and I had recovered some of our supplies from our hidden cache, but not all, because we might need more in the future. We removed some food items, medical supplies, a few pistols and ammo, but that was it. We'd returned and placed the supplies in my shanty.

I'd had my talk with Marty a few days after we'd finished our new camp, and while she'd delivered a good sermon, I'd believed little of it. Oh, I'm sure she was honest enough with me, but she'd killed my dogs and I could never forgive her for that. I think I wanted to catch her lying to me, but I didn't. I finally ended the conversation with a warning, if she touched my last dog I would literally skin her alive. She knew I meant it and I could see fear in her eyes.

We then issued side arms to each person and Tom gave a good weapons safety course. "If you want to kill something, just point this end at your target and pull the trigger. Never point the business end of any weapon at anyone or anything you don't want to kill. Always keep your finger away from the trigger until you see something that needs killing. Now, since all of you have pistols, let me warn you. The first time I catch one of you playing with it, I'll take it away. A weapon is not a toy, it's used to kill, and while you don't need a gun to kill a person, it makes it whole lot easier than using a knife, club or rock. Any questions?"

"What do I do with this thing? I mean, where do I keep it?" Alisa asked.

"Each of you will get a holster and you're to keep the pistol on you at all times, even when you sleep."

I handed a box of ammo to each woman and said, "Your pistols are all Colt All American 2000's, which is only a fair weapon. There are only seven major parts to this pistol and each magazine holds fifteen rounds. It's a semi-automatic, which means it will fire as fast as you pull the trigger. Now, a lot folks have complained about the quality of the pistol you're holding, but I've discovered if you keep it clean and don't over oil it, it's a reliable enough weapon." Tom and I knew the weapons were of fair quality at best, but we'd purchased a couple dozen a few years back at two hundred dollars a pop and kept them. We'd purchased a few cases of ammo at a discount at the same time, only our budget just wouldn't allow us to purchase a better weapon.

When I made eye contact with the women, I saw serious questions in their eyes, so I continued, "Now, Tom and I will help each of you load a magazine, show you how to operate the safety, and provide you some basic shooting information."

We moved among the woman and began teaching. In less than an hour we'd completed our training and while condensed, we'd covered the major headings.

Vickie, with a grin on her face asked, "When do we get to shoot our pistols?"

I frowned and replied, "We don't have enough ammo to prac-tice with, and I wish we did. Have any of you ever fired a weapon before?"

As expected, Vickie replied, "I used to hunt rabbits and squir-rels with my dad, but it's been a few years. We'd always get a mess of rabbits. Why, one time the two of us shot over twelve rabbits one morning."

I knew Marty had been taught to shoot by her husband and now Vickie admitted she'd done some hunting, so that left only two to be concerned with, Alisa and Carol. I'll have to keep them under a close eye until we need their help, and then I'm not sure how much good they'll do.

CHAPTER 9

The next morning dawned cold, with clouds so low it looked like I could reach up and touch them, but they were dark and that concerned me. I walked into the woods, did my morning toilet, and made my way to the fire.

"Looks like snow," I said sitting on my heels.

Tom laughed and then asked, "When was the last time you saw snow around here?"

I chuckled and replied, "Okay, even if it does snow, it'll not amount to much. I don't know the temperature, but guess it's below freezing."

"I agree. Listen, we need to do a little scouting."

I picked up my cup and poured some coffee as I replied, "You and I are thinking alike. We've been a here a while, and I'd like to know if we've been spotted or if anyone else is in the area."

"Finish your coffee and we'll run a recon. I think the women will be safe enough, don't you? I mean there are six of 'em and I'll leave Dolly with 'em."

"I'll speak with Sandra before we leave and make sure she's got a handle on it. Do you want to take any of the daughters with us? It might help to give one of 'em some experience."

After a dry chuckle, Tom said, "The only one out of the whole group that has any grit that I trust is Vickie. We can take her if you want."

"Okay, Vickie it is. While I talk to Sandra, you give our new troop a briefing of why we are going and what's expected of her. Make damned sure she understands when to shoot and when not to shoot."

"I'll brief her, so don't worry about it."

An hour later we were walking an ever enlarging circle, moving slowly as we looked for any sign of others. So far we'd found nothing, but then Tom stopped and motioned for us to get down. I fell in the grass and saw Vickie do the same. She'd not been a problem yet, at least after I'd told her we were not to talk as we walked. At first I think she thought we'd just stroll down the road talking, picking flowers, and scratching our asses. I'd broke that illusion for her with just the tone of my voice. On a more positive note, the temperature was going up and the threat of snow was gone.

Tom, turned his head and indicated he'd seen movement. I knew we were close to an old timber road that ran parallel to the fence line, but I saw no movement.

Long minutes passed and then I heard a loud curse followed by a laugh. An unknown voice suddenly ordered, "Cut the chatter and laughing! You two keep playing grab ass and I'll see your whiskey ration cut tonight."

"Chill, man, there ain't nobody around but us and we're the meanest bunch of bastards in the state."

"I said shut your damned mouth, Thomas, and I mean now."

I glanced toward the road and saw a long file of men moving away from our position, heading north. Some were wearing parts of military uniforms, but most wore jeans and civilian jackets. I looked at Tom and he motioned his open palm toward me and then motion downward with his hand, indicating he wanted me to wait and not move. Five minutes after the main group passed, a single man passed. I knew right then I was dealing with a prior military unit.

Twenty minutes after the drag man passed, we move to a huge pine tree about two hundred yards away. It worried me that such a large group was operating in the area.

"I must have seen the point man's movement, but I never saw him clearly." Tom said just above a whisper as he shook his head.

"I counted fifteen and you?" I asked.

"Sixteen counting the drag."

"Who were those men?" Vickie asked, keeping her voice low.

"I have no idea." I answered honestly and then continued, "But, we'll treat them like the enemy until we learn different."

"Most were armed with shotguns, crossbows and arrows, and one man even had a compound bow." Tom stretched his legs out in front of him.

"I saw five long guns," I replied.

"Long guns?" Vickie asked.

"Rifles or shotguns."

She gave a sheepish grin and said, "I counted five of them too, but I didn't see any pistols except on two or three."

"What now?" Tom asked, but he knew the answer.

"We hang back and follow them. No need to get close enough to see 'em, we'll stay in the woods and follow their tracks. That many men will be easy to follow."

Vickie started to speak, but didn't, so maybe she was learning. Nonetheless, I knew what she was thinking, only it would have to wait until we found out more about these men.

We moved parallel to their tracks for over five miles, when I noticed about four thin fingers of smoke rising in the distance. Tom must have noticed it as well, because he raised his balled fist to stop us. Then he pointed at himself, motioned the direction of the house, and finally pointed to his eyes. *He's going to scout the house out and wants us to wait,* so I nodded in understanding. He moved forward.

Vickie was kneeling on the ground and not once did she move that I could see. She'd picked up the routine quickly, so all my worry had been for nothing.

A few minutes later, Tom returned and pointed back down our trail. I took point and covered about a half mile before I angled into the woods to our right and finally stopped under a large post oak tree. We all knelt.

"What did you find?" I asked.

"Huge compound, with a lot of men and women, and even guard towers. It's not a place I'd want to try to get into or out of. I even saw a few machine guns, old M-60's, mounted on two of the towers and one sandbagged bunker near the gate. One joker was walking around with what looked to be a flamethrower, so I backed off."

I thought for a few minutes and then said, "It could be an old reserve or guard unit that stuck together for safety after the fall. If so, the leader is likely a full colonel with a lot of experience in commanding a combat unit in the field. I don't like this, not at all." I scratched the side of my face and then asked, "Did you see a flag flying?" Hoping the unit still supported 'Old Glory.'

"Not that I saw, but to be honest I didn't stay there gawking at the place very long. What now?"

"I'm not sure, so let me think about this on the way back to camp." I was concerned, but not overly shocked. I just never suspected someone had a base camp this close to us, and I felt strongly inclined to move our current camp.

As we moved the wind picked up and a light rain began to fall. Tom and I pulled out ponchos, but Vickie didn't move.

Tom asked as he turned to her, "Don't you have rain gear?"

"No, not a thing. Hell, I didn't have anything where we were living, but I'm okay."

Tom handed his poncho to her and said, "Here, use mine." Vickie hesitated, so he added, "I'll be alright, because I have my hoodie."

As soon as she took the garment, Tom reached into his pack and pulled out a dark green wool hoodie, that would not just keep him dry, it would also keep him warm. Wool insulates even when wet, so we both carried one in our pack.

One thing about Tom, he was a true Southern gentleman most of the time, unless he was mad about something; then he was a different man. I'd once attended an awards program where he'd been presented a silver star for some heroic act he'd performed in Iraq during a combat tour and when I later asked him about it, he'd simply replied, "Those Iraqi's made me mad."

Lightning filled the air and thunder cracked sharply as we cautiously made our way back to camp. The temperature dropped a bit and I could see each breath I took. I glanced at the other two, looking for symptoms of hypothermia, only they looked fine. Vickie was tired, of course, but not one complaint from her. *You'll do and I'm glad to have you as part of our team*, I thought and then my mind moved to the group we'd just seen. *We need to move camp and do it quickly.*

Once back at camp, I pulled the women near as Tom pulled guard. I explained what we'd found on the recon and that we needed to move out of the area. The only problem that concerned me was where were we to go? So, I asked the women and waited.

"We want to stay in the woods, if we can." Sandra added, as soon as I'd finished speaking.

Carol frowned and said, "My old place is in the woods, but I'm not sure how safe it is."

Sue suddenly grinned and said, "How about Jackson?"

Alisa shook her head and said brusquely, "Sue, do you know how stupid what you just said sounds? Jackson? Do you really want to live in Jackson with no police? Hell, I wouldn't live there with the police."

Sue lowered her head. "I'm tired of living like an animal in the woods. We can make peace with people and stop the killing. I think it'd work."

"If we moved to Jackson, you wouldn't have to worry about living anywhere for very long." I said, and then quickly asked, "Any other ideas?"

"Maybe those men you saw were friendly." Sue said as she raised her head and smiled.

"And," Vicki said, he eyes narrowed in anger, "maybe you're a damned fool! I saw those guys and they were hard looking men. I have no doubt in my mind they're killers, just by the way they moved. They'd kill John and Tom, and then use us for sport! I think we—"

To defuse the situation I said, "That's enough! We can't risk contact with them and it's not likely they're friendly anyway. Since things ended we've been alone, and I want to stay that way if we can. Small groups can move, hide, and be fed easier than large groups."

Sue crossed her legs and arms, glared at Vicki, so I added, "Look, I don't care if all of you like each other or not. However, I suggest very strongly that each of you try to avoid arguments in future, because we must be able to depend on each other or survival isn't possible. And the first serious problem I have, both parties will be banished, understood?"

Sue stood, and in the heat of anger asked, "You'd banish people over an argument? I thought we had the *right* to argue! This *is* America, right? I *know* my rights!"

Dolly, not liking the tone of Sue's voice, growled.

I gave a light smile at her stupidity, because this woman needed to wake up and smell the horse apples scattered all around us. "No, this is *not* America, or at least as we remember our country! We have *no* government, so *you* have *no* rights." I felt my anger growing so I continued, "*I am the leader* and what I say goes, or you can leave right this minute."

I knew if she left, Tom would go with her, so I was as surprised as her at my words. I didn't care if Sue left, and took her liberal attitude with her, but Tom I needed. But, I'd already spoken, so I waited.

After many long minutes she sat in the dirt and lowered her head.

I wasn't sure what to say next, so I did like I had in the military, I issued an order. "Let's get all our gear packed, horses ready to go, and get some food in us. We're leaving today."

Five hours of hard riding placed us a little over ten miles. While the trip had been rough, we'd not moved as quickly as I'd have liked due to the shortage of horses. *Starting tomorrow, the horses will carry our loads and all of us will walk,* I thought while dismounting in a light drizzle. Turning to Tom, I said, "Circle this place and let me know what you find. We'll hold off on a fire or food until you get back."

"I'm cold now." Sue said, and glared at me.

"Honey," Tom said, "John is right. We can't have a fire, until I make sure this place is safe. So take your pretty little butt and sit under a tree until I get back."

Tom pulled his horse to the left and disappeared into the drizzle, while Sue stomped off in the direction of a huge oak tree. I had a silent chuckle and then pulled the saddle from my horse.

Ten minutes later, Tom returned, shook his head and said, "Not good. I spotted movement and followed trail for a bit. About a half a mile north is a house with a group of men moving in and out. I have no idea how many are there, but more than we can handle."

I turned to the women, all of which were now under the oak with Sue and said, "Two hour break for the horses, then we'll load our supplies and start moving, only this time we'll walk."

"Walk? Why do we need to walk when we have horses?" Sue asked as she stood with her hands on her hips.

Annoyed by her question, I managed to answer with an even tone, "Because we can't keep riding double on the horses. If we walk we'll be able to cover more ground and right now we need more distance from our last camp."

It was then I saw movement from the corner of my left eye and when I turned I was able to see a man moving in the brush. I bent down, as to pick up my saddle, and in just above a whisper I said to Tom, "Movement."

Tom walked toward the women and didn't appear to have heard my warning, but I knew he had. He was moving to a better firing position. As he approached, Sue turned and started moving away from the tree. I wanted to warn her not to move, but there was nothing I could do.

From the brush behind me there sounded a rifle shot and Sue collapsed in the mud at her feet, unmoving. I swung around and fired my shotgun, heard a scream from the brush and then rushed into the trees. The area was suddenly alive with rounds ricocheting from rocks and trees, as the air filled with the loud booms of shotguns, sharp cracks of rifles, and lesser pops of pistols. I heard screams of pain and yells as orders were given from the brush. And then, it grew quiet.

I guess the whole thing had lasted less than five minutes, but combat was like that at times, and it was usually after a battle that fear struck me hard. Knowing the women would be scared and unsure what to do next, I swallowed my fear and yelled, "Stay where you are until I check things out."

I quickly circled our temporary camp and saw bloody tracks of two men moving away from us, four bodies in the brush and one man yet alive. He'd taken a round about seven inches above his belly button, so he wasn't a threat. I disarmed him and then moved to the oak where I'd last seen the women. Tom was on his knees beside Sue, crying hard, so I knew she'd been killed. I spotted Marty's body near the tree and didn't bother to check her pulse, she'd taken a round in the center of her face. I waited a second for my nerves to settle and then called out, "Everyone come to the oak where you were when the shooting started."

Sandra was the first to walk from the trees, with Dolly at her side, and she smiled at me briefly when she saw I was safe. Then, Alisa and Vickie came, both in tears.

"Where's Carol?" Sandra asked as the two neared.

Vickie, upset, replied, "She was hit in the chest and she's in the woods. W... we tried to move her, but she's too heavy."

"You all stay here, while Sandra and I check her out. Tom lost his wife, so I need all of you to be ready to fight in case those men return. Dolly, stay."

Vickie nodded in understanding, but Alisa was still crying when we left.

I followed the trail for about 100 feet and found Carol lying on her back. She'd taken a slug from what looked like a 30.06 in the chest and was bleed copiously. Sandra took one look, gazed into my eyes and shook her head. I knew then the injury was just too severe for us to bother with, so I said, "Medicate her."

"It won't do any good, because I can't stop the bleeding."

"I guess I didn't say what I meant, over medicate her. We can't help her and I'll not see her put through hours of pain just to die in the end. End this, so we can move." I realized I sounded cold, but I had the safety of others to consider.

Sandra opened her medical bag, removed the medication bottle and a hypodermic needle. A few minutes later, she stood and met my eyes. She was crying, but not making a sound, and I knew what she'd just done was hurting her. I pulled her into my arms and whispered, "Baby, we did the right thing. She would have died anyway and we need to move. Do you understand?"

She nodded and I heard a weak, "Y... yes, let's move."

Once back at the tree, I took Vickie with me and gathered up the weapons and ammo dropped by the dead men, and discovered the injured man dead. Most of the ambushers carried shotguns, so we kept them, but one had carried a compound bow with about two dozen arrows. I placed it behind my saddle and tied it securely.

Tom was standing now, his face streaked with tears, and while I felt his pain, we had to move. "Tom, we need to move and do it now. Are you okay?"

He nodded, but I knew he'd be useless on point or walking drag, so I turned to Vickie and said, "You cover our rear. I need you to stay about a 100 feet behind us and when we stop, you stop. As we move, check the sides of our trail and at times our rear. If you see anything, try to move quickly to the main group. If you can't or don't have time to move, shoot and we'll get the idea quickly enough." I then handed her one of the shotguns taken from the dead men, along with a vest full of shells.

"Tom, we need to move. You understand that, right?" I asked.

"I'll move."

"Aren't we going to bury our dead?" Alisa asked as she wiped the tears from her cheeks.

I was growing tired of having to explain everything to the new women, so I replied, "No, we are *not* going to bury any of our dead. In a few minutes those men will be back with others, likely a larger group, and I'd like to be far away from here by then. Now, there has been enough chatter, so let's move people!"

Darkness found us still moving and I guided the group away from any lights I could see, but there were not many. I couldn't trust anyone, so I avoided everyone. At one point, I moved back beside Tom and asked in a low voice, "You doing okay?"

"No, not really. You'd figure a tough old war dog like me would be used to death, but the death of a loved one is difficult."

"Tom," I said, feeling his grief, "if you need to talk later this evening, I'm here for you, buddy."

He gazed into my eyes and said, "I know that, only I'll be okay."

I broke eye contact and moved to the point position once again.

Near dawn I moved into some heavy pines and oaks, where I said, "We'll rest here for five hours, then move again. I want two people on guard at all times. We'll all pull two hour shifts and since there are only five of us, I'll pull the first shift with Tom, and I'll help cover the last shift. I want the changes after that to be Sandra and Alisa, then Vickie and I will cover the last hour. If there are no questions, no fire and if you want to eat, eat it cold, and then get some rest."

I was concerned about not having a fire, because it was per-fect weather for hypothermia, between 35 and 40 degrees and still drizzling rain. I sat beside Sandra under a large oak and pulled a pair of dry socks from my pack.

"Lawdy, I miss a good hot bath." Sandra said, and then gig-gled.

I slipped a sock on my right foot and pulled her close as I said, "Hopefully, God willing, there will come a day in the not too distant future you can have that bath."

"I hope so, but rough days are still in front of us. Have you given thought to where we are heading?"

"Right now any direction is good, because we may have men on our back trail. I'm not certain of that, but I suspect we do. Those men who ambushed us yesterday and Patton's men may not be able to follow our tracks in the rain, but both are looking for us."

I released her and slipped the other sock on my left foot and placed both boots on. As I laced them, she said, "Who would have thought America would turn into a place like this? I mean, we were the world leader in everything, but now we're a country of blood-thirsty animals."

"We're about as low as people who can communicate can get right now, except most of us are simply attempting to survive. Most kill others out of fear, because it's safer to kill people you don't know than to let them live. Now, let me get to where I'll pull guard, because I don't like spending time here."

Sandra leaned forward and kissed me on the cheek. Pulling back she said, "John, be careful, and remember I love you."

I stood, gave her a tired smile and said, "I love you too, now you try to get some sleep if you can." Seeing her smile, I moved toward Tom.

Tom was under a large Pine tree and alert, which was good to see.

I sat beside him and asked, "Do you know this area?"

"Hunted it a few years back, oh, maybe five years ago. From what I remember, there aren't many people here."

"I'm sorry about Sue. I know we argued, but I liked her a great deal."

He gave a dry chuckle and his eyes watered as he said, "She just never understood why people could not sit down and discuss things in a rational manner until they reached a happy agreement. Sue saw the good in everything and never really had a chance once the end came, only I think she knew she'd not survive. Her and I argued all the time about things, but I loved her, John."

His voice had started strong, but gradually lost its power as he spoke until at the end I could barely hear him. I patted him on the shoulder and said, "I'm moving to the other side. You see or hear anything, let me know."

The time passed uneventful and five hours later we were moving once more.

Again we traveled all night, and near dawn the next day, I moved deeply into some trees, found a small clearing and said, "Tom, check around us and take Alisa with you. We'll have a cold camp until you get back." They both moved without a word.

It was still drizzling rain and I prayed we had no river or creeks to cross, because they'd be swollen by now and we'd be trapped on this side. I'd just pulled my canteen from my horse when a man I didn't know stepped into our clearing. Dolly jerked the leash in Sandra's hand and started growling.

CHAPTER 10

He was thin, like most of us, about six feet tall and dark eyes. While his clothing was a mixture of military and civilian, he wore an old feedlot ball cap on his head. I noticed a shotgun hanging loosely from his left shoulder by a strap.

"If you move, I'll kill you." Vickie said with narrow eyes, and I saw the shotgun in her hands.

Raising both hands slowly, the man said, "I'm no threat to you. I'm lookin' for my dog is all, so go easy with that scattergun."

I pulled my pistol and commanded, "Move to the log and have a seat. Vickie, you take his shotgun as soon as he's on the log."

As soon as the man was disarmed, he turned to me and asked, "What unit were you with?"

"What makes you think I'm prior military?"

He chuckled and replied, "I been watching y'all since you walked in here and I know military when I see it. My names, Cotton, James Cotton and I'm a retired E-9. Spent my whole career in the 82nd Airborne. I served in Vietnam near the end of the war and Desert Storm."

I didn't know or trust the man, so I replied, "Well, good for you, Mr. Cotton."

"You're a tight lipped man, I see, and that's good. So, now you have me, what'll you do next?"

"Maybe shoot you."

"No you won't, or I don't think you will, not once we talk."

"Keep quiet."

Dolly growled a warning.

"Okay, but your man and the lady with him will be back in a few minutes. They'll tell you what they found. They found a farmhouse, it's mine, and it's flying 'Old Glory' from a flagpole in my front yard. Listen to me son, I'm a patriot and love this country."

I flipped the safety off my shotgun and said, "Shut your mouth."

Dolly stood waiting my command.

Cotton smiled, but said nothing.

Tom walked into the clearing glanced at Cotton and said, "We've a farmhouse near, it's flying our flag and a U.S. Army flag, but I didn't see anyone around."

"That's because I'm here, Tom." Cotton said and then broke out laughing.

Tom stared at the man hard for a few minutes and then asked, "Top?"

Still smiling, Cotton nodded and said, "It's me, son. How have you been? I'm glad you're still alive, but we need to talk when we get a chance." He then glanced at me.

"Do you know this man, Tom?" I asked.

"I spent part of Desert Storm with 'em, and he was our top sergeant. He's a good man and no threat to us."

I shrugged my shoulders and then said, "Give Top back his shotgun, Vickie."

Looking at Dolly, who was sitting and watching him closely, Cotton said, "Uh, would you do something about your dog? I don't think she likes me much."

"Dolly, come." As soon as she was at my side I patted her head and said, "It's okay, girl."

Cotton took the gun from Vickie and then said, "I'm just an old man now, not a top sergeant. Well, not like I was before anyway."

I met his eyes and said, "Once a top sergeant, always a top sergeant."

Cotton lowered his head, but didn't say anything. I suspected he was remembering his days as the top enlisted man in the unit and I respected him, because I knew exactly the kind of cloth he was cut from and would be until his death.

"Top, can we go to your place or do you want to talk out here?" Tom asked.

Raising his head, Top said, "My place. These ladies can have a bath, eat some hot food and sleep in a warm bed."

"How many others live with you?" I asked.

Standing, Top said, "Since Angela died, it's just me and Jesus, son. However, I'm rarely alone and I'll explain all of this later."

As we moved toward the farm, the women grew excited about a hot bath, food and sleeping in a real bed. The noise got to the point Top commanded, "That's enough chatter! We don't have any idea who we share these woods with right now. The next woman who opens her mouth before we get inside my place will not get a bath today."

I moved up beside Top and said, "We might have some men on our tails."

He waved his hand as if it meant nothing and then asked, "Are there more than a thousand of 'em?"

"Closer to fifty or so."

"Don't worry about 'em then. Now, when you open the gate at the fence that goes around my house, do not wander off the walkway approaching the porch. There are mines in the front yard, and I have an alarm system that I can never remember the code for, but it's loud. I have two big mix-breed dogs in the back-yard, but I'm sure they'll be no problem for your Dolly."

I saw the American flag flying on the flagpole and gave it a salute, as did Tom. Sandra gave me a look of pride, and I think she felt the deep love I still have for this great nation.

We walked into the house and the living-room looked like an armory, with ammo stacked in boxes and weapons mounted in a dozen display cases.

"Y'all follow me back to the kitchen and I'll warm up some coffee."

The kitchen table was huge, about twenty feet long, and there were a good dozen chairs. The second thing I noticed was a shortwave radio and clock on a counter-top. Top caught me looking at the radio and said, "It works and I use it all the time. My power comes from solar panels on the roof and generate enough juice to even have lights, but I don't use 'em much. Now, y'all take a seat."

Tom sat and asked, "Who do you talk with on the radio?"

"Friends of mine, but we'll get to that in a minute." Top moved to an electric coffee pot and turned it on.

After we were all seated, Top said, "I communicate with the local patriot forces in the area each evening at 1800. I can contact them anytime, but I'm not to do that unless I have an emergency."

"Patriot forces, who's that?" Sandra asked.

Dolly'd been smelling boxes and containers, so I motioned with my hand for her to sit, which she did instantly.

"Men and women, most are veteran's of one war or another, who have gathered together to take this country back. We've members from all branches of the services, including airborne, special forces and Seals. We're mostly young men and women, however some are older than me, but the thing to remember is, we're an organized group of about two thousand."

Tom gave a low whistle and said, "That's a lot of folks."

Top grinned and said, "I'm the Command Sergeant Major, we have a commander, executive officer, and all the rest. We've even establish a table of allowances for supplies and such. If you didn't know better, you'd think we were a military unit."

"How'd this commander get his position?"

"Frank's a retired airborne infantry brigadier general with three combat tours in Iraq and Afghanistan, so we thought he had the most experience for the job. The exec is a retired special forces light colonel, and he got the job because no one carried more rank than him while on active duty, except Frank. All of our positions are based on the individual's prior military rank and experience. Now, keep in mind we're scattered to the four winds most of the time, but we do gather now and then to clean the area of riffraff."

"What about supplies, gear and fuel, Top?" I asked.

He gave a cackle and said, "When the local reserve unit was told to secure all supplies and leave, the unit didn't do that and stayed together. Most of the supplies are stored in underground storage bunkers, but our supply commander has the keys."

"Fuel?" Tom asked.

"We don't have a great deal of fuel, but some. We have some tanks and other heavies, including two rescue choppers that belonged to the Air Force, but we've never moved any of them. Once a month we start each one, check the idiot boxes on the consoles and then shut 'em down."

"Is this area safe?" Sandra asked looking over the rim of her coffee cup.

Top's eyes narrowed as he said, "It was until a couple of weeks ago, when we spotted what I think was another military unit scouting our lands."

"What makes you think it was a military unit?" I asked.

"They moved like a military unit, with a man walking point and one on drag, and they didn't bunch up like civilians do when on patrol. I heard no talking and all communications was done using their hands."

"What kind of weapons did they carry?"

"All weapons were military and I even spotted LAW and M-60 machine gun in the group, which worried me, because that means they're being well supplied from some place."

"Maybe one of the pentagon generals maintained control of a large group. Or is that even possible?" Sandra asked.

"Anything is possible, but when things went to hell right after the fall, people scattered just so they could find enough to eat. Nobody lives in large cities or towns now, because they'd starve to death. I don't think there is a huge group living anywhere," Tom said, glanced around the table and then asked, "Right?"

Top replied, "I doubt the cities are populated, but it's possible to a limited extent."

"I don't see it. There is no food in the cities anymore, so folks have moved to the country. Top, do you think those men you saw noticed anything?"

"No, I don't, but only because they didn't come close enough. About three miles from my farm they turned north. Our special forces guys trailed them that day, the remainder of the night, and returned saying the group had finally turned east."

Unexpectedly the radio erupted, "Falcon 6, Falcon actual. Falcon 6, Falcon Actual."

Top moved quickly to the radio, picked up the microphone and replied, "Actual, this is six, over." Then, turning to the women, he smiled and said, "Actual is the general."

"Six, we're under attack from a large unknown force." Gun shots could be heard over the radio and then, "We may have to escape and evade in your direction, copy?"

"Roger, copy." Top said, and then shook his head as he looked around the room. While I could see his concern, there was nothing we could do to help.

"Six, move to the trail and help those you can moving your way. I suspect—". A loud explosion filled the speaker.

"Actual, this is Six, over." Top repeated numerous times, but there was no response. Placing the microphone on the counter, Top ordered, "Grab your gear, and I want everyone to follow me! Let's move people, lives may depend on how quickly we get to the trail."

All of us followed the man out the door, down the sidewalk and into the woods. On the way out the door, Top grabbed his shotgun, a vest full of shells, and his boonie hat. Now he fumbled to don the gear as he ran full speed, down a meandering trail that reminded me of a cow path.

After we'd covered about a mile, Top stopped on a hill and I could see a much wider trail winding through the woods below. In a voice near a whisper he said, "Tom, you and I will move to the side of the trail and pull anyone off who is wounded. But, before you move from your cover beside the path, wait for my okay, because it might be a bad guy. Understand?"

"Sure, Top, you'll clear 'em and I'll pull 'em from the trail."

From the strain showing on Top's face, I began to wonder if coming with the man had been a good idea from the start. If a force of over two thousand could be wiped out, I didn't want any group large enough to do that job on my ass. Only he said most of the men were scattered, so I'd have to wait to see how many had just been killed.

Turning to the rest of us, Top ordered, "Spread out and provide security as we assist the wounded. No shooting unless I fire first." Then, patting Tom on the shoulder he said, "Let's move to the trail."

Long minutes passed before I spotted movement on the trail. I flipped the safety off on my shotgun and waited. I spotted three men moving toward us. Two of the men were supporting an injured man in the middle and the injured man's head was hanging loosely. He was covered with blood and I could hear him moaning with pain as they neared.

"Stop!" I heard Top call out.

"That you, top sergeant?" The man on the left asked as his rifle came up.

"Williams, stop and I'll send a man to you."

Tom moved from the brush and approached the three in the road. I wasn't able to make out what was being said, but soon the small group entered the thicket. Tom moved back to the road, picked up two handfuls of dirt and slowly sprinkled it on the boot tracks. Within a few seconds the trail was clean, but only the last fifty feet or so.

Top and Tom soon walked toward us and I noticed the three from the road were with them. Lowering the injured man on his back, Tom said, "Sandra, take a look at this man and let me know his medical condition. "

"Barnes," Top said, "are you and Jones injured?"

Sandra moved to the injured man's side and started her examination.

"Not a scratch on either of us, but don't expect anyone else to come down this trail. The attack was fast and brutal, and over in just minutes. If the three of us hadn't been near the barn when it happened, we'd not be here right now."

The one I now knew as Jones said, "I don't think the attack took more than five minutes and from what I saw there were no survivors, except us."

"How'd Tompkins get hit?"

"We'd just reached the woods when he went down from rifle fire. So they know some of us got away."

"I covered the tracks and blood back a ways, Top, but I couldn't cover it all." Tom added, and I could see concern in his eyes. He knew as I did that an experienced tracker would find where they left the road and even this very spot. Most civilians don't understand that even covering tracks leaves signs they've been doctored to an experienced eye.

Sandra looked up, shook her head and said, "This man is dead. It looks like he bled to death or maybe had a weak heart."

"Damn!" Top swore and then added, "Let's get back to my farm and decide our next move, but I suspect we don't have much time. I think the attackers are already on the blood trail."

"Okay," Top said, "Barnes, I want you and Jones to leave within the next few minutes. I need the two of you to locate Willy Williams and let him know what's happened. I want him and his men to find out who the attackers were. Tell Willy to try and locate a main staging area or camp, because it's payback time."

"Come on, Jones," Barnes said, "let's go now."

"What about us, Top?" Tom asked as soon as the two men left.

"We're going to gather up some ammo, water, and other gear and move to my safe house. Follow me back to the farm and I'll show y'all what needs to be taken with us. When we leave, I'll wire the house to explode if anyone comes in without the proper password for my security system. There is no way we can fight off the number of men that wiped out the general and his staff."

Once we followed him to the farm and into the room, he said, "All that stuff on the left wall goes, because it's additional food, water, and medical supplies. The ammo on the north wall will also go. Other than that, we'll leave it, because the safe house is pretty well stocked. I never leave food or ammo for anyone."

I picked up a crate of ammo and said, "Lead the way Top, I'm right behind you."

Picking up two huge boxes of MRE rations, Top said, "Follow me and don't step off the trail for any reason. It's mined and I have traps all over the place. If we start taking gunfire, fall straight down, because the sides of the trail might just kill you."

As we moved down the trail about twenty minutes later, I heard an explosion and looking back, I saw a huge fireball rolling toward the sky. *Guess they were close to our asses when we left,* I thought.

CHAPTER 11

The safe house of Top's really wasn't a house at all, but rather a cave with a narrow entrance that led into a huge cavern. I was surprised at all the gear and crates of all sizes lining the walls. However, the place was as large as house and once we were all inside, Top moved a little switch on the side of the wall and a steel door on rails closed to block the entrance.

He flicked another switch and lights came on. Grinning he said, "Some of the boys from an Air Force civil engineering squadron, Prime Beef they call themselves, did the electrics for me and it's powered by batteries. The batteries are charged during the day by the sun. I'm most likely the only man around with a solar powered cave."

"Why a cave? Looks to me like you're trapped in here." Sandra said.

Top laughed and replied, "Not at all. See, if you follow the cave back far enough it leads out, but on top of this hill. I have the exit well camouflaged and booby trapped, so that end is safe. The steel door in front will protect us against most fire, except maybe a LAW or tank cannon. Small arms won't even dent it."

Tom smiled and said, "This thing would protect you from just about everything. I love it, but the best part is, it's comfortable all year round and doesn't need heating or cooling."

"Yep, even if an atomic bomb went off in Jackson, I'd be safe from the fallout, because there is over 150 feet of soil over this cavern. Of course, solar flares and such won't bother me either, and I have gas masks with a complete chemical/biological suits if they attempt to flush us out with chemical or biological gases."

Vickie, who'd been quiet the last few days, asked, "Do you have more than one of those chemical get ups? I mean in a size that would fit a woman?"

Top chuckled and then said, "I have plenty, so don't worry your pretty head. Listen, we could live in this place for at least five years, if we really had to do the job, but I think we'd end up killing each other way before that time. It's an excellent command bunker and that's really what it was designed to do."

Moving to a radio sitting on a table, Top said, "The antenna is in a huge pine on top of this cave and it's super hard to spot, even when you know where to look. Let me see if I can reach anyone." He turned the radio on.

Picking up the microphone, he said, "All stations, all stations, this is six over." He glanced at his watch and I knew he was earlier than he usually checked in with others.

"Six, this is Bravo one, over."

"Go ahead, Bravo."

"Six, we have reports of Falcon six being overran and destroyed, copy?"

"Roger, copy, what's the status of Falcon Six Actual?"

"KIA, Kilo India Alpha, and recon found no WIA, repeat no Whiskey India Alpha, over. All KIA and accounted for."

"Have Whiskey Whiskey doing a recon at this time. Will advise on results. Notify all units to move to safe locations, over."

"Copy move to safe locations. Will do immediately. Watch your ass, Top. Bravo one, out."

"Roger that, Bravo, out."

Turning to us, Top said, "For those of you who don't speak military, the commander and his entire staff have been killed, with no wounded left alive. That means the men who attacked killed every man there. I informed the radio operator that Captain Willy Williams is doing a recon on the site and will advise everyone on what he finds. Willy is a prior green beanie, so he's good and knows his stuff. He has a number of combat tours under his belt too, which helps."

Tom sat on a crate and asked, "What now?"

Meeting Tom's eyes, Top replied, "Now we wait while we gather information about the attackers. Once we have enough intelligence to make a decision, we'll decide what to do at that point. In the mean time, eat, sleep and get some rest, because this will take a couple of days."

Sandra gave me a weak smile as we moved to one of the walls of the cave and sat in the dirt. There were chairs near a table, but I'd given them no thought.

"Are you doin' okay?" She asked.

"Pretty much, but not sure if joining these folks is the right thing to do or not."

She gazed into my eyes and replied "They're veterans who still fly our flag, they're fighting to regain control of at least this part of the country and besides, I'm not sure how much longer we could have made it on our own."

"Well," I chuckled, "I understand the lingo and how things are done in this group. What worries me is we've joined a group, or tribe, as my old college professor discussed once. He predicted if the United States as we knew it was ever busted up as a sovereign nation, the survivors would group together in tribes for survival."

"Interesting, because that's exactly what has happened. I think it's easier for a tribe to survive than loners. Tribes can send men out to scout, gather food, and guard the village, while loners can't do all of that at the same time. Did he say what would happen once the tribes were formed?"

"Uh-huh, he said eventually we'd be engaged in wars to see which tribe was the strongest. We'd be almost like the red man was before the first white men came. Each tribe would lay claim to certain land and if others trespassed, they'd be killed." Dolly moved to my side and placed her head in my lap. I started scratching her ears.

"Well, it sounds like Top and his men have a vast area they claim as home."

"I don't think this attack was over land boundaries. Most likely, the attackers did the job for more ammo, food, medical supplies and equipment. Or, just to remove a threat."

"But, why would one military styled tribe attack another, if you share the same beliefs?"

"Well, we may not share the same beliefs. Listen, just because the attackers were a prior military unit, maybe, doesn't mean they feel any sense of loyalty to the old United States. Hell, it could be their commander wants to be the only real power in the local area. He may actually picture himself as a king or dictator or something. I don't have a clue."

"We can always leave."

I put my arm around her and pulled her close before I replied, "Baby, I want you safe, and the attack on our home not long ago showed that Tom and I can't do the job. Eventually one of us will be killed or wounded and there is no way one man could protect all of us now."

"We women can fight."

"Sure you can and have proven it, but y'all lack the combat experience that Tom and I have. Experience is the main difference, and often that's all that will keep a person alive in combat. Tom trusts Top and I think his trust is well placed."

Suddenly tired, I said, "I'm going to take a short nap. Wake me at supper time."

Sandra laughed and replied, "It's good to know some things just never change."

Two days later, about an hour before daylight, Top walked from the cave to where I was sitting on a rock pulling my shift of guard. He sat beside me. Dolly raised her head, but didn't growl or even move. She then lowered her chin to my right foot.

I glanced at the man and asked, "What's on your mind, Top?"

"Just got off the radio with Willy and what he found has me worried."

"Did he find a big base camp for men in the group he followed?"

"Well, no, it's not that. The estimated size of the group is less than ours, but it seems he moved in pretty close and spotted three individual's dressed in complete uniforms. It was night and at first he was unable to get a good look at 'em. Eventually one of the men moved near a lighted window and he was able to make it out clearly enough."

Must be some men who have access to some old military uniforms, I thought, but asked, "Are you going to make me keep guessing or tell me what he saw?"

Top gazed into my eyes and said, "Willy swears he saw Russian uniforms, and the language spoken was Russian, too. It has me worried. I surely hope the Russian's haven't invaded us."

"How does he know they were speaking Russian?"

"He speaks the language fluently. All army special forces personnel were required to speak at least one additional language, but it wasn't unusual to have a man that spoke three or more. According to Willy the Russians were complaining about the crudeness of the base camp, poor food, no women and the lack of vodka. Then, one of the men said something like he had to check his men for the night."

I thought for a moment and then asked, "Was he able to determine their rank?"

"Company grade officers. One was a captain and the other was a lieutenant, but neither were elite forces and both wore infantry insignia."

"Well, the way I see it is, those two either have Russian troops to oversee or they're part of an advisory unit sent here to assist someone, but why?"

"We know that the men who attacked the general used AK-47s and a few carried SKS assault rifles. Willy confirm that when he trailed them."

"How far away are these guys from us right now?"

Top thought and then said, "I'd say pretty close to twenty miles north by east."

"So, what are we going to do about this?"

"I want you, Tom, and a couple of your women to move near the base camp. If possible, try to get one of the girls to draw out a single soldier, which may be out of the question. I'm sure with all the killing going around, lone soldiers don't take strolls down country lanes in Mississippi right now."

"If we can't isolate one?"

"Try to capture one if you can do the job and if that proves too difficult, set a number of booby-traps and then get out. Oh, and leave your dog here. I want her with us, because she may give us our first warning things are about to hit the fan."

"I don't have any problems with my orders, but why don't we just attack 'em in mass and wipe 'em all out?"

"That's being considered as we speak, but I think the boss is wondering what other arms the Russians have given this unit. If they have small arms, why not some bigger stuff too, unless the Russians are adviser's only. Could be the Russians are simply checking the political water, so to speak, to see if they can influence one unit by indirect and direct assistance. We need a hell of a lot of intelligence before we can risk an open attack."

"When do we leave?"

"As soon as you get what you think you might need from our supplies and gather up your troops. I've indicated on a map your target and gone over it with Tom already. Watch your asses out there, because they'd love to get their hands on one of you. I'll take over guarding now."

I started to reply, but changed my mind and nodded in understanding. I then made my way inside the cave.

Two hours later we were moving slowly down an old logging road when a sudden crack of thunder almost made me jump out of my skin. I glanced up and saw dark clouds circling overhead and knew we were in for rain. Thanks to Top and his supplies, we wore real military camouflage face paint and I knew it'd not wash off in the rain. Hell, it was hard enough to get off when you wanted to remove it in a shower.

I was navigating using our compass as Tom counted our steps. Behind us I had Vickie loaded down with a week of MRE's for us and extra ammo, while Alisa brought up the rear. As far as I was concerned, Alisa was unproven, but we all have to start sometime and this was as good a time as any. During our walk away from the cave, I'd warned her that it was very likely there'd be no talking the entire time we were on patrol, but if there was, it'd be at a whisper. Each of us carried a 12 gauge pump shotgun and sidearms. Tom also had his deer rifle with scope slung over his shoulder by a sling.

I had a weapon that was lightweight and silent along as well, the compound bow I'd taken from one of the men when Carol and Sue had been killed. I carried it on my backpack, but if I needed it in a hurry, I only had to remove two "D" rings. The arrows I carried in a pouch dangling from my web belt. Compound bows are good weapons if a sentry needs to be taken out quietly or when hunting for food. There are obviously more places it can be used effectively, but I'd use it where it would offer me a safe way to kill silently.

The first raindrops had just hit my face, when Tom abruptly stopped me and cupped his hand behind his ear. I listened, but heard nothing. I shook my head to indicate that I heard nothing. He stood still for a minute, then motioned for all of us to leave the road and move into the bushes that were thick on both sides. Once in position, I slipped my safety off and listened intently for any sound. Finally, I heard a noise and it sounded like a big truck, maybe a deuce and a half. I glanced at Tom and he shrugged.

A two stroke motorcycle was riding point on a convoy that was larger than I'd suspected. Anything that required gasoline was rare and to see a good dozen or more big trucks confused the hell out of me. Where in the world was all the gas coming from?

The trucks were moving toward Top and bunch, but that meant little, because I had no idea of their actual destination. I tried to spot uniforms, but the sides of the trucks were down against the rain. The motorcycle rider was dressed in an olive drab rain-suit, which told me nothing.

Almost a hundred feet from us I watched as one of the trucks began to slide in the mud and then it stopped, its right front tire in a ditch. I heard loud yelling, the passenger door opened, and out stepped a man in a uniform I'd only seen in books or military pamphlets—Russian. The man's insignia indicated he was a master sergeant and like a senior NCO in any army, he was chewing ass as he stepped into the mud. I suspected he was chewing the driver's rear, but really didn't know because I didn't know one word of Russian.

Moving to the center of the road, the top sergeant stopped the next three trucks. He yelled and the tailgates fell and about thirty men, all dressed in Russian uniforms, dismounted. A rope was attached to the rear bumper of the stuck vehicle and the other end was attached to the front bumper of a truck in the roadway. Some of the men took shovels and cleared the mud out from under the wheels of the stuck truck, while the rest moved to the front.

Then, as if it had been practiced many times, the sergeant moved to the center of the road and began to give orders. I heard what I assumed was one, two, three, pull, because at the last word the rocking of the truck started. Less than two minutes later, the truck was back on the road. The sergeant waved to the men, grinned and then climbed back inside the cab. A few minutes later the trucks all left the area.

We waited a good hour and then Tom said just above a whisper, "We need to warn Top the Russians are coming, or at least I think they are."

"I don't want to do that," I replied.

He gave me a surprised look and then asked, "Why not?"

"Top has been around, so they'll not catch 'em unprepared or am I wrong?"

"Of course he'll be ready, but not against that many men."

"All he has to do it close the door and go out the back way. They'll use some time getting in the cave, unless they have RPG's or C-4 along."

Tom thought for a moment and then said, "I'd forgotten about the door. I've known Top a lot of years, and if a person can be ready for a fight it'll be him."

"Enough talk, let's continue the mission." I stood, opened the compass and found my compass heading once more. As I moved toward the trees, I could hear the boots of the others as they walked behind me in the mud.

We continued to move toward our target until the rain grew heavier and then I moved into some pines and oak trees. Once stopped and our heavy packs were lowered to the ground, I said, "Vickie, you'll share a shelter with me and you two share. This way we have one veteran with a rookie. We need to get two shelters up, so we can get out of this rain."

When the two women looked confused, Tom pulled out two casualty blankets and said, "We'll use these. They're not as good as a tent, but will keep us fairly dry, unless the wind blows pretty hard."

A few minutes later, we had two lean-to's up and as I crawled under mine, I noticed the temperature was dropping. I said nothing, because we'd have no fire unless needed in an emergency the whole length of our mission. The light of a fire can be seen and smoke smelled for long distances, so we'd have a cold camp unless the weather got much worst. I expected one of the women to complain about the lack of a fire, but they said nothing. We had some surplus poncho liners and they were the best we had for blankets, but they'd work fine. I'd used them often enough in the 'sandbox,' as we called Iraq.

Tom approached and handed me two MRE's, gazed into Vickie's eyes and said, "That's it until breakfast. It won't fill you up, but it'll keep you alive. A lot of calories in one meal, but since we don't have the heaters you'll be eatin' 'em cold."

"What's the guard schedule?" I asked.

"One on and we'll rotate every two hours. First will be Alisa, then Vickie, you, then me."

I nodded and turned my attention to my meal. I groaned when I saw I had the beef stew meal packet, because it always gave me indigestion when eaten cold. It was an excellent meal when hot, but I detested it cold. I opened my accessory pouch and removed a spoon, multi-grain snack bread, and lemon tea. I filled my canteen cup with water and added the lemon drink mix.

I felt someone watching me and when I glanced up, I saw Vickie was confused with her meal pouch. She'd been watching me, and I could see she had no idea what to do next. I also noticed she had the beef brisket, with garlic mashed potatoes and crackers, and considered seeing if she wanted to trade, but figured it wasn't worth the effort. It was simply a meal to keep me alive until I could complete my mission.

I showed her how to open the pouches, what was in them, and that was pretty much all there was to it. I did watch as she took her first bite, met my eyes and smiled. *She must be starved to like these damned things cold,* I thought as I opened my entree. As I ate in silence, I realized that, to the women, this trip must be pretty rough. For someone who has gone from living in a house and cooking on a stove, to backpacking miles into the woods and then eating under a sheet of plastic in the rain, it was a huge change. I'd always felt that was one of problems with our society in the old days, we'd grown soft as a people. Gone was the determination and pure guts our forefathers had when they carved a nation out of virgin wilderness. Toward the end, folks were too lazy to even talk, and were text messaging their spouses while they sat on the sofa beside them. Now, those folks were either dead, wishing they were dead, or living like animals, holed up someplace.

It was then that Tom stood, slowly turned a complete circle and whispered, "Movement, all around us."

I slid the safety on my shotgun to off.

CHAPTER 12

"Chill, we're on your side!" A voice called out from the rain. "How do I know that?" Tom replied.

"I'm Willy Williams! Top and I go back a few years!"

Tom gave me a big grin and said, "Come."

From the rain walked a mountain of a man, wearing a green beret on his head at a cocky angle. He was loaded for bear too, with two pistols, three grenades, shotgun and two knives that I could see. His clothing was a mix of civilian and military with his trousers being jeans.

Soon a squad of ten other men joined him and Tom asked, "How'd you find us?"

Willie laughed and said, "I wasn't looking for you, but Top sent me a radio message and asked me to scout this area. Seems one of his teams reported a good size convoy heading his way and he wanted confirmation. Only, we've seen nothing. I'd have walked right by you, except one of you stood while I was looking in this direction."

Tom grinned and said, "I stood, but at any rate, the convoy is for real and we've seen it. I counted one motorcycle and thirteen trucks, and all may be manned by Russians."

"Jinks!"

"Yo!"

"Return to camp and send a message to Top. Let him know the convoy has been confirmed by the team he sent from his base camp. Stress to him the number of vehicles and the fact the Russians are now in the ballgame. Tell him to expect at least ten men per truck, or over 130 men to attack. Send it in code, too."

"Will do, Willie."

"Once you send the message, wait for a reply before you return. Top may have to escape and evade, but he's a crafty old fart. Now, get."

As Jinks took off at a trot, I asked, "Is this area clear?"

"From what I've discovered since I scouted the group that killed the general, these jokers never get off the main roads or well traveled trails. I know the Russians and they'll have some local good ole boys with 'em when they travel, as guides. They understand that no one knows the area better than the locals."

"Willie," I asked as sat on a log, "Why are the Russians here? I don't understand all of this. Don't they understand that by attacking us, and this is no advisory function, they'll simply unify us?"

Willie chuckled and replied, "The Russians have craved our country for years, and now is about the only chance they've had to get it. They're smart too, fully understanding they needed to wait a couple of years for hunger to kill large numbers of us and for diseases and tribal wars to start. With less population and weakened by disease and conflict, I suspect they think we'll be easy pickings. What they don't understand about the whole situation is the American people and how we'll come together to fight a common enemy."

"Wouldn't they do that in Russia?" Vickie asked.

"No, not these days, or I don't think they would. See, what most folks don't understand about Russians is they're a different people now than in 1945. Russian unity grew while they were fighting the Germans and then petered out after the war. They've seen so many people executed over the last sixty plus years, they no longer care who in the hell is in charge. They just want to be left alone to eat their cabbage soup."

"Do you think it's safe to have a fire?" I asked, seeing my breath as I spoke.

"I'm sure a fire is safe here, but by the time you rest overnight and then move on, I'd say no. You'll be too close to your target by then."

"Have you spotted any Russian dog handlers?" Tom asked.

"Not yet, but that doesn't mean they don't have any. See, I have no idea of the type of unit you saw in the truck, but I assume they're infantry. I doubt they're Spetsnaz, because they operate in smaller numbers, much like our green berets."

"What's that Spets thing?" Alisa asked from the darkness.

Willie grinned and said, "It's Spetsnaz, but let's get a fire going and we'll join y'all for supper. As we eat, I'll explain how the Russian Special Forces operate."

The next morning, before Willie left with his men, he went over the map and explained to us what we'd find near the base camp. It didn't sound good to me, and I said as much.

He smiled and said, "Look, you're not attacking the place, so just wait a few days and see if a lone man or a couple come out for some reason. If they do, nail 'em and take 'em back to Top. It'll be as easy as fallin' off a stump." He reached into his backpack and pulled out three Claymore mines.

"Why do you have those?" Tom asked.

"As you know, if we run into a larger force, they're really good to use with an L shaped ambush. But, Top asked me to give 'em to you. He said for you to put 'em out each night and they'll add a little security to your night positions. He also said for you to not bring 'em back, so I'd guess he wants you to use them before you return."

Tom gave a devilish grin and said, "Have you seen what these things can do to a man or a vehicle? Why just one will tear your ass up!"

Willie slapped Tom on the back and said, "I've seen what a claymore can do. Listen, we need to get moving. You be sure to use these before you start the trip home and tear up some ass." He then winked at me.

As soon as they'd left, Tom said, "Okay, everyone touch up your makeup and let's get ready to move."

"Makeup?" Vickie asked, and then giggled like a little school-girl.

"The camouflage on your face, hands and neck. We always reapply it in the morning, because some will have rubbed off over night."

I heard her giggle again and mumble, "Makeup."

Near noon, we spotted movement near a road we had to cross. Tom went forward to scout and returned a few minutes later. He pointed at the two women and motioned for them to stay, and then indicated by pointing at me and then the direction he'd come that I was to go with him. He then pointed to my eyes and I gave an okay by using my thumb and index finger. It was clear he wanted me to look at what he'd spotted.

We moved forward slowly, but the trip was short, and when I glanced at the area Tom pointed out, I spotted an old eight-wheeled Stryker parked beside a sandbagged machine gun nest. I saw no weapon mounted on the top of the light personnel carrier and suspected they had removed it for some reason. I waited, and a few minutes later two men exited the vehicle and made their way to the machine gun, where two others waited. Tom and I watched for over thirty minutes before he touched my arm and we moved back to the women. Once there, we moved away from the Stryker and went deeper into the woods.

Stopping after about a mile, Tom squatted on his heels and said just barely above a whisper, "I think this is the best opportunity we'll get to take a prisoner. I counted four men, no weapon on the Stryker, and an M60 used in the machine gun nest. One of the men was wearing a Russian uniform, so that's the one I'd like to take back to Top, if we can."

"Typical crew for a Stryker, without a gun of any sorts would be two men, but they could do the job with just a driver in a safe area. The M60 usually has two men as well. How do you intend to get a prisoner?"

Tom explained his idea and I had to admit, I thought it was a solid plan and could think of nothing better. Once his briefing was complete, he said, "Eat and relax a bit. We'll move into position two hours before dark. Alisa, move out about fifty feet and guard for a couple of hours. You'll be relieved by Vickie."

The day passed slowly, with me taking catnaps, nibbling on the contents of an MRE, and not talking at all. Finally, it was late afternoon when Tom whispered, "Saddle up."

Our trip back to the Stryker was uneventful, but my senses were on high alert for any smell, movement, or sound. We stopped at almost the same spot we'd used before. Tom and I moved forward, leaving the other two behind, mainly because we weren't sure they'd be quiet enough. At the vehicle, like soldiers all over the world, they were shooting the shit and relaxing. That was a good indicator to me and I thought, *looks like they have no idea they're being watched.* After a few minutes, I saw the Russian pull out a bottle of something from the Stryker and he passed it around the group. We remained in position for well over an hour, then moved back to the others.

We remained in position until well after midnight, then moved directly behind the machine gun position and placed a claymore mine. I made sure all four metal legs were in the soil and the front was toward the enemy, by feeling the embossed text on the front of the mine. I then ran the line off a ways to Tom. Tom was to detonate the claymore when one of the soldiers woke and moved to the forest for his morning pee. I would then capture the lone survivor, just after the claymore exploded, and the women would rush the machine gun to kill anyone yet alive. I hoped things went as planned, but suspected they'd go to hell, and quickly. In combat, few things go as planned.

Earlier two of the men moved into the Stryker to sleep, most likely, and two remained at the machine gun. But, from what I could see from the moonlight the two at the gun seemed asleep a little later. I was wrong, and in just few minutes one of the men moved off about twenty-five feet and took a leak.

The night passed slowly as I watched the men. Occasionally one would walk around the vehicle. I could tell they didn't have much experience, because more than once I was tempted to kill them both with a knife. I was sure I could do the job, only we had a plan and I'd stick to it.

Just as darkness was turning into gray, I heard a two-stroke vehicle coming up the road and figured it was someone passing on the daily orders or carrying messages. Soon, an old beat-up dirt bike rode up and the driver turned his machine off and dismounted. All this time the machine gunner had his weapon on the man. Finally, I heard a voice say, "Point that damned thing in some other direction, will ya!"

The barrel immediately swiveled off the man, which told me the gunner knew the man or recognized the voice. The other guard said, "Hank, how've ya been?"

"I'm doin' fine. Where are the other two?"

The guard pointed to the Stryker.

"Wake 'em up. The colonel wants ya to return to camp and you're to come with me. Now, get 'em up and movin', because I've a busy day ahead of me."

"I'll wake 'em, but Ivan will be pissed. We were told to stay here a week and he was in the vodka pretty hard last night."

"He's been pissed before, so wake 'em."

The guard chuckled and moved to the vehicle.

A few minutes later I could hear cursing and the two men came out with the guard exiting last. Both men moved to the woods to pee and I noticed the Russian was standing right in front of the Claymore mine. I remained in position and the American was close enough to worry me. The last thing I wanted was for him to take a leak on my head, but he missed me by inches.

As I watched my guard zipping up his pants, I heard a loud explosion, followed by screams. I came up off the ground, knocked the man to the ground with the butt of my shotgun, and he lay unmoving. I heard screams and cries for help, then saw Tom running toward the machine gun. I heard one long burst from the gun, of maybe five seconds, heard a couple of shotgun blasts, and then silence.

I stayed in position, knowing if I moved too early someone might just shoot my ass. As I waited, I removed a roll of duct tape from my pack and taped my prisoners hands behind his back. I quickly taped his feet too.

"John, all secured! We have one wounded."

I made my way to the machine gun and saw Tom working on Alisa's legs. Blood was pooling under her and Vickie stood by unmoving. By looking at her eyes, I could tell Vickie was going into shock. The machine gunners head was almost completely gone and the ammo man had been hit in the stomach. Both were beyond caring and the cyclist was twitching and jerking as he screamed.

The blast from the Claymore really messed the bike rider up, and there was no way he'd survive. I pulled my knife, knelt beside him and cut his throat.

I stood and then ordered, "Vickie, look in the vehicle and see if they have any blankets. Also check for first aid supplies while you're in there."

"I'll . . . I . . . I'm going."

I squatted by Tom as he worked and asked, "Serious?"

"I think the bone in the left leg is broken and the bleeding won't stop."

"What about the right leg?"

"It's a clean in and out injury. I imagine it hurts like hell, but this leg has me worried. I'm going to use a tourniquet and see if that works. I'm using a direct compress now, but it's not even slowing down, so I suspect the femoral artery has been damaged."

"Vickie, is there a stretcher in there?"

"Yea, do you want me to bring it out?"

"Bring it and what you've found." Then, turning to Tom I said, "We need to load her and get moving. I'm sure others heard the explosion."

"Did you get a prisoner?"

I nodded and motioned with my thumb, "He's back in the trees. Let me get him, while you take care of Vickie."

When I neared the prisoner, he looked up at me with huge frightened eyes and they grew larger as I pulled my sheath knife. I hadn't cleaned it since I'd cut the throat on the cyclist, so the blood was fresh on the long blade. I squatted beside him and said, "I'm going to cut the tape at your feet, but you try anything and I'll kill you. Do you understand?"

"Yes," was his weak reply.

I cut the tape and then said, "I'm going to help you stand. Once you're on your feet, don't take a single step, or I'll blow you in half with my shotgun."

He nodded, so I helped him to his feet.

"Now, move toward the gun and do the job slowly."

As we walked by the dead Russian, I noticed him staring at the body, or what was left of the man. The Claymore had blown him in half and only the upper half was in the grass. I wasn't surprised; after all, the mine threw 700 steel balls that are about one-eighth of an inch in diameter, and that would ruin anyone's day. As we neared the machine gun, my prisoner took in the damage done. Both of the dead suffered from the Claymore, but it was the shotgun blasts that killed them. I noticed the prisoner looked at the dead cyclist a long time, and he understood where the blood on my knife came from. I wasn't sure how the gunner lived long enough to fire at all, but he had, and knew Tom would tell me more later.

"Stop," I ordered and my prisoner stood still. I saw Alisa was on the stretcher and the tourniquet seemed to be working.

Tom stood and said, "The bleeding has stopped, but we need to get her to medical help as quickly as we can. If the tourniquet stays on too long, she'll lose the leg."

I gave an ill-felt smile and said, "Load her in the Stryker and we'll drive to Top, or as far as we can get with the fuel in this thing." Turning to the prisoner, I asked, "How much fuel in the vehicle?"

"I guess you'll need to see for yourself, won't ya?"

I swung my shotgun hard and felt the barrel take him along side of his head. He fell to the ground unmoving. I handed my weapon to Tom and then pulled the prisoner inside the Stryker and taped his legs together. I considered taping his mouth too, but changed my mind for no real reason. I searched him thoroughly and discovered a small .38-caliber pistol, a sheath knife, two grenades in his coat pocket, and a pig-sticker on a cord around his neck. I took these and placed them in my coat pockets.

I saw he was a youngster of maybe 25, close to six feet tall, and like most of us he was thinner than he should have been. He wore his blond hair cropped close to his scalp and his face was cleanly shaven, showing a scar that ran from his left ear to his lips. He also wore glasses, which I removed and placed in my pack. I started to walk away, but as an afterthought, I squatted and removed his boots. I then threw them into the woods. *He may run away, but by God he'll run slowly barefoot,* I thought.

Vicki and Tom entered with the litter and placed her on the left side against the wall. Tom pulled the safety straps over the litter and then connected them. As soon as he'd tightened them I asked, "Is the machine gun in good shape?"

"Yep, and there is a box of ammo with the gun and some more against the other wall here."

"I'm going to get it, and on the way back you can ride shotgun for me."

Tom chuckled and replied, "I hope you do better this trip than you did the last. If I remember correctly you got us blown up!"

"We weren't blown up, but it was pretty close," I replied and then made my way to the gun. A mounting bracket was in place on top of the Stryker, so when I returned it was a simple process to install the gun, wipe the fresh blood off, and load a new belt of ammo.

I climbed down from the gun, turned to Vickie and said, "If the prisoner so much as passes gas, kill 'em. Tom will be keeping watch from above, while I drive, so it's up to you to keep us safe."

Vickie pulled her pistol and said, "You drive, and let me take care of our boy."

A few minutes later I cranked the engine, noticed an almost full tank of fuel, and off we went. While I knew the top speed advertised for the vehicle was 62MPH, I wanted to move much slower than that, so I kept it around 20MPH. *If I keep the speed down, I'll get more miles per gallon of fuel and not likely drive into an ambush either. I don't need to be racing down a road I don't know or have any idea who I'll run into,* I thought as I enjoyed the ride.

Tom was suddenly behind me and said, "Stay on this dirt road for close to 20 miles, then turn off on a dirt road to the right. The map says it's county road 380. We go down that a couple of miles and come to a creek. The cave should be up on the left."

"Got it," I replied.

"I'm moving back to the gun."

The morning was clear with no clouds to be seen and the road was in fair shape, with few ruts or potholes. I knew no one had worked on it for years, but it might mean the difference between Alisa living and dying. As I drove, I constantly scanned the area through my viewing ports, which were fairly limited in my opinion. *Can't see much using these damned ports,* I thought.

Mile after mile was covered quickly and an hour later, as I slowed down to turn on county road 380, I heard a loud explosion, and then Tom opened up with the machine gun. My man was good, firing short bursts to avoid burning the barrel. Dust and debris flew by my viewing ports, and I heard a few loud pings as small arms fire struck the vehicle. I looked out of the ports, but saw no one.

The bastards missed, this time, I thought and goosed the vehicle to increase our speed. I knew if anyone ambushing us had anything heavier than small arms, we were dead meat.

Two more explosions were heard, our machine gun kept a steady and well spaced beat, so I made a split-second decision.

CHAPTER 13

I slowed down to almost a crawl, turned to the left and entered the woods. Once in the forest, I kept my speed low, to avoid trees and boulders, but also so I could watch for the bad guys. Almost instantly our gun on top went quiet.

I'd just dodged a huge pine tree when I heard Tom say, "Those boys back there weren't expecting a Stryker to come down on 'em. I think we surprised the living shit right out of most of them. I don't see any damage to the vehicle and everyone inside is safe."

"Do you think Top is safe? If not, then this trip might be a waste of time."

Tom laughed and then replied, "Didn't you see the vehicles hidden in the trees back there? Hell, I'll bet over two hundred men shot at us, but with your piss-poor driving and weaving, we only took a few rounds. I think it was the convoy we spotted earlier."

"That means one of two things. One, they've attempted to enter the cave and weren't able to do the job or two, they've not even tried yet." At this point we hit a bad rut or narrow ditch, because I bounced all over the place and Tom cursed.

"I think it'd be smart if we kept moving and approached the cave from the opposite side. They may have placed some ambushes along the road, but right now I need to get back to the gun."

"Roger that, so I'll arrive at the cave on the west side and all should go well," I said, but thought, *I hope they don't have a bunch of men near the cave or we're dead meat.*

Tom reappeared, leaned over my shoulder and said, "Don't get too close to the cave, because Top might just shoot our asses. Stop short, maybe a 100 yards and we'll walk the rest of the way."

"I'd not given that much thought, except with Alisa hurt like she is, let me stop the Stryker and then one of us can move to the cave with the prisoner. We have no idea if someone is watching the place or what."

"I'll stay with Alisa, but hurry, because I don't like having the tourniquet on that leg very long."

"Get back to the gun, we'll be where I intend to stop in a few minutes. Once I'm out with my boy, keep me covered as I head to the cave."

"Roger that, but relax, because I don't think they've found the cave yet. If they had, they'd be gathered up closer to the place."

He moved from my side and I drove just a little faster. I knew if the blood flow to her leg was stopped for too long, the leg would be lost. That thought scared me more than just a little, for two reasons. I wasn't sure any of us knew how to properly remove a leg or had the necessary surgical equipment, and I'd yet to see anyone alive since the fall with a missing limb.

Ten minutes later, I stopped on the outside edge of a grove of tall and ancient oaks. When I moved from the drivers seat to the interior of the vehicle, I saw our prisoner glare at me, but he wisely kept his mouth closed.

Turning to Vickie, I said, "I'm taking the prisoner and moving for the cave. I want you to unass this thing and move over into the trees. Stay close to here, but help cover me as I take our boy to meet Top."

I squatted by the prisoner and pulled a rope from my pack. Tying a slipknot in the end, I placed it over his head. I then cut the tape to his legs and helped him stand. I finally let the rear ramp down and warned, "Walk in front of me and go where I tell you to go. You zig when you should zag, and I'll blow you apart with this .44 magnum I have. Do you understand me?"

"Ya, I hear ya."

"Start walking straight for about a hundred yards. I'll tell you when to turn."

We were within twenty yards of the cave entrance when I heard an order, "Stop, that's close enough!"

We stopped.

"Who are you and what are you doing here?"

"My name's John, and this bastard is the prisoner Top requested I get for him."

"Stay, the both of you, until I can get to your position."

As I waited, I watched my prisoner opening and closing his hands, which to me meant he was growing afraid and that was good. If Top had an intelligence branch, they'd soon know all this man knew, so if he had half a brain he'd spill the beans right off.

"Okay, I'm behind you. Move to the closed door and on the right, up high, you'll see a red button. I want you to push that button and then step back."

As we moved I thought, I should have blindfolded our prisoner, but other than our walk to the cave, he didn't see much. It's unlikely, if he escapes, he'll even know which direction to run.

At the entrance I pushed the button and stepped back.

The door moved and began to open. I heard the guard at my back command, "Enter and do the job slowly."

We entered and Top looked up from where he sat on a wooden box. He grinned and said, "Hank, he's okay and one of us. Go finish your guard, but you did the right thing."

Dolly growled at the man until I said, "Dolly, hush."

"Howdy, Top, I brought you the prisoner you wanted."

"Good God, son, you ain't the only one left are you?"

"No, the others are near a Stryker we borrowed for a while. One of the women has a serious leg injury."

"Jones, take the prisoner and form a detail of three others. Once you're ready to go, take the man to Colonel Parker and ask him to send me a full report."

"Brown, Light, and Carrier, you come with me."

I turned my prisoner over to Thompson and then asked, "Can you loan me a few men to return to the Stryker? I'd like to get our wounded in here as soon as possible. There was a bleeding problem and Tom had to use a tourniquet."

"Smith, you and James come with me. We won't need any packs, just web gear and rifles."

I turned to Dolly and commanded, "Dolly, go to Sandra." I smiled as she made her way to my wife.

Minutes later we arrived at the vehicle with Tom still guarding with the machine gun. Vickie was in a prone position near a huge oak. Alisa looked pale and her breathing was shallow and weak.

Top immediately took charge, "Take everything of value from his vehicle, then rig it with a booby-trap. Pull the radios, cushions, and I mean anything we might need. James, I want this rigged so it explodes as soon as it starts. Smith, grab the far end of the stretcher and I'll get this end. We need to get this young woman back to the medics. Let's move, people!"

Hours later, as Sandra and two other medical types worked on Al-isa, I sat against an empty crate and ate my first MRE meal of the day. Tom was beside me, eating as well, but he had little appetite.

"You need to eat," I said.

He shook his head and said, "I'm more tired than hungry right now. After being up all night before I blew the Claymore, it's taking a toll on my ass."

"Well, at least eat the entree and then get some sleep. If the bad guys blow the door off this place, you might not get to eat again for a long time."

"I've thought of that, but if I don't get some sleep, I'll fall on my ass if we have to escape and evade from this joint anyway." He placed his meal in the dirt beside him.

"Get some rest."

As he moved to the sleeping area, I saw Sandra approaching me as she wiped blood from her fingers with a towel. Hospital gloves were now a thing of the past and no one used them, because no one had them.

She stood in front of me and said, "If I remember correctly, your blood type is O negative, right?"

"Yep and it's fairly rare compared to the other blood types. Why?"

"I need some blood from you, because if we don't get some fresh blood into Alisa she'll be dead by morning."

"How are you going to do this? I mean, do you have the equipment to give her my blood?"

"We have the necessary needles and surgical tubing, but you're the only one we know of with the right blood type."

I stood, gave her a goofy grin and replied, "You know I'll do it and be glad to help, if it'll make a difference. But, why is my blood so rare?"

"Less than 7% of Americans have O negative, so it's pretty damned rare, so you're likely the only one here besides her that has this blood type. Worldwide, the percentage depends on the ethnic group or race, but it's still damned hard to find. Now, if you'll come with me, we'll try our best to save this young woman's life."

I could remember giving blood before the fall of our nation, and the civilians would be working up a sweat as they waited for the needle. Most military folks, active duty or veterans, never seemed to fear the needle much. I guess after a hitch in the service, you've had so many shots and other needles in you, it no longer scares you. *I hope my giving blood helps,* I thought as I followed Sandra.

A little later, as Sandra taped a piece of gauze pad over my 'wound,' I said, "What are her chances now that you have the blood?"

Her face grew serious and she lowered her eyes before she replied. "Not real good. If we have to remove the leg, she'll die on us. We just don't have enough blood for surgery and I'm sure she'd die of blood loss and shock."

"Take some more of mine, then."

"I already took a pint and that's all you can safely give. If we had a way to give your plasma back to you, then you could give more. We don't have the equipment to return your plasma, so we can't do more than what we just did for her." She replied, and then leaned over and kissed me. I felt my desire start to flame, but she pulled away from me and smiled.

"I need to get you alone," I whispered with a big grin.

She grinned right back and said, "Won't happen G.I., not with all these folks around and we can't leave the cave, especially with all the unfriendly people out there."

"I love you."

"I love you too, but there is a time and place for everything. Now, go drink some water and eat a bite. Then, get your tired ass to bed, because you're about to fall over."

I slowly stood, felt a little weak, more than likely from being tired than giving blood, and made my way to where Tom lay. In a few minutes I entered the deep void of sleep.

I awoke feeling sore and irritated, with a slight headache. I stood and made my way to a partitioned area we used as a toilet. Top had some of the Air Force Prime Beef civil engineers rig up some toilets that worked pretty good. They were constructed from 55 gallon drums cut in half with a sheet of plywood on top. A circle had been cut from the wood if a person had some serious business to attend to, but for a pee, we had a funnel made from aluminum that was mounted on a metal tube that carried the urine into the drum. Once a day, someone emptied the drum using a two wheeled dolly.

I finished my morning toilet and walked toward Top, who I noted was bent over a topographical map, and Willy Williams stood beside him. As I neared, I noticed blood all over the left leg of the jeans Willy wore.

"...and right about there is where they ambushed us, Top."

"That's right where John and Tom ran the bullet gauntlet in the Stryker, right?" Top met my eyes.

I looked the map over and saw Willy's index finger at the turn off from the main road to county road 380, so I said, "Yep, right where the dirt county road meets the main macadam road. I didn't see shit driving, but Tom told me he'd seen at least 20 vehicles parked in the woods as we sped through the place."

"We didn't see any vehicles at all, so I suspect they've moved on, but they had us in a perfect L shaped ambush, or would have, until one of their men fired early."

"Did you charge their positions like you're suppose to do?" Top asked.

"No, because there were only ten of us to start with, and I lost half my men right off the bat. Four died instantly and the other died later, but we pulled back and then moved deeper into the woods. That was the day after we left y'all, John."

Top scratched his chin and then asked, "How are the other four men?"

"Ralph the radio operator and Butler had no injuries at all, while Mike took a grenade fragment in the left arm, but it was more of a graze than a real wound. In Iraq we'd say he got an easy purple heart. Our medic, Wilcox, is the one who bled to death."

"And you?" I asked looking at his leg.

"I'm fine, and the blood isn't mine. Our wounded man had a severe injury to his neck, and we couldn't get the bleeding to stop. He'd taken a bullet to his left carotid artery and there was simply nothing we could do for him in the field, so basically he bled out. I think he took the neck injury as we were un-assing the area of operations, haulin' ass actually, and the original wound to his arm was small."

Top was quiet for a minute and then said, "John, I want you and Tom to join Willy's team. We have other Green Berets and SEALS, but they're busy right now and on the other side of where I need you guys. And, John, take your wife along too, as the medic."

"Well, I don't know," I started in a serious voice and then continued, "if I like the idea. Does it mean I have to wear one of those silly girl scout beanies?" I broke out laughing.

Everyone laughed and once we sobered up, Willy said, "I think you have what it takes to earn a green beret, but remember, we only take five out of a hundred."

I laughed and replied, "Next you'll be singing the Ballad of the Green Berets, by Barry Sadler."

Willy laughed and said, "I know the words!"

Top cleared his throat and said, "Okay guys, let's get back to the work at hand. Willy, I want you to take your group and do a recon on the area. Sneak and peak is all, and avoid any enemy contact if you can. It'll give me some intelligence and allow your new members to break into the unit. John, take your German Shepherd with you, because I don't think she'll listen to any of us."

"She'd listen to you, but I think she'd actually be an asset for our small group. My dad told me of dog handlers in Vietnam and I watched 'em in Iraq. They saved a lot of lives."

Top grinned and said, "Yep, I know all of that, but the main reason I want her to go with you is because she doesn't eat when you're gone. She sits by the entrance like a dog waiting for a small kid to get off a school bus. Besides, I think she needs a walk in the sun."

Willy laughed and said, "That's what my uncle called an easy mission in World War Two, a walk in the sun."

"Did he experience a lot of those walks?" I asked.

"Not a one, but he said he heard of 'em."

"Get your men ready to move, Willy, and see if Sandra can leave with Alisa hurt like she is right now. If need be, leave without a medic, because all of you have had basic combat first aid training and you green beanies even kept a goat alive, or so I heard."

"Yep," Willy said proudly, "I kept mine alive during training, but I ain't treated another goat since."

We broke out laughing again and after a few minutes, Top slapped Willy on the back and said, "Saddle up, it's showtime."

Hours later, near dusk a light rain began to fall and the temperature dropped dramatically in just a few minutes. Before we'd left, Willy explained some rules, and Tom and I found it a normal mission briefing. When we could talk, breaks to be taken and how often, food breaks and so on. It was old hat to us, but I could tell Sandra was confused. Now, with darkness closing in, she seemed a bit scared. She was a smart woman and not many would want to spend the night deep in Injun country with no help on standby. We were on our own and if the shit hit the stump, some, if not all, of us could very well die.

We were sitting back-to-back, facing the four compass headings, with each of us keeping an eye on our surroundings. We'd been informed by Willy there would be no sleep tonight or tomorrow. Three Claymore mines were rigged in triangle position around us. We were to return to the cave late tomorrow, so I figured a little missed sleep wouldn't kill any of us.

The Night was long and I grew bored near 0300 and almost nodded off, but when I checked on Sandra and found her awake, I was determined to stay awake no matter what it took.

A few seconds later, Dolly growled and looked to the west. I didn't say a word, but I heard all four safeties slip off.

CHAPTER 14

I heard movement moving from the north moving south and Dolly once again growled, so I whispered a low, "Hush, girl."

From the movement I heard a voice say, "I heard a dog growl."

"Jonas, you're full of shit. Why in the world world would a dog be out here? Hell, most cats and dogs have been eaten up by now."

The moon was full, with a few fast moving clouds overhead, and the tree limbs overhead covered us from most of the faint light. I saw silhouettes of what looked to be a squad of men moving through the trees. Tom touched me and when I glanced at him he tapped his balled fist with his thumb. *He's going to fire a Claymore when they get closer. Lawdy, I hope these men aren't the point for a much larger group*, I thought.

Then, when I glanced back at the men, they'd disappeared.

They either smelled us or caught Tom's thumb movement, because they've gone to ground, I thought as I got ready mentally and physically for the shooting to start. I brought my shotgun into position as I thought over and over, *Start the dance, start the dance, start the dance.*

Tom tapped me and when I looked at him, along with Tom, Sandra, and Ralph, he placed his index fingers in his ears. I knew the Claymore was about to blow.

Seconds later the cool and quiet night air erupted with an earth-shattering explosion, followed instantly by loud piercing screams. I heard shotgun and rifle shots, and actually saw a small branch fall from the tree overhead. It fluttered to the ground uninterrupted. From the muzzle blasts in the darkness, I counted ten men still shooting, which meant more had survived than I'd thought. Obviously, the angle of the Claymore when we placed it caused us to miss most of them. *Hell, how did we know where they'd show anyway?* I thought and felt fear gnawing on my stomach like a small animal. I knew from experience once the firing started I'd be okay. I always grew scared when any battle first started and usually ill following a fight. Puking was not uncommon.

Two loud explosion followed, one after the other, and then it grew quiet. I'd heard a *fizz* and then felt Tom's arms move twice just before the explosions, so I'd known he'd tossed grenades. Long minutes passed with only the occasional scream or wobbling cry of the wounded. Still, we remained in position and waited. We waited for the wounded to bleed more and for the seriously wounded to die. I'd learned on my first tour in Iraq that an injured man often knew he was dying and would try to take a few enemies with him. The minutes ticked off as slowly as hours in my mind.

I scanned 360 degrees around us and spotted movement to our north. I picked up a Claymore clacker and waited for them to get nearer—my wait was a short one. When I could make out the shapes of men moving toward us, I squeezed my clacker, heard the resulting explosion and grinned.

Once again, men screamed and cried out in pain. I heard one voice screaming for his mother over and over, until the victim gradually grew weaker, and the voice grew too faint to be heard. I felt nothing for my enemy, no emotions at all. They'd come to kill me and I knew it, so the most they could expect from my ass was a quick death. If that makes me a cold and hard man, so be it. War, and we are at war, is not the place to be filled with progressive ideas of deep loving compassion and soul touching tenderness. It is a time to kill or be killed—so I'm deadly in battle. However, with that said, I'm usually compassionate with injured prisoners in a rear area, but only to a certain point. I'll never risk the lives or safety of anyone with me for a prisoner, and you already know what I'll do to a prisoner if I need information. Most of the time I'm up front in battles and prisoners just slow a unit down, so I take no prisoners.

"Two hours until daylight, so we wait." Willy whispered, and then leaned his back against mine.

Sandra whispered, "Ralph is down."

"Hard?" Willy asked.

"Breathing, but I can't tell in the darkness."

Pulling a poncho from my pack, I handed it to her along with a small light doctors use to check patients. I'd picked up the light from a man I'd killed a few weeks back and right now it'd come in handy.

Still whispering, Sandra asked, "What am I to do with this poncho?"

Before I could answer, Tom replied, "Drape it over your head and when you check Ralph, make sure the sides are covering his body. Don't let any of the light out of the poncho."

Many drawn-out minutes passed before I heard Sandra whisper, "He took a rifle slug to the upper left shoulder and it's clean through his body, while a single pellet struck his head. I pulled the pellet out and it didn't go in far, maybe a quarter of an inch. The bleeding from the shoulder will stop shortly."

"Gonna live?" Willy asked.

"Yep, but he'll be a hurtin' sonofabitch when he comes around. I'll give him some morphine when that happens."

"Good. He's the only member of my old team still alive. It'll be light in a few minutes, so let's get ready to check the damage done."

I scratched Dolly's head and fed her part of an energy bar I had in my shirt pocket. She gobbled it down in seconds. "Dolly's a good girl," I whispered and felt my love for her touch my soul. Suddenly my mind flashed to Newt and Skillet and my happiness instantly vanished, replaced with grief.

As we waited, over time the moans, groans and cries of the wounded grew fainter and weaker until all was quiet.

CHAPTER 15

With the coming of full light, Willy whispered, "Okay, John, you and I will check those people. Sandra stay with Ralph and Tom, but all of you keep your weapons ready at all times. We'll take no chances."

I took Dolly by her leash and moved toward the site of our ambush.

The first three men I saw had been torn apart by the mine, and they'd died instantly. The next two had serious head injuries and I could see a small fragment from a grenade stuck in one man's forehead.

I moved to where Willy was squatted over a man and heard him say, "You've taken shrapnel in your gut and you know what that means, right?"

Dolly growled a loud warning and I knew she wanted a piece of the downed man's ass. I kept her leash tight and commanded, "Sit, Dolly. Stay." I smile with satisfaction as she sat.

"I. . . I'll die."

"Yep, and there isn't a thing I can do to help you."

"Kill. . . me. I . . . hurt. . . too much." The injured man pleaded and I could see deep pain in his eyes. His forehead was covered in sweat and he was pale.

Willy looked at me, crossed himself, and then pulled his knife. Turning to the man, he asked, "Are you sure you want me to do this?"

"Yes, I. . . can't take this. . . pa. . . pain." The man then arched his back and gave a loud moan. I saw his fingers clawing the dirt, leaving miniature ruts in the soil.

For God's sake, kill the man! I screamed in my mind.

Willy's knife flashed quickly and entered under the man's left ribs, and once the blade was buried to the handle, he jerked the knife hard from side to side, twisting it as he did so. The injured man screamed, jerked a few times and then quivered violently. A minute later his eyes lost focus and I heard a loud sigh—he was dead.

Pulling his knife from the man's chest, Willy cleaned the blade on the dead man's shirt. He looked up at me and said, "I hated doing that, but he'd have died anyway. I just hope God forgives me the mercy killings I've done over the years."

"I see you're Catholic, so confess the act to a priest."

"I haven't seen a priest in years, not since the fall. I've been praying, but not sure if that works or not."

I gave a low chuckle and replied quickly, "I'm not Catholic, so I have no idea if it works or not, but we Southern Baptists been praying straight to God for years. And, by the way, I'm not laughing or making light of your religion, mostly I'm laughing at the differences. I think God knows all of our hearts and he'll judge us accordingly."

Willy cleared his throat, so I felt he was uncomfortable discussing religion, and then he said, "Let's check that batch you smoked on the north side."

We found ten more bodies and all were as dead as a bottle of Christmas whiskey. It was as we were about to turn and return to Sandra that Dolly moved forward in a leap. She barked twice and I knew immediately someone was in the area. I reached down and released her leash from the collar. She shot into the woods.

I heard two loud gunshots, followed instantly by a loud scream. Tom and I hurried forward, but not too quickly because we had no idea what Dolly had treed. After moving into the woods about twenty yards, I saw Dolly hanging from the arm of a man in a Russian uniform.

Willy screamed a command in Russian, and the man glanced at us and shouted a reply.

"Call the dog off." Willy ordered, and then brought his shotgun up to cover the Russian.

"Dolly, come!"

As soon as she was by my side, Willy spoke slowly and it sounded to me as if he were telling the man to do something, step-by-step. The Russian dropped the pistol from his right hand, unbuckled his belt and tossed it to the side, and then fell to his knees. He placed his hands on top of his head, lacing his fingers together.

Pulling a roll of duct tape from his pack, Willy said, "Watch this joker closely as I secure him. Any fast moves, blow his ass away."

He then moved toward the man, holding his shotgun at the ready. As he secured the man's hands behind his back, I heard them talking in Russian. Then, Willy helped the man stand and made his way toward me. The prisoner was limping and I saw blood dripping from his arm where Dolly had been holding him and from between his legs. Dolly's tongue was hanging out and she was panting hard as I praised her, "Good girl. You're a good girl, Dolly."

Beside me now, Willy said, "This sumbitch says he doesn't speak English, but he's a liar. He's a senior sergeant and if he was with these others, you can bet your ass he speaks some of our language."

"What now?" I asked.

"Well rig up a stretcher from two tree limbs and some shirts from the dead. Then, Ivan here and one of us will take turns packing Ralph back to our base camp. We need to hurry too, because everyone and his brother heard our battle."

When we returned, Sandra was placing an IV in Ralph's arm and Tom grinned when she saw the Russian.

"Sandra, while Tom and John rig a stretcher for Ralph, can you take a look at our guest?"

"Sure." She replied, and then stuck a long forked stick in the dirt beside Ralph and hooked the IV on one of the branches. While we moved off to get the shirts and tree limbs, I could hear the conversation.

Willy rattled off some Russian and the man sat in the dirt, and then stretched out on his back. His hands were still tied behind him.

"How do I do this safely?" Sandra asked.

Will grinned, put his shotgun on the ground and then pulled his pistol. Walking to the prisoner, he knelt beside him and place the gun barrel against the side of his head. "Now, check the bleeding at his groin first, then the arm. If he moves suddenly, you'll hear my shot. Treat him for blood loss, but no painkiller or antibiotics at this point."

I returned with two bloody shirts in my hands and a few seconds later, Tom placed two limbs beside the clothing on the ground near Ralph. I buttoned the shirts down the front and then ran the limbs down the long sleeves of each. We placed Ralph on the shirt buttons and the job was complete. While it'd not hold up for miles and miles, I suspected it would last long enough for us to get the man back to our base camp. If not, we'd make a better one using a poncho.

I watched as Sandra unbuttoned the prisoners trousers and lowered them, along with his green cotton boxer shorts. She gave a light chuckle and said, "Looks like our Dolly tore his scrotum open, and he's a puncture wound to his penis. He's bleeding badly, but the injury is not serious. Once back at camp someone will sew it closed for him."

She placed a bandage against the bleeding bag and taped it in place.

Tom commented, "Rough wound, and our boy almost lost the family jewels."

"Now, let me check his arm."

Willy spat out some more Russian and the man rolled over on his stomach. Pulling her sheath knife, as the green beret sat on the prisoners back, she sliced the shirt up the entire length of the arm. When she pulled the material away from the arm, I grimaced at the damage done.

The forearm muscle was torn loose at the elbow and flapping, and a huge chunk was completely missing from his upper arm. The bite to the upper arm had to hurt and it was bleeding profusely. Sandra placed a bandage on both injuries and then taped them in place.

"He's good to go."

Willy asked, "Can he carry an end of the stretcher?"

"I don't know, really. The medical side of me says he shouldn't, but I think he can for a while anyway."

"Get saddled, we're moving," Willy ordered and then spoke to the Russian. The prisoner moved to Ralph's head and squatted by the stretcher.

Tom went to the front of the stretcher and as soon as they lifted Ralph, we began to move overland toward Top. I felt uneasy, but had no real reason to feel the way I did.

"John, take point, I'll pull drag. We'll take no breaks on the way back. Make a beeline to Top, but don't compromise safety for speed. I love Ralph like a brother, but I'll not risk our lives for his. Next on the stretcher will be Sandra, me, then John and finally back to Tom. If the Russian tires, tough shit. Rotate on the stretcher every twenty minutes."

I stepped off at a slow but steady mile-eating-mile rate and scanned the area closely as we moved. A few times I stopped the group, only to spot a squirrel scurrying up a tree or a rabbit making a mad dash to safety in some thickets. The return trip, as far as all were concerned, was too slow, but uneventful.

Once we entered the cave, Top smiled, moved to the prisoner and asked, "Where'd ya find this vodka slurping sonofabitch?"

Willy grinned and said, "Last night his group almost walked through our over night position, so I popped a Claymore, and then John popped another. This is the only survivor out of two squads."

"He looks to be bleeding a little."

I laughed and said, "Dolly almost tore his balls off and bit his tallywhacker, too. The muscle of his forearm was ripped from the elbow."

Top winked at me and said, "Remind me not to piss off Dolly. One of the men killed a deer late yesterday, so give our canine hero a big raw steak tonight. I feel anyone that can capture a real live Russian should be rewarded. Does this bastard speak English?"

Willy replied, "He claims he doesn't, but if he didn't, why was he with a bunch of American's? I suspect he's working as an adviser."

"Don't worry about it. Someone in intelligence will go to work on him shortly. Oh, by the way, your Stryker is now history."

"How'd that happen with it mined?"

Top chuckled and said, "Late last night a group of close to ten men loaded the thing and cranked the engine. I swear, when the explosives went off, it shook this cave. From the spot we use for guard duty the flames must have been 200 feet in the air."

"Well," I added, "it had well over three quarters of a tank of gas left, and I think your boys may have placed too much C-4 when they booby-trapped it."

"At first light we did a recon and from body parts found, it must have been a squad."

Tom grinned and said, "You know, there ain't no good way to die, but that was likely one of the fastest ways I know of. You're here one minute, and in small pieces the next."

"As we say in special forces, you're in hell before you know you've died."

"Ganton!" Top suddenly yelled.

"Yo!" A huge black man of about twenty-four yelled back.

"Gather up your men and get this Russian bastard out of here. Ask Colonel Parker to work this guy over hard. I figure he knows a little something, only don't expect too much, because he's just a sergeant."

"Will do, Top. Okay, y'all heard the top sergeant, saddle up."

"What of my injuries? Will you not treat them and give me something for my pain?" The Russian suddenly asked in perfect English.

Before I could react, Willy backhanded the man so hard he fell to the floor. Then pulling his knife, he placed his foot on the Russian's chest and said, "You told me you didn't speak English, you lying bastard. I hate a liar with a passion! You denied speaking the language so you could listen to our conversations."

"Sir," Top yelled, "don't kill the worthless piece of shit, he may know something that will save lives. He's a valuable prisoner, Willy!" Top pleaded, and moved to Willy's side. He placed his hand on the captains shoulder and added, "He's not worth it, Willy. Let it go."

Sheathing his knife, Willy said harshly, "I want no medication given to this man or any enemy we capture from now on. We don't have an endless supply, so save it for our own."

"Well said. Ganton, get this scumbag away from us now!"

"You cannot deny me medical attention, because it is part of the Geneva Convention. As a POW I demand medical treatment!"

Top grinned and said, "Ivan, the United States government signed and agreed to the Geneva Convention, not us. See, America no longer exists as a sovereign nation, so we don't have to adhere to a damned thing. I think your trainers may have forgotten to tell you that part. I don't think this is your lucky day."

Ganton moved to the prisoner and said, "Let's move. You burp or look cross-eyed and one of us will stick a knife in your gut."

I pulled the duct tape from my pack, threw it to Ganton and said, "Cover his mouth with this once outside, and he'll be quiet on the trip.

Sandra was suddenly by my side and when I looked at her she looked like hell warmed over. She hadn't slept in close to thirty-six hours, so she had a right to look rough. I started to speak, but she said, "We have to take Alisa's leg off in just a few minutes."

"Do you have what you need?"

"Pretty much, because it doesn't really take any special tools except for a bone-saw. I just wish we had more of her blood type."

"Ganton, stop!" I called out as the man started to leave the cave with our prisoner. Then turning to Willy I asked, "Is blood type on Russian dog tags?"

"No, they don't have the same information on theirs as we do, but it should be on a card in his wallet."

Top must have read my mind, because he ordered the prisoner brought to us. Then he smiled at the Russian, pulled his pistol, and then asked, "What is your blood type? If you answer me, you will receive full medical treatment. If you refuse to talk or lie to me, I'll kill you where you stand."

"My blood type is O negative, why?"

Willy, who'd opened the man's wallet, pulled out a small card and said, "Yep, O negative and his name is Adrik Chirkoff. He's also a senior sergeant."

"What kind of name is Jerkoff?" Tom asked and then broke out laughing.

"That's enough of that, Tom. Ganton, our Soviet visitor has just volunteered to give two pints or more of blood." Top said, but I could see he was wanting to laugh as well.

Sandra instantly shot back, "He can't give—"

"Yes he can and he will. After you take blood from him, treat him properly and give him a painkiller. Take as much as you can without killing the man."

The Russian grinned as Ganton led him to the area where the blood would be taken.

"Top, he's already weak from the loss of blood. If I take two pints it could very well kill him. If I take more than two, he'll die." Sandra said.

"I fully realize he may die, but I'll not let one of my people expire if I can avoid it at any cost. And, young lady, there is something you need to learn about war."

Looking puzzled, she asked, "What's that?"

"Shit happens. Now, draw your blood from Adrik and try to save Alisa's life. I've forgotten about the Russian already."

I sat on an oak log someone had pulled in to use as a sofa and opened my MRE. I was hungry and tired. I'd just taken the first bite of something that was suppose to be an omelet, when I noticed Sandra approaching me.

When in front of me she asked, "Honey, I know you're tired and so am I, but can you help us remove Alisa's leg?"

I gave a dry chuckle and replied, "Well, the sight of blood doesn't bother me, but I'm afraid my medical experience may be a bit low. I was trained in combat first aid and can keep anyone, but the most severely wounded, alive long enough to get to a doctor. I think I'm lacking in the skills you need."

"I'll be doing the actual surgery, but I need someone to hand me the tools as I work. Besides Willy, who will assist, and Tom, who'll be there too, you're the only one I know that can help."

"Hell, I thought we had a doctor or nurse practitioner here?"

"Had, is the key word now. Top sent the nurse off to help some men who'd been severely injured in an ambush."

"Baby, you know I'll help if I can." I placed my meal by my foot and started to stand, when she said, "I knew you would, because that's the kind of man I married. But, sit back down, she's still in what we'd call pre-op. We have to give her something to put her out, shave the skin around the amputation spot, and some other things. Right now, I just need an answer."

"How long do I have to eat?"

She gave a dry chuckle and said, "You have about ten minutes. Willy is getting her ready now and from the way you veterans eat, I suspect you can eat and still have eight minutes to relax. As soon as you finish the meal, come join us." I watched as she turned and walked toward the small group assembled around Alisa.

Well, she was wrong, I finished the entree and side-dish in three minutes. I stood, wiped the dirt from my hands, and thought, Lord, let Alisa live. She's a good woman and deserves better than what we're about to do to her. However, thy will be done.

CHAPTER 16

To be honest, Alisa looked more dead than alive when I neared the table. Her skin was pale and the medication they'd given her must have been working, because she was completely out of this world.

"How much blood did you take from the Russian?" I asked.

"Three, pints and that's all we have for this surgery. We had to use your blood earlier today." Sandra replied and then continued, "Now, wash your hands well with soap and water, then pour a little alcohol on them. We'll start in a few minutes."

I was fascinated by the surgery, but was lost most of the time, because Sandra would ask for this or that tool and I had no understanding of why she needed it. Things went well, until Sandra pushed the sharp bone cutting blade of the bone-saw across Alisa's leg.

An earsplitting scream filled the cave and Sandra yelled to be heard, "Willy, more morphine!"

Alisa attempted to move from the crates we were using as an operating table, and her body flailed in all directions. She made the most inhuman babbling sounds and screams as pain radiated through her body. Sandra quickly pulled the saw away and backed from her patient.

Willy swung into action and in just a little time Alisa fell back, with no sounds from her at all.

"Is she dead?" I asked.

"No, not even close. It's the morphine. It's good shit for surgery and lays a person low in no time." Willy said, and then winked at me.

Sandra returned to the leg and added, "It used to be sold in a diluted form called laudanum over the counter of most general stores. The difference in laudanum is it had a heavy dose of alcohol mixed with it as well."

"Sounds too dangerous to offer over the counter," I said, and watched her grasp the saw firmly with both hands.

"Big addiction problem in the late 1800's, especially following the War of Union Aggression. The north had all the drugs, except for what the south could smuggle or steal and as a result, the addiction problem was bigger in the north. Read your history, honey, and you'll learn laudanum and opium were as popular in the days of the cowboy as beer is today." Sandra said and then ordered, "Hold her down, Willy, this leg must come off now."

A few minutes later the leg fell to the floor of the cave with a dull *thud*. Alisa hadn't moved again, and I felt she'd been blessed. I knew the shock alone of Sandra cutting the bone could easily kill.

"John, hold the loose flap of skin up as I use stitches to close the flap over the raw end."

As I held the skin in place, I asked, "What's the odds of infection, if she survives the surgery?"

"Well, she's got a better than average chance of survival, really. We'll use some triple antibiotic ointment on the injury, give her the rest of the blood, and hopefully in a few days she'll be fine. But, even in a hospital like we had before the fall, there were no guarantees."

"How's the Russian?"

She shrugged her shoulders and said, "He was unconscious the last time I checked. He'd already lost a lot of blood, and we took too damned much from him. I'm not sure if he'll make it or not."

"I guess you didn't have to medicate him, huh?"

"Huh-uh, he passed out from blood loss."

"It'd be an easy death."

At that point she smiled at me and said, "I can finish this alone. Go wash your hands and then get some sleep; you look rough."

"I'll do that, if you'll lay beside me in a few minutes."

"Oh, don't worry about that, because my ass is draggin' from being up all night. Only, this had to be done now and not later, or Alisa would have died."

I leaned forward, kissed her on the cheek and then made my way to the washbasin.

The next morning both Adrik and Alisa were still among the living, but I didn't think the Russian would be with us much longer. I sat in the dirt of the cave and shared part of an MRE with Dolly. As she ate, I scratched her ears absentmindedly. I did a whole lot of thinking about nothing the hour before, simply allowing my mind to jump from subject to subject without attempting to control it. My mind jumped from making love to Sandra, to the last time I'd seen my father, and then to a circus I'd seen as a small child. I enjoy my nonsense thinking because after doing it for an hour or two, I always felt refreshed.

Top walked over and sat beside me, placing his coffee cup on the ground.

"What's on your mind, Top, or is this a social call?"

He smiled and replied, "Absolutely nothing is on my mind right now. Actually, it's been a good day, so far."

Suddenly interested, I asked, "And why is today going so well?"

"Just got off the radio with G2 intelligence, and the American POW you brought in is singing like a robin these days."

"Does he know much?"

Top nodded and said, "He's full of more shit than a Thanksgiving turkey. The problem now, or so they tell me, is he won't shut up."

"How'd they get him to sing?"

Top laughed loud and hard, but after a few minutes he said, "They had one of our men who'd been sentenced to death for being a spy. He was guilty as hell and admitted it, so we had to make an example of him. They held off the execution until the new man arrived. After your POW had been there a few hours, playing Mister Hard-ass and refusing to answer any questions, they brought the condemned man out, forced him to kneel, and then shot him in the back of the neck. He fell right next to the POW's foot. G2 said he hasn't stopped talking since the execution."

I grew sober and then asked, "What will they eventually do with him? I mean, we don't have a POW camp or even a way to house prisoners."

"I honestly don't know and don't want to know. I suspect they'll kill him, once they milk all they can out of him. We don't have the manpower to watch POW's or even a prison."

"I'd suspect that's exactly what they'll do, so we can expect the same if we get captured, or so I guess."

"I think you're correct with that guess. Anyway, he informed G2 the Russians are here only as advisers, and the large convoy you spotted was taking them to various units. They usually work in two men teams, totally different than our Green Berets."

"Did he have any idea why the Russians are supporting this one group?"

Top cleared his throat and replied, "Yep, because they're the biggest unit in the states right now, with close to 10,000 men and women."

"We can't take on that many folks!"

"Relax a bit, son, because they ain't all in Mississippi. They're scattered all over the country and from what we were told their communications system is terrible. The Russians have been supplying the units with helicopter, parachute drops and even LAPES."

"LAPES? Isn't that where a C-130 flies a few feet of the ground, a parachute opens behind the cargo, the load then flies into the slipstream as the chute catches in the wind? The parachute drags the contents of a pallet or two down rollers inside the aircraft and then to the ground."

"That's pretty much how it works, but it raises a hell of a lot of dust."

I shrugged and said, "Hell, if it works, it's worth the risk of dust. But, how will all of this impact us as a unit?"

"It won't impact us any time soon, because their units are too scattered."

"Anything on the Chinese? I can't imagine them not getting involved, too."

"The POW said they're here, too, which is the main reason the Russians sent advisers. Both are attempting to get a piece of the American pie."

"Top, if the Chinese get serious, we'll be in a world of hurt. Hell, there must be a zillion of them."

"Son, the problem with the Chinese is they can't support or supply too many troops here, and even after all the deaths over the last few years, our population will fight the Chinese hard. If America has a common enemy, it's communism, or it was until our last president came into power."

"He claimed he was a liberal."

"He was and still is, if he's alive. The man changed laws to fit his needs, totally ignored our Constitution, increased mandatory immunizations, raised gas prices, which led to higher food prices, had chips implanted in some folks, tried his luck at gun control, kept all the minorities pissed at each other, and even made it illegal to show support to any Christian faith. He spent more money on his many cars than he did on meals for our troops or helping veterans. After his sexual affair with his male staff member broke open, all of us could understand his pushing so hard for gay rights."

"The gay issue meant nothing to me and I didn't care if they were recognized or not. I still feel that way. My Bible tells me it's a sin to live such a lifestyle, but God will judge them, not me. I'm not gay, so what others do behind closed doors doesn't impact me at all," I said, and honestly meant my words.

"You're right, God will judge, but we've always had gays around us and I know I've served with many without knowing. If I'd known, it wouldn't have made any difference to me because I evaluate people on job performance, not sexual orientation."

"How'd all that racial stuff hit you? I mean, since you're a black man."

Top laughed and then said, "Personally, I've never let the liberal media guide my thinking or my actions. Especially just before the fall, when some of media kept the racial shit stirred up every time there was a killing of a person of any color. See, they rarely reported when a Hispanic person killed a white, or if a black killed a black, or if they did, race never came out. I knew all of the facts were not being told in anything they reported. I may be a member of the black race, but I think for myself."

"And, professionally? Did it bother you?"

"Lawdy no, son. The army never tolerated racists, no matter their color, during the time I served, but they had a problem with it in the years past. By the time I'd entered, we were all seen as 'green' and of no particular race by the army. I learned as a young kid that some black folks can be racists as well, so it ain't just a white man's problem. See, I think racism is taught in families and that family can be of any color."

"What straw on our governments back caused the final collapse, or do you have any idea? I've given it a lot of thought, but can't pinpoint one particular issue or act."

Top stretched his legs out in the dirt in front of him, thought for a minute or two, and then said, "I think when we granted the right for millions of illegal aliens, or undocumented aliens as the politically correct liberals used to say, to stay in the country, we committed economic suicide as a nation. Many of those we allowed to stay had no jobs, few had skills that were needed, some were out and out criminals, and our unemployment rate was already over fifteen percent. We already had more folks on government assistance than we had working, so how could the people working support such a financial burden? That led to the government borrowing all kinds of money, knowing they couldn't pay it back and couldn't even make the first payment on the loan. Hell, we were still sending foreign aid to countries and should have stopped that to pay our loans or help our own people. To this day, I don't understand how we, the American people, could have been so stupid. Our leader led us right down the path, and openly, but very few challenged him."

"Well, it's all water under the bridge now, with survival on everyone's mind."

"Yep, it's a done deal, but I seriously doubt you and I will ever see this country back as we remember it."

"Let's say we do come together as one people, what kind of government do you think we'll have?"

"It all depends on the political thoughts of the man or woman who is able to unify us as one again. I pray nightly that our Constitution will be re-instated, our rights protected, and states are given more power individually than the Federal government. A big federal government caused our fall, as sure as I sit here talking with you."

I chuckled and then said, "The kind of government you're describing is exactly what the Confederate States of America wanted and the real reason for the Civil War."

"I'll not discuss old Southern politics with you, but I do know the war wasn't fought to free the black man. I think the Yankees fought to keep the South in the Union and that was the only reason for most of them. Lincoln simply tacked the Emancipation Proclamation on the wall once he saw he'd win the war. Slavery had always been a thorn in the side of our country and I guess he thought it was an excellent time to put the issue to bed, and it was. But, the slave issue was pretty much over by the war, except for the actual freeing the folks."

"How do you figure that? Hell, thousands of black folks were still slaving away every day from dawn to dusk in all kinds of weather. And, no plantation owner wanted to lose his property." I was confused by his statement.

Top smiled and said, "The invention of the cotton gin spelled the end to slavery. See, it could do more work in a day than a whole bunch of slaves could do in a week. Plus, with slaves costing between five-hundred and a thousand dollars or more a head, they would soon be rendered too expensive. Compared to the new cotton gin, or one of the many illegal copies, slaves were no longer cost effective. The owners could cut the costs of running a plantation a great deal using a gin, because slaves required housing, food, clothing, and other items just to live. Other machines were to come that reduced the need for excessive manpower to run any plantation."

"You mean the war was fought for nothing? All those men lost their lives, on both sides, for a lost cause?"

"No, they didn't die for a lost cause, no matter which side they were on. The right of a state to leave the Union had to be established, especially since the only state that had any real legal right to leave the Union was Texas. When accepted into the Union, Texas made it clear they wanted the option of leaving if need be or things didn't work out."

"I'll be damned, I didn't know this." I was amazed by Top's intelligence of history.

Top shrugged his shoulders and replied, "Our school teachers, before the fall, did as well as they could, but they were limited by what they could and couldn't teach. If it wasn't on the lesson plan, they weren't allowed to expand on the lesson. Most of us in America grew up learning incorrect American history, and often our history was written by those who'd never been to the place they were writing about or even alive at the time."

"That's not history, that's opinion!"

"Well, your words ring true, but what I just told you is fact. My wife was a school teacher for thirty years, and she bitched about the lessons all the time. Now, enough bullshitting. I want Willy and his team, which includes you, to do a recon north for a few days. Rumor has a Russian unit up that way and we need to see if they're in our area of operations."

"And, if they are in our A.O.?"

"Look, listen, and then come back here. If you're seen, consider your mission a failure. We want to get in, see what's going on, gather some intelligence, and get out without them being aware we were there. Got that?"

"Uh-huh, it's sounds simple enough, but I doubt it will be."

"You do what Willy orders and all will turn out well, unless someone walks into your night position like the last time. Things like that are rare, but they do happen from time-to-time. Oh, and before I forget, leave your wife behind this trip. Our nurse is tied up right now and won't be coming back anytime soon, so I need her here. Take Vickie with you so you're not short."

CHAPTER 17

Today, a day later, I'm on point and moving slowly through a cypress swamp, keeping an eye out for gators and snakes, and looking intently for the bad guys. I step over a log, but before my raised foot strikes the water, I see movement. Looking at the waters surface, I see a huge cottonmouth swimming away from me. While not really scared of snakes, the image makes me shudder. I keep moving forward as I try to get my heart rate back to normal. *Damn, gotta use a little more caution than I have been. But, it shows we're quiet enough if the snake didn't know we were approaching*, I thought.

Off and on we change point until darkness, when Willy whispered, "We'll spend the night here."

Vickie's eyes grew large, because we were still in the swamp and no dry land was visible in any direction from where I stood.

"How can we sleep here?" She asked.

"Sit in the water or climb a tree," I replied.

Willy grinned, and whispered once more, "I'm using a tree, but only because gators can't climb trees."

Vickie smiled and didn't say much, but I felt she thought she'd be safe in a tree, so I added, "Snakes can climb trees and are often found in trees. Also, if you use a tree to sleep in, secure yourself or you'll fall out once asleep."

Her smile quickly disappeared as the rest of us selected trees to spend the night in. I wasn't worried about snakes in the water, but being attacked by hungry gators and some were very aggressive. What most folks don't realize about a swamp is it comes alive with movement and noise once the sun goes down. I noticed we all selected trees that covered the four main compass points of north, south, east and west.

Once in my tree, I tied myself to the trunk and cleared the limbs and moss from the area directly overhead. I removed an extra large hook that easily screwed into the tree trunk. In the days before the fall, I'd used the same hook to support my bicycle many times. I hung my shotgun from the hook and placed another hook on the other side to hold my backpack. I removed a small bottle of insect repellent and applied it liberally to my exposed skin. The last thing I needed was come down with a West Nile Virus or malaria.

From near Vickie's tree I heard a faint, "Shit!" and then a splash in the water. The original splash was followed by a number of louder splashes that sound like a fight going on. *Gators fighting over what Vickie dropped,* I thought, and grinned. She'll learn, if she lives long enough.

I have no idea what she'd dropped, but it'd stay there until morning or gators ate it. I heard gators stirring in the water below and the sounds of thousands of insects, frogs and maybe even the boogieman. Strange noises come from swamps at night, and we heard them all this night.

Once the moon came out, I could see swirls in the water when snakes and gators moved, and moonlight reflect off the small waves. Suddenly I heard a loud scream that equaled any woman I'd ever heard in a horror movie, but I quickly identified it as a panther or other large cat. While most in Mississippi thought no such animal existed, some of the good ole boys have been saying for years they did, and I believe them right now. While not overly concerned, I felt for my shotgun in the inky darkness under the canopy of my tree. Feeling the warm metal, I relaxed a little.

The night was long, but I dozed off and on most of the time. When morning came, a thick white mist cover the swamp like a veil. I climbed down my tree and waited in the knee deep water for the others. Soon, Ralph, Tom and Willy were at my side and a very tired Vickie walked to us a few minutes later.

Whispering, Willy asked, "Get any sleep?"

Vickie shook her head.

Willy gave a crooked grin and said, "Okay, Tom, you take point and stay out about 30 yards. Vickie, you pull slack and cover the rear. Let's move."

Well, I thought as we started moving, *at least the water is warm and the sun is shining.*

Shortly after noon, we exited the swamp and moved into some oaks. Three Claymores were placed, a guard designated and the rest of us got some much needed sleep. I must have fallen asleep instantly, because when I opened my eyes next, Tom was squatted beside me. He whispered, "Your turn."

It felt good to be out of the swamp, so I moved under a large pine and placed my shotgun in my lap. I placed one of the Claymore clackers near my left leg and did a lot of thinking about nothing. It bothers me that our country is in pieces, and I pray one day I'd see it unified again, but Top didn't think it'd happen again in our lifetimes. *A man has to have hope, or there is no reason to live,* I thought.

It was then I heard a noise of some kind of machine, and it was in the air. In just a split second I recognized the familiar sound—helicopter! I moved to the others and touched each one on the foot. They came awake instantly.

Willy listened for a few seconds and then pointed at himself and Tom. He then pointed to a nearby clearing and finally, using his index finger and his middle finger pointed at his eyes. They'd go see what was flying around overhead. They moved to the edge of the clearing.

From what I could hear, the "whop-whop" sound of the bird was continuous and didn't vary, so that meant it was moving in a straight direction. However, it was getting closer and louder. If we were lucky it'd fly right overhead and Willy could identify it.

A few minutes later the sound was was gone and silence returned to the woods.

Returning from the edge of the clearing, Tom whispered, "I made it out to be a Chinese Habin Z-9. Mainly by overall design, the horizontal tail fins near the tail, and enclosed tail rotor. What do you think, Tom?"

"All I can say for certain is it had a red star on the tail boom. I don't know much about aircraft of foreign countries."

"Were they looking for us?" Vickie asked, and I could see the sleep had done her little good.

"No, the aircraft wasn't flying a search pattern and I think it was simply moving from one spot to another." Willy replied and then ordered, "Saddle up, we'll keep moving until dusk."

Damn, I thought, *I should have had a bit to eat before I went to sleep.*

The rest of the day was perfect, meaning we'd seen no one, and when we stopped near dusk, Willy pulled out a map. Under cover of a poncho and using his flashlight, he got our location, plotted a course and then said, "We'll move on in five hours."

As he folded the map, Ralph asked, "We're close, aren't we?"

"Less than five miles from where Top suspects a base camp may be located. Tom, you're on guard as the rest of us eat, so move up under a tree. Before we eat, get the Claymores out and then we'll all eat back to back."

I was tired, sleepy, hungry and not in a real good mood as I pulled out an MRE and read the label in the dying light, 'Chili with Beans.' I groaned, knowing they'd be fighting in my gut in an hour or so. However, I had to eat, so I opened the pouch and started eating. I must have been pretty damned hungry, because the meal was excellent, and a few minutes later I was asleep.

I had the last shift of guard and woke the group almost to the minute five hours had passed. All moved into the bushes to take a leak, and I smiled when I realized there was no sound. Most soldiers in the old days coughed, cleared their throats or spoke as they did their morning toilet, but we were as silent as death. Only the quiet and cautious were still alive now, the others long dead.

Once saddled up and ready to move, Willy pulled out his lensatic compass, looked at the glowing dial and said, "I'll lead and John, you pull drag. We'll move slowly due to poor light, but keep the noise to a minimum." He then slung his shotgun over his shoulder and pulled his pistol. He knew he'd not be able to keep us on course and carry a long gun.

It was slow going even with the moon out, and I fell so many times I felt like a complete fool. Then, less than two hours later,

Willy stopped. He signaled for all of us to stay, but must have changed his mind, because he then pointed to me and motioned for me to come with him. As I moved forward, the others spread out on the ground and if seen from above, they'd have resembled a star. I noticed the Claymores were not placed, so Ralph must have expected us to leave in a hurry.

Willy and I moved forward very slowly and often he'd stop to listen. I heard nothing and saw even less due to the trees blocking the moonlight. After close to ten minutes we spotted a small clearing in front of us. I saw right off it wasn't natural, because I could see stumps and the trees had been removed close to the ground. *Shit,* I thought, *a mine field. I hope he doesn't want to cross the damned thing; there is an excellent chance it surrounds the whole complex.*

Pulling his knife and then reaching behind him, Will cut a small switch. Whispering to me he said, "Not likely they have any pressure detonated mines, but there could be some trip flares or Claymores with trip wires. Stay in my footprints."

I nodded, and then he slowly moved forward crouched over. As he advanced, he was constantly moving the switch he'd cut from the tree in a figure eight in the air, about six inches above the ground. Suddenly he stopped, turned ninety degrees and moved his switch once more. I knew he'd just discovered a trip wire. He moved forward once more, now on a new path.

I don't scare easily, but moving over a minefield knowing if I made a mistake I could very easily die, frightened the living hell right out of me. My rear was puckered so tightly I could actually feel the pressure, as I could feel the sweat running freely down my forehead. The temperature was cool, but my sweat was from fear and not heat, and more than once I wanted to go back. Except, I couldn't, because the only safe place was right behind Willy. I wouldn't make it ten feet until something would explode or go off.

Finally, we moved from the clearing into some trees. Willy squatted, as I did once I reached his location. "Just on the other side of these trees is where the base should be. We'll move until we can see lights, then we'll crawl to where we can see the place. If it's large enough, they might have dogs, so that could be a prob-lem."

He pulled out an old pill bottle and then a small plastic bottle. He handed them to me, so I asked, "What?"

"One is pepper and the plastic bottle has ammonia. Both are hard on dog noses if they get after us. Sprinkle a few drops of ammonia on our back trail and then a few feet later some pepper, but only if dogs get to be a problem. Any questions?"

I immediately thought of Dolly, who I'd left with Sandra and smiled. "No."

Just minutes later we neared another clearing, and off in the distance I saw more lights than I'd ever seen in one place since the fall. Willy got down and once I was prone he whispered, "Crawl forward, but stay behind me. When I stop, move to my side."

Crawling is slow business, especially when you don't want to disturb the grasses or draw attention. I'd seen a number of high towers, which I suspected held searchlights, and maybe more than just a few machine guns. Someone in a tower, if looking in our direction, would see any grass moving as we crawled. No, he might not actually see us, but the movement would get his attention.

After a long time, Willy stopped and motioned me forward with his left hand. Once in place, I saw we were next to a road and the base was right in front of us. Pulling a small tablet from his pocket, Willy began sketching the camp layout and from the dim light of the base, I saw the first thing he drew was the compass directions on the paper.

As he drew his illustration, I scanned the base and marked as much of it as possible to memory. The first thing I saw was a runway, which worried me, then six towers from where we were positioned. I saw no aircraft parked in the open and no building large enough to house anything very large. I saw a guard with a huge German Shepherd walking between two high fences right toward us, but the man looked bored as hell to me. I elbowed Willy and pointed.

I felt a light breeze on my face and knew the dog couldn't smell us, so all we had to do was remain still and all would be fine. The man followed the fence-line and when it turned about 90% he started his stroll down the other stretch. From where we were, I saw no housing or barracks or much of anything else. I felt Willy tap me with his hand, and we moved back into the woods.

Over the next three hours, we completely circled the base and gathered as much information as we could. From what I could see, the place was well defended, had excellent lighting from someplace, and was something we'd want to avoid. Well, in my mind I wanted to avoid it.

Willy touched my left arm and I saw a guard with a dog approaching, but this time he was outside the double fences. The dog suddenly stopped and sniffed the air. I slipped the safety on my shotgun off.

The guard wanted to move on, except the dog didn't like the idea, and I suspected our scent was in the air. Willy touched me again, and at that exact moment the dog starting barking. The dog handler removed the leash the animal ran right at us.

Willy's shotgun sounded once and the dog fell, whining loudly. Willy began to crawl backward as he said, "Let's move, and fast!"

A siren suddenly blared, indicating the base was under attack, which was far from the truth. Once in the trees, we moved as quickly as possible in the darkness. I heard a loud pop, followed immediately by a *hiss*, and knew flares were being sent high into the sky. More pops followed.

By now the sun was slowly coming up, turning black to gray, and I was concerned, knowing the Chinese chopper could have came from the base we'd just visited. *Sonofabitch, how did those guys get all that gear and supplies? Do they have other choppers on the base?* I thought, and then realized something else. *Shit,* we *have to go back through that mine field!*

Suddenly, I heard dogs barking behind us and knew they had our scent. They were far enough behind us that I hoped they'd not reach us until we'd navigated through the mines. *We don't have the time to do Willy's circles of figure eights to get to the other side,* I thought, and hated the thought of running blindly through the field. If if we just run, one or both of us will be either killed or injured, and if captured one equals the other, because we'd die in either case.

When we stopped for a short breather, Willy said, "When . . . when we get . . . to the mine field . . . you go first."

I was gasping for breath so hard I was unable to get my words out, but I was thinking, *Me! Hell you led me through the thing at night!* So all I did was nod.

The barking grew louder so I managed so ask, "A. . . ammonia?"

"Not . . . yet. Run."

A couple of hundred yards later we ran out of woods and stood on the edge of the minefield. Willy, either seeing or sensing my hesitation said, "Stay to the right. . . of the cloth I have tied in place. . . on the trip flares."

Straining my eyes, I saw small pieces of cloth tied in spots. I moved to the first piece of cloth, actually expecting my ass to get blown away any second. By the time I'd moved to the fourth piece of cloth, I had some hope and felt some confidence. Turning to look behind me, I saw Willy removing the material. Smart bastard, Willy is. The dogs will lead the handlers right into this field, I thought, and then increased my speed because the barks were much louder now.

I'd just stepped from the field when I heard two gun shots, followed by the loud boom of Willy's shotgun. I stopped but was slapped on the shoulder by Willy as he said, "Into the trees."

Dropping down behind a large log, Willy yelled, "Get over here, because the mines will start to blow in a—"

A loud explosion shattered the morning stillness, followed almost immediately by a second. I heard the yelps of injured dogs and the screams of injured men. When I raised my head, I saw two men down, along with their dogs. At least fifty others stood near the opening, afraid to attempt a crossing.

Whispering, Willy ordered, "When I fire, empty your shotgun into the group. Ready?"

I nodded, and when he raised and started shooting, I joined the party. Men screamed and blood and bone flew in all directions, as bodies began to fall. As much as I dislike the task, I aimed a few shots at the dogs, hoping to keep our trail clear.

Shooting them brought tears to my eyes, but we had to survive, no matter how much it broke my heart.

We emptied our shotguns and as we reloaded, Willy said, "Back to the others now, and we'll not stop until we get there."

As I stood, gun in hand, I saw no movement toward us, but could clearly hear the cries of the wounded, animal and human. It was a sound that would haunt me forever.

We pushed ourselves hard as we ran toward our group. Branches and thorns tore at my face and hands, sending blood down my cheeks like tears. I glanced at my hands and they were covered with bloody trails. However, I knew to slow down could very well mean death, so I kept running.

As we neared where we'd left our group, Willy slowed down to a walk and said, "Slow and easy now. We run into the place, and they'll shoot us to hell and back."

A few minutes later, I heard Tom say, "Stop."

"It's us, Tom," I replied.

"Been hell around here the last few hours."

"Saddle up and let's move due north, we'll talk later."

"Yep, we need to hunt a hole for a couple of days." Ralph said, and as he spoke I watched a black dot appear on his forehead, his eyes grew huge, and then the back of his head exploded, sending blood, brains and bone in all directions. Then I heard the shot.

"Down!" Someone yelled.

I thought the command was bit late as a bullet struck my left calf, and sent me to the grass. I heard one of our Claymores explode, followed by screams, then a whistle. A group of men moved toward us, so Willy discharged another Claymore and tossed two grenades. Explosions filled the air, along with more screaming. I peeked over a log, spotted two men moving forward and fired my shotgun, laughing for no real reason as they fell.

Willy made his way to my side, sliced my pant leg open and said, "Graze to your thigh. You're goin' to have to run with this."

"I can run, just give the order."

I heard Vickie scream and when I looked at her position, she was standing and firing as fast as she could pump in a new round. Tom, I couldn't see, but heard his firing.

"Get up, we need to make tracks! Form on me, now!" Willy yelled.

I saw a big chunk of wood fly into the air from my log and heard a zing as a bullet ricocheted into the trees.

I made my way to Willy, and as a group, we began to run in single file deeper into the woods. After a couple of hundred yards, he dropped back beside me and said, "I need you to slow down and cover our rear. While you're doing it, sprinkle some of the ammonia on our trail and then in about a half a mile drop some pepper."

"I don't hear any dogs!"

"You will in a bit, because that's the fastest way to track us. Now, do as I said, because I don't have time to argue with you."

"I got it."

As Willy turned and started running, I pulled the container of ammonia out and sprinkled it on our back trail. I wasn't sure if it'd work, so after about a hundred yards I stopped and added some more. I ran until I figured I'd covered nearly a half a mile, then broke out the pepper. Once I'd completed the job, I ran to catch up. Nothing makes a man feel more vulnerable than being on drag with a shitload of bad guys on your ass, and you have to stop to sprinkle pepper on the path.

Finally, when I caught up with the group, I discovered they'd slowed down to an easy mile-eating jog that could be ran for hours without wearing a person out. I got into the rhythm of the run, and every few seconds I'd spin around and check the trail behind us. A few short minutes later, I heard the dogs.

CHAPTER 18

I kept listening to the loud howl of the dogs and was growing damned anxious when suddenly it grew quiet. All I could hear was our gentle footsteps as we jogged down a narrow trail. We would have to stop in a bit, because of the weight of all the gear we packed, and running in boots is no easy task.

We came to a small stream, maybe ten feet wide and a foot deep, and Willy walked into the water and said, "We'll move in this stream for a couple of miles. Then, once we've covered the distance, we'll turn south. Once we've cover about five miles moving south, we'll rest a bit."

"I. . . I don't think. . . I can do it." Vickie said.

"Okay, then sit your sorry ass down on that big rock over there and wait for the bad guys. When they get here, just tell 'em you don't want to play anymore." Tom said, and then added, "But, for me, I'm going to run until my lungs explode, if that's what it takes."

I shook my head and heard Vickie ask, "Why are you shaking your head?"

"I'm pissed at myself. I never would have brought you along if I'd known you were a quitter. See, I don't like quitters at all, and I never thought you'd turn out to be one when things got a little rough."

"Damn it, I'm tired, John!"

"Well, by God, I think we all are, but why are you the only one who wants to quit?" *I want her pissed,* I thought, *so she'll start moving. Once she gets moving, she'll keep going then.*

Willy suddenly said, "I ain't never had a woman worth a damn on any group I've ever led. I thought you were different, but I can see now that none of y'all are worth a shit in the field. Come on guys, let's move."

We took out jogging upstream and a few minutes later Vickie passed me with tear-stained cheeks, but she was moving. I disliked running in water because it was loud and there was no way to mask the sound. I figured once we left the water and stopped, I'd use the remainder of the ammonia and pepper to cover our trail. After that, we were on our own.

When we finally stopped, Willy and Tom rigged a Claymore mine to detonate by a trip wire and I sprinkled my dog protection on the ground. It'd work for sure, but not if they had unlimited dogs. I watched as Willy pulled an empty soup can from his pack and placed it on the ground near his foot. He then pulled out a white phosphorus grenade and some clear fishing line. He must have felt me watching him, because he looked up, smiled and said, "This is nasty. I'll rig this thing so that when someone comes walking down the trail, or even a dog, and hits the fishing line, it'll pull the grenade out of the empty can. The pin will already be pulled, so it'll explode before most realize what has happened."

"I've seen 'em before with frag grenades," I replied, but Willy Pete, as we called white phosphorus, was nasty and the resulting burns were terrible. Nothing could stop the burning as long as it had oxygen. The army taught us to pack the burn with mud to smother the air, but that was only until a doctor could be found.

"I don't understand." Vickie said.

"This soup can will keep the handle from flying off, so the grenade will not explode as long as it stays in the can. Once someone moves the fishing line, the grenade will be pulled from the can, the handle will fly off and then one hell of a hot explosion. Enough talk. Let me get this rigged and then we need to be making tracks." He then secured the can to a bush.

No one said anything to Vickie about her wanting to quit earlier and not a word would ever be said, as long as she kept up. She just needed a verbal kick in the ass to get her motivated and the army did that all the time, only now we *were* the army.

We'd covered about a half mile when I heard the Claymore go, and a few minutes later the Willy Pete grenade ruined someones day. I grinned and kept jogging, but as I spun around to look at our back trail, I could see white smoke from the white phosphorus grenade high in the air.

We jogged until dark, then moved under the low limbs of a big cedar tree and had a silent meal. We were out of Claymore mines and only had two grenades left, so we had no solid night defenses. I'd heard nothing of dogs the remainder of the day and imagined the dog handlers were still cursing us. According to Willy, the pepper and ammonia would bring tears to the eyes of the dogs, but not cause permanent injury, only their noses would start to run and render them useless.

I'd fallen asleep quickly, due to fatigue from running, but awoke shortly from a touch to my shoulder. I could see nothing in the darkness and I knew better than to speak, so I listened. I heard a faint noise, like a branch or limb brushing against clothing. I grew concerned when I heard it once more, but on the opposite side of the tree.

"Damned cheap-assed Chinese batteries!" An unknown voice spoke near our tree.

"I'm having the same problem. My NVG's work fine for about twenty minutes, then they start to lose power." A different voice replied.

I knew NVG's were night vision goggles that allowed the user to see in the dark, and I'd never thought of anyone following us having the capability, which deeply concerned me. It looked like darkness was no longer a friend. But, if the batteries kept dying on them, they'd soon take them off and move without them.

"Shit, these things are worthless if I can't see in 'em! Anybody have an extra battery?"

I heard four voices reply with a short, "No," and knew there were five folks looking for us, but it was unlikely they'd see us, even with NVG's, under the tree. When I glanced around, all in my group were hugging the ground and well hidden.

"Jones, shut your mouth and keep the noise down. My NVG is starting to weaken as well, so we'll head back to base. More than likely, they've moved north toward the Russians. And, Jones?"

"Sir?"

"I want to speak to you as soon as we get back."

I had to stifle a laugh, because I knew a good old fashion ass chewing awaited Jones for poor noise discipline in the field. I'd had a few of those in my early days in the army, and they were not pleasant.

I sat under the tree wound up as tight as a three dollar watch and didn't relax until a good hour after they'd left. Eventually, I dozed off.

Morning arrived with rain in the air and the threat of a serious storm from the west. I heard no more movement or barking dogs around our area, so it looked as if we'd lost them. Nonetheless, we'd still move like they were on our asses, and I figured Willy would make a beeline to Top and the cave.

We applied our makeup, closed our packs and clean up any tracks we could find in the area. Willy motioned us to gather around and once we were in position he whispered, "Straight line back to the cave. We'll move fast and only stop for five minutes each hour. With luck we should be there by noon."

An hour later, as we moved singly over a small clearing in the trees, I heard a chopper and before I could shout a warning, I heard machinegun fire. Vickie, who was out in the open, collapsed and was unmoving. I glanced overhead to see the aircraft climbing and turning to the east to line up another attack on us.

"Tom, let's cross the opening now and on the way we'll grab Vickie. We'll only have one chance before the chopper lines up for another approach."

"Let's move, now!"

We took off at a dead run, stopped by Vickie just long enough for each of us to grab an arm, and pulled her into the trees. Tom then picked her up and threw her over his shoulder like a bag of grain and we took off running.

I knew once the pilot saw Vickie's body was gone, he'd target the trees with his guns, because that's where he'd seen her headed. We'd not gotten far when tree limbs began to shatter and fall, as bullets tore huge holes in the ground and the sound of ricochets filled the air. Tom fell to the ground and then moved over Vickie, protecting her with his own body. A few seconds later the bullets stopped, and the sound of the aircraft grew fainter by the second.

Willy appeared from the dust, squatted beside Tom and asked, "Are you okay?"

"I'm fine, not a scratch."

"We need to treat Vickie, if she needs it and get moving. I'm sure they'll have a patrol out in this area within the hour. Hell, if they've got radio communications with the base, it might be much shorter than that."

Tom rolled Vickie on her back and I saw a head injury, which looked slight, and blood on her left thigh. Once he cut her jeans, I noticed a long furrow on her left thigh. She'd been very lucky, because bullets from machine guns usually blew apart what they hit. Tom wrapped both injuries and picked her up once more.

"We'll take turns carrying her and switch about every fifteen minutes. Hand her and your weapons to me right now. We'll switch carrying the weapons, too. Now, let's move."

We made it to the cave a little over three hours later and I was tired, hungry, and sleepy. Once past the guard, who Top had informed of our expected arrival, I made my way inside and received a loving welcome from Sandra and Dolly. After being kissed by both, I made my way to Top, who stood grinning by a table talking with Willy.

". . . and a Habin Z-9 flew cover. The same type of aircraft wounded Vickie, and I suspect it's based at the facility I sketched. What bothered me the most, Top, was the patrol looking for us had NVG's."

"Damn, not good. Are you sure they had NVG's?"

"I heard them bitchin' about the poor batteries they were using and how the power would start to go after less than thirty minutes."

Top thought for a moment and then said, "I don't think the NVG's are a serious threat then, because it sounds like the Chinese are issuing obsolete batteries, which makes them less than dependable. The damned chopper is serious business though, and I'll notify intelligence of all of this."

"Top?" I asked, and when he met my eyes I said, "We lost Ralph and couldn't bring his body back."

"Son, I understand, and I know Ralph doesn't care. This isn't like the old days, when we could call a chopper and remove our wounded and dead when we left an area. I only expect our wounded to be brought out and not even then if we suspect they'll die anyway. Since we have to pack our injured out, it only makes sense to save those that will heal to fight another day. By the same token, I want no wounded left behind either, if you get my drift. I find no fault in your thinking. Now, Willy, see your team is fed and allowed some sleep."

By Top's last comment I knew the conversation was over, so I picked up an MRE and moved to the sleeping area. I sat down and Willy joined me a few minutes later. I took a few bites of my entree and then asked, "You doin' okay with Ralph's death?"

"It's rough on me, but I'll be okay in a few days."

"If it means anything, I'm sorry. One thing for sure, he never felt the bullet that hit him."

Tears rolled down Willy's ebony cheeks and his voice quivered slightly as he replied, "He was one of he finest men I've ever known. He once had a loving family and nice home, but the fall ended all of that. He'd started working with me after things went to shit, and when we returned to his place one evening, his family was gone."

"Gone? Where'd they go?"

"We took one of my dogs, a big mix breed named Wolf, and found 'em dead about a half a mile from the house. His wife had once been beautiful, but her face had been completely destroyed by a knife blade, and she'd been raped a number of times. They'd cut her throat when they'd tired of her."

"That's a damned shame."

"They shot the boy and girl, but only after they'd raped the 'em both. She was only six and the boy four, but it'd made no difference to those animals. We found the prints of four men and the dog was kept close to me as we tracked 'em."

"Were you ever able to locate them?"

Willy gave a loud sigh and replied, "Yep, we found 'em about three hours later, and they were drunk as skunks. Ralph and I took them prisoners."

"Good," I replied and then fed my face a few minutes before I realized we had no place to keep prisoners. "Did he kill 'em?"

"No, he didn't, but I would have and never batted an eye either. He brought them before Top and the commander. All four were found guilty in what passes for a courts martial. Hell, they all fessed up to doing it, and were sentenced to death. Top thought the punishment should equal the crime, so each man was impaled on a red hot spike. I guess I don't need to tell you where the spike entered, huh?"

I chewed my food for a minute and then said, "Willy, to rape anyone, but especially kids and one a boy to boot, they deserved what they received. I hope the sumbitches suffered a lot before they died."

Willy leaned back on his blanket, closed his eyes and said, "Oh, believe me, those men suffered. Lawdy, did they suffer."

I stopped talking as I finished my meal, because I suspected Willy had told me enough, and I knew he was tired. With the fall and lack of police, scumbags ran around the countryside taking what they wanted. Families were murdered, rapes were common, and stealing turned into a way to survive each day for them. It was the old adage that only the strong survive. Now that we'd gathered into groups we had some defense from criminals, but the survivors, those that had survived to this point, had reverted back to a time before cavemen. The only real way of dealing with them was to kill them.

I must have fallen asleep, because I awoke later with Dolly and Sandra beside me. I sat up and watched men and women as they reported to Top or one of the other senior sergeant's. I felt movement at my side and when I looked, Sandra smiled.

"Are you doing okay?" I asked, and returned her smile.

"Tired is all. The Russian died the day you left, and Top had some men remove his body." She sat up beside me.

"Lack of blood?"

"I think that's what caused his death, but we didn't do an autopsy to determine the actual cause of death. Hell, it's not likely we'd have found much anyway, because we're not equipped to do much. We're just a step or two above basic first aid."

I dreaded the answer, but asked, "How's Alisa?"

"She grows stronger each day and is conscious most of the time now, but I still have to give her pain pills. She's a strong woman, and a real asset to us."

"Any sign of infection?"

"No, and I don't expect any. She's still on antibiotics and will be for another two weeks. At some point this week we'll remove the drain tubes from her stump."

I put my arm around her, pulled her close and kissed the top of her head. "Sandra, I love you, and want you to always remember that."

"Well, I love you too, so don't forget."

I raised her chin with my thumb and index finger and when her eyes gazed into mine, I leaned over and kissed her deeply. I felt my desire kindle and then flash into a strong flame.

A loud explosion rocked the cave and the air filled with dust and smoke. Men and women screamed, but I heard Top yell, "They're attempting to breech the door!"

CHAPTER 19

"Willy, get your team and Johnson's team out the back way! Go! Jameson, Wilson, and Prentice, your group is to follow the first teams out the back next. Turner, you and your group stay with me. Take weapons and your packs only! Move, People!" Top yelled, and I saw him move toward the booby traps that lined the entrance.

Willy stood, quickly cast his blanket aside and yelled, "Team 7, form on me!"

Sandra ran to the medical supplies, picked up two bags and slipped them over her shoulder. When she joined me, she had her shotgun in her hand.

"John, take point and if possible, when we exit, head due east!"

"Willy, we'll follow your group!" Johnston shouted.

"Yo!" I screamed as bullets began to strike the steel door on the entrance. I turned my flashlight on and move deeper into the cave. Dolly walked calmly at my side.

It wasn't until I neared a rope ladder, that I realized I was at the exit. Top had not mentioned disarming any booby traps, but I would make sure before I stuck my head up. I figured any traps would be near the entrance and not on the ladder. I waited until Willy and the team neared.

"Willy, hold the ladder as I go up. Once at the top, I'll scan for booby traps and if it's clear, I'll let you know."

"Go." Willy took hold of the rope.

The distance to the top was about thirty feet, but I wasn't worried about falling. It was when I reached the top that I discovered the exit was covered with a woven mat, which felt like it was covered with dirt. I pushed hard and the mat fell to the side, sending dirt to my face and rocks to those below. I wiped my eyes as clear as I could using one hand, and went up one more rung on the ladder. I slowly raised my head, but saw nothing except trees. Very slowly, I exited the hole and then began to search for explosives or trip wires, but found nothing. I leaned over the hole and using my right arm, which was extended into the cave, I motioned for them to come up. I pulled Dolly up using a rope and while she didn't like it, she didn't resist once in the air.

One at a time I helped the others from the hole, until Johnson's first man exited and I told him, "It's all yours now."

Willy said, "I'll take point, but John, I want you at our rear. Stay back about a hundred feet."

As we moved, I could hear gunfire and yells from the front of the cave, but it sounded to me as if they'd not been able to enter yet. I noticed Vickie, Sandra, Tom and Willy moving in front of me and wondered how far Vickie would be able to walk. She'd taken a light head wound and graze to her thigh, so she still had to have some pain.

Once, as we walked, we went to ground when a Chinese chopper flew high over our position, but for the rest of the day we saw no one. Tonight, as Sandra shared two MRE's she'd brought with us, Tom whispered, "In the morning we'll tag up with another group, if they haven't been attacked, and rest a bit."

"Who are they?" Tom asked.

"Our intelligence folks, or G2, so I suspect they'll want to know what is going on with Top. Each group was sent to different base camps so we could inform them of the attack on the cave."

"Do you think Top is okay?" Vickie asked.

Tom gazed into her eyes, then broke away and said, "No, I don't. I think they've all been killed."

Vickie lowered her head and said, "That's why I came along with you. I suspected the others in the cave would die." Then turning to Sandra, she asked, "Do you have anything for pain?"

"I can't give you much, because if I give you something strong and we have to run, you'll never make it." She reached into her medical bag, took out a pill bottle and let one white pill fall into her palm. "Take this, it's a light painkiller."

"Enough chatter." Willy ordered. "Guard will be Vickie, Sandra, Tom, John and then me. One hour shifts, then we start all over again. We'll start moving an hour before daylight. I want total silence the rest of the night."

I remembered how, before the fall, American's were soft and loud. Can you imagine a group of five sitting in the dark and not speaking for over ten hours in those days? It's hard, and even harder not to move much. Movement is usually spotted before a person is, so most of us stretched out to catch some sleep. I slept well, until I felt a touch to my shoulder and saw Tom in the moonlight. I moved to a position to watch over the others and got as uncomfortable as possible.

I was still sleepy and knew sitting on pebbles and sticks would annoy me just enough to keep me awake. Additionally, I didn't lean against a tree trunk or even try to get comfortable. I had to watch over my friends closely, or all of us could very well end up dead. Besides, they trusted me to keep them safe, and I'd damn sure do whatever it took to not let them down. Dolly, who was at my side, lowered her head to her paws as I scratched her ears slowly.

I was about to wake up Willy when I heard a slight noise and the night sounds disappeared. I slipped the safety switch on my shotgun to off and listened again. Leaning slightly to my left, I touched Willy on the ankle, and I saw his eyes open. In the moonlight, I cupped my hand behind my ear and saw him nod. He understood the night sounds were gone.

We sat in silence for well over an hour, before he whispered, "Wake the others. When they're awake, I'm going out there."

I nodded, knowing he could see the movement, and moved to each person, touching their leg. At the sounds of safeties switching to off positions, Willy said, "Don' shoot my ass comin' back in."

Fifteen minutes passed, and I leaned to Tom and whispered, "I'm going out—"

"Tom, I'm at your 1400 position. Come to me now." I heard Willy say in slightly lower than normal tone.

When I met Tom's eyes, he shrugged and moved toward Willy.

A few minutes later I saw Willy nearing, and he was helping a man to our position. Behind him came Tom assisting another man and finally, a man I didn't know walking under his own power.

Willy and his group moved to us and he said, "It's Top, Smith and Skinner. The cave fell to the attackers and those inside went out the back, and had to escape and evade. These guys were moving to G2 when they collapsed."

"Where's Alisa?" Vicki asked, and I could hear the fear in her voice.

"She's dead, and so are many of the others. When the door blew open, it struck her and she died instantly. The survivors went out the back and fled to the four winds."

I heard Vickie crying softly. I suspected Top or one of the men inside killed her to prevent her capture. If captured, she'd have been used repeatedly and then killed. Of course, I knew Top would never tell anyone what really happened, because he was too professional to do that. I also knew it'd bother him for some time to come.

"Which of you is the most seriously wounded?" Sandra asked from my side.

"Smith took a round to his left lung, and I patched 'em up with part of a zip lock bag. Don't laugh when you see it, because all I had at the moment was duct tape and the bag, but I managed to seal the would airtight, so he could breathe again." Top said.

"And, Skinner?"

"I'm not hurt at all, but I carried Smith most of the way and I'm worn out. I ran out of fuel right in front of y'all."

Sandra was digging in her bag as she asked, "And, how about you, Top?"

"I took a knife blade in the upper left shoulder and have a concussion for sure, but the head hurts the most."

"Of a rating of 1 to 10, with ten being the worst, rate your pain."

"Fifteen."

Handing something to Top, Sandra ordered, "Take this and it'll help the pain a little. I can't give you anything stronger without it putting you to sleep. Now, if you gentlemen will excuse me, I have to cover myself with a poncho and check Smith."

Suddenly a bright light appeared from the general direction of the cave, followed long seconds later by a muffled blast. Top laughed lightly and said, "Someone opened a case of special grenades, I fear."

From the size of the light, I knew most of the ammo had gone up along with other supplies, including gasoline or other flammables stored. The blast would have killed anyone in the cave at the time.

Sandra pulled he poncho off and said, "This man is dead."

"Internal hemorrhage?" Top asked.

"Most likely, but we'll never know for sure."

"Well, Top, let me start with you and give you both the once over."

Willy suddenly ordered, "Tom and John, move out a ways and guard this place."

"Yo!" Tom said and as I stood, I heard Top say, "They couldn't have followed us, because they were too busy looting the cave."

"I want guards out anyway."

I glanced at Dolly and said, "Come."

Near daylight, just as a false dawn was on us, we returned to camp. Willy said just above a whisper, "We've got to move, and quickly. At some point today both Top and Skinner will come down with a fever. Once that happens, we'll go no place."

I gulped part of an MRE Top threw to me and was glad to have it. I was tired, but knew if we could get to G2, I'd get some much needed rest. A few minutes after I'd placed the empty MRE in my pack, I heard Willy say, "Saddle up, we're movin'."

As we moved just slightly faster than a walk, I thought, *What kind of future does our country have now? In the past it was always Third World countries who suffered from internal strife and wars, but we've gone from a world superpower to third world nation in less than two years. Hell, the last I heard, we didn't even have anyone making a move to pull us together or take over as a leader. How can this continue, or will it be as Top predicts, someone will eventually take control?*

Near noon, as we took a short break, Willy pulled out a map and went over it with Top as they squatted near a large oak. A few minutes later, as he folded the map, Willy said just barely audible, "We should be there in less than an hour. They know we're coming, because Top radioed them before he left the cave."

Tom asked, "How do we know they got the message?"

Whispering, Top added, "They replied, so they're expecting us."

Sandra neared and asked, "How's the head, Top?"

"Headache, but I'll live, but the shoulder is throbbing now." He looked feverish to me.

"Once we reach a safe house, I'll fix you up good as new." She said, and then handed him another pill.

"Let's move, people," Willy commanded, and our break was over.

A little over an hour later, as I walked point with Dolly, she suddenly stopped and gave a low warning growl. I'd been expecting to run into a guard or someone, but I saw nothing.

I whispered, "What is it, girl?"

She continued to growl and jerk on her leash, so keeping the leash firmly in hand, I moved with her, allowing her to make her way toward the threat.

"That's close enough!" Came a loud command from a female. I suspect the voice wasn't much over a normal tone, except we'd been whispering so much it sounded like a shout to me.

I stopped and said, "Sit, Dolly."

"Who are ya and what do ya want?" The same voice asked.

"I'm looking for intelligence or G2 as the army calls it. I'm with Top and pulling point." I hoped telling her that much wouldn't get me killed, but we were long overdue at the safe house.

"Where did Top send his last radio message from?"

"I suspect the cave, since we don't have any other radios that could transmit the distance to y'all here. Only to be honest, I don't really know. Look, I'm tired, hungry, sore and not in the best of moods, so either shoot my ass or wait for the main group. Right now, I don't really give a shit which you do, either."

A strikingly beautiful woman stepped from the trees, and I've seen more cloth on a babies diaper than she had on. She was well proportioned, with deep blue eyes, long red hair and just a tad over five feet tall. Of all things, she was wearing a camouflage bikini, and it reminded me of the guns and ammo ads I used to see in magazines before the fall. The publishers obviously were using sex to sell their products and it'd worked too, except the buyers were usually men. Well, this woman would have sold a mountain of guns.

I must have been staring intently or drooling because she laughed and said, "Ya look like ya ain't seen a woman before. Hell, how long ya been livin' at the cave?"

"Not long, and it's not the fact you're a woman, but how you're dressed. Surely that ain't the uniform of the day?"

She gave a deep sexy laugh and replied, "No, not hardly. I've only got two other sets of clothin', woodland camo fatigues actually, and they're washed and hopefully dried by now. It was my turn to pull guard, so here I am."

"I have a small group on my tail and they're good people. We have one man with untreated injuries and another that's had to put off her treatment for a spell. Is your position considered safe?"

"We're as safe as it gets these days, but nothin' is certain. Your dog is well behaved."

Lawdy, woman, you'd make a small dog break a huge chain just to lick your palms, I thought, but said, "Her name is Dolly, and she was trained for security before the fall."

"I like that, 'the fall,' because it fits."

"What do you do with G2, or do you guys call it intelligence?"

"G2 is fine, and I'm a linguist and photo interpreter. I was on active duty when things turned to hell, so here I am. Most of us here are prior army, but I was Air Force."

I heard a slight noise behind me and when I turned, the group was approaching slowly. I had to admit, they looked like death warmed over.

I realized I'd not asked her name, so I asked and she replied, "Kate. If ya folks will follow me, I'll get y'all to the house."

As the group neared, I saw every eye on Kate and knew her bikini had caught their attention. Willy met my eyes, winked and whispered, "I'd follow her right into the flaming gates of hell."

Sandra shook her head and while she didn't say anything, her eyes narrowed as she gazed into my eyes. I gave a silent chuckle, walked to her side and said, "Her uniforms were dirty."

"Wipe the drool from your mouth." She whispered, and then laughed.

Like a fool, I reached for my mouth, but found it dry, so she gave another laugh. I shrugged and replied, "I am a man, remember?"

"Well, I can see right now, I need to get you alone so we can verify that statement. It's been too long, John."

I took her free hand and held it in mine as we walked. After a few steps I said, "I'm human, baby, and I was pretty shocked when she stepped from the woods dressed like that."

Once again she laughed, and after a few seconds said, "I wish I'd seen your face! It isn't everyday that a beautiful half naked woman holding an M16 rifle steps from the trees to ask questions."

I gave a blank look and asked, "She had a weapon?"

Top, who'd been walking behind us, burst out laughing and said, "Yep, she did and a sidearm, too."

"What kind of pistol?"

"Uh, well, I don't remember. I got to her hips, saw a holster and well, followed her legs all the way to the ground."

The three of us laughed and it felt good, it felt real good.

CHAPTER 20

The safe house was anything but a house, and was actually a well camouflaged barn that'd been emptied of hay and critters. It was ancient too, the wood unpainted, and the color reminded me of bark from an oak tree. As we neared, men and women were seen with weapons in their hands watching our approach cautiously. Finally we entered the structure and I was surprised by the desks and a couple of old manual typewriters I saw. Off in the corner appeared to be an old personal computer, but I knew it was worthless.

A man who looked more like a college professor than anyone involved with intelligence or the military made his way to us and said, "I'm Colonel Thomas Parker and the chief of intelligence. Top, it's good to see you again and you, too, Willy."

"Sir, do you have any medical facilities or supplies?" Sandra asked.

"Yes, we have both, and I see you have the need too. The last room on the right is our examination room and it'll have to do, because it's all we have. As for supplies, you'll find most of what you need in the room."

As Sandra, Top and Vickie made their way to the room, I heard my wife say, "Top, you first, so I can look you over better and give you something for the pain."

Willy introduced us and as we shook hands, I noticed for a man I'd thought was a bookworm, he had a solid handshake.

Parker said, "I want all of you to follow me into my office where we can talk in private."

Kate, standing with the butt of her M16 on her right hip and her hand holding the barrel, winked at me as I walked by her. *Lawdy, now that I don't need. I suspect she's teasing me, and right now that's the last thing I need,* I thought, and then entered the office.

"Pull up a chair and let's discuss what has happened and why." Parker pulled out a well worn leather chair and sat.

After each of us telling what we knew and with Willy handing him a copy of the sketch he'd taken of the base, Parker grinned. He studied the sketch for a few minutes, reach down to the bottom drawer on his desk and opened it. He removed a folder and sat it in front of him, and then pulled out a bottle of bourbon whiskey, along with some cheap plastic picnic cups. Pulling the cork on the bottle, he placed about two fingers of whiskey in each cup.

"Gentlemen, please, take a cup of whiskey and let me tell you what I know up to this point."

He waited as each of us took a sip of the drink, and I smiled as the amber colored alcohol burned a trail to my empty stomach. I then placed my cup on the corner of the desk. Dolly looked at me and I patted her softly on the head.

Parker opened the folder on his desk and said, "The Russians and Chinese both have military advisers in our area of operations, with the Chinese being our biggest threat. From what we've been able to find out so far, the Russians have sent no aircraft, missiles or tanks. The Chinese, on the other hand, have sent all three but in limited numbers, which to me indicates they are clearly here to stay. Right now, I think both countries are simply testing the waters to see if an invasion or other military action is feasible or even worthwhile. Our intelligence is not very good, so I may be wrong about all of this."

"Hell, colonel, just the land would make it worthwhile." Tom said.

"No, I don't think so, because our once waving fields of endless corn and wheat are no more. The Chinese would have to bring in farmers, protect them, and even supply their own seeds. The agriculture of our country died along with our government. It just wouldn't be cost effective for them take our lands. I'm afraid the airlift and security costs wouldn't justify the end results."

Willy said, "Political influence is my guess. If they can back an American leader, get him to gather up a large group of followers, and perhaps unite the whole country, they'd have a thumb in the pie once we became productive again."

"Why hasn't the United Nations protested the simple fact both countries are here?"

Parker gave me a smile a professor would give his favorite student that was close, but not really on the mark, and said, "The United States of America owed both countries billions and billions of dollars, and they're both claiming they have a right to be here since the United States no longer exists. They're laying claim to our land since we defaulted on the loans."

"Why they're here really doesn't mean a rat's ass to me." I said, and then continued, "The question is, how do we get rid of them. I think we should try to find out where they are and how many are here." I picked up my whiskey and threw the remainder of the drink back, giving a light cough as the alcohol burned my throat.

"Excellent idea, John, and my thoughts exactly. I have a number of teams, both here and at other locations, researching that information as we speak, but our access to solid intelligence is limited. See, we have a few computer geeks who've modified some old computers to access the internet. Now that we have that in place, we're attempting to hack websites that will provide us with a little more needed information."

"Hell, there aren't any internet access providers still around these days." Skinner said.

"No, they're all out of business, but we were able to gain satellite access using a provider from India. However, I'm not at liberty to explain how that was done. The computer folks located an old satellite dish, made some magic changes to some things, and lined the dish up properly. It works, and well."

"What good is a computer without power, or do you have a generator?"

Parker smiled and replied, "We now use solar power, because running a generator made too much damned noise. We've gained access to a few military sites of both countries, but I can say no more about the project. You gentlemen do not have a need to know anymore than what I've just told you."

"What now?" Willy asked.

Standing, Parker said, "I suggest all of you get a bath in the river behind the barn, eat a good meal, and get some sleep. If you need medical attention, you can use your medic or see one of mine."

"Who do we see about the food?"

"We have a small kitchen behind the barn in an old storm cellar, and it serves our purposes most of the time. It's manned around the clock, so someone will feed you. Just have Kate show you were it's at, but don't clean it out of food." Parker said and then laughed. I knew right off he's been in the military and knew how much a hungry soldier could eat.

When we entered the main area of the barn, Kate was standing by the doorway with a rifle in her right hand. Hearing us, she turned. She was standing in such a seductive pose I decided to leave the group, "I'll see if Sandra wants to eat and be right behind you."

Sandra was finishing up on Vickie when I entered the small room. "If you're about finished, we can grab a bite to eat."

"Sure, just give me a few minutes."

A few minutes later, as she washed her hands in a basin filled with pink water, she said, "Top and Vickie won't be joining us for a meal. Both were given morphine and will be asleep in a few minutes. I also gave Top some antibiotics and started an IV with fluids. He has a slight fever, but it'll get worse before it gets better. The knife injury I'm not so worried about as I am his head. He told me when the door flew off the entrance to the cave, a part of it struck his head. That confused me, because I thought the door killed Alisa."

Now, I don't make it a point to lie to my wife, but felt she didn't know what I only suspected so I said, "A solid steel door is heavy and that one must have weighed a ton, because it was mounted on rollers. The door may have blown off, struck Top in the head and then fell on Alisa. Her death would have been instantaneous."

"I know enough about combat to know strange things happen, and it's not a big deal anyway." She dried her hands on a bloodstained towel that any hospital before the fall would have thrown away.

At the cellar, I saw nothing of Kate and I relaxed a bit. I suspected she was simply teasing me, but I didn't like it at all. There wasn't enough room in the shelter for all of us to eat, so we took our aluminum trays and moved under a large pine tree. The meal was simple but tasty. We had stew, cornbread, and believe it or not, milk served in an aluminum cup.

I took a long drink of the milk and then asked, "How'd they get milk here?"

Willy laughed and then said, "The colonel has two cows hidden back a ways, and they're guarded all the time. He only issues milk to fighting troops and guards, which I've heard pisses off his G2 folks. I also heard a rumor that he even makes cheese, but I've never seen any of it."

"Well," Skinner said, "it's damned good and much better than the bourbon he gave us."

"I wondered about that too, the bourbon I mean," Willy said as he looked over the rim of his aluminum cup. "Where in the world does a man get good Kentucky sippin' whiskey when for all practical purposes the state of Kentucky doesn't exist anymore?"

"He has some connections, and that's all we really need to know. Hell, he's got a working computer, so whiskey should be a snap." Skinner added, and then took a spoonful of stew into his mouth.

Sandra, who'd been silent and didn't know about the computer before now, said, "Lawdy, I must have fifty thousand unanswered emails." She broke into a loud horselaugh, and we all joined in for a few seconds.

Seeing a confused look on Skinner's face, I asked, "What's the matter?"

"The meat in this stew isn't beef."

"Nope, it ain't." Willy said, but didn't add anything else to his comment. I noticed the trace of a slight smile on his lips.

He's baiting the guy, I thought, and then grinned.

"What is it?"

"You got a soft stomach?"

"Hell, no, I'm an airborne Ranger. If it's slower than me, I can eat it."

"How about you?" Willy asked, as he met Sandra's eyes.

"Nope, my stomach is strong enough. We've had to eat cats, bugs, and even snakes since the fall, why?"

"Now, I ain't one hundred percent sure, but it tastes like dog meat to me."

Dolly growled and I touched the side of her head and said, "Stay, you're okay, baby."

"Dog?" Skinner asked, as he placed his tray in the grass beside him. I guess he was suddenly full or didn't like the idea of eating Fido. He looked pale and weak to me, so I quickly turned to Sandra, wondering how she'd react to Willy's comment.

She took a big spoonful of stew, looked over at Willy as she held in near her lips and said, "Bullshit." She then began to eat her stew.

"Ask the cook then."

My wife smiled, met Willy's eyes and said, "I grew up on a farm and I know what this meat is, believe me. It's not dog, horse, cat or some other domestic animal, because I've eaten all of them since the fall."

Willy grinned and winked at me before he said, "Okay, Missus Know-it-all, what in the hell is it then, if not dog?"

"This meat, sir, is 'possum."

Tom asked, "You ain't serious? You mean that rat lookin' gray thing with the curled hairless tail?"

"Yep, Tom. You, Sandra are wrong, but close!" Willy said.

"Close?" Sandra said.

"It's really rat."

Skinner, the big badass Ranger, suddenly gained his feet and moved for the woods, his tray forgotten.

Tom gave a blank look and took a bite of the stew before he said, "Hell, this stuff ain't half bad, huh?"

We broke out laughing again and after we sobered up, Willy said, "Actually, I have no idea what it is, but I'll eat it anyway."

Sandra looked in my direction and said, "Don't ask Mister Survival, hell, John will eat anything, and I do mean anything at all. I guess it really doesn't matter where the protein comes from as long as we get enough to stay alive. I'm positive some of the greens in here are dandelion greens and water cress."

I said, "Right after the fall we had all kinds of stored foods and supplies, but I wanted to save most of it for hard times. Then, when Tom here and his wife joined us, the stockpile doubled." I noticed Tom lowered his head when I brought up his wife, but death was part of life and he had to learn to accept her death.

"So, was she lying about all the different stuff she'd had to eat?" Willy asked.

"Nope, in order to save our foods, I'd bring in everything from worms to deer for supper. Now, I'll eat damned near anything, but I'm not crazy about cat, insects of any kind, or bird eggs with embryos, and we had all of them at some point."

Kate suddenly appeared, and I noticed right off she was dress in her woodland battle dress uniform and the bikini was gone. Seeing Willy, she walked to him and said, "Colonel Parker wants you and your team right now."

"Any idea what's on his mind?"

"Not hardly. Colonels don't usually tell junior grade sergeant's much of anything. He just said to find you and have the team come to his office."

Willy stood and said, "Let's drop the trays off in the kitchen and then go see the colonel. Skinner!"

"Yo!"

"Bring your ass over here. I think we have a mission brief to attend!"

"I'm comin', but if one of ya starts talkin' about eatin' dog or that other shit, there'll be a fight."

We laughed, and made our way to the kitchen.

This morning, an hour before dawn and after a night of good sleep, we were once again on the move, only we had an additional team member—Kate. According to the colonel, she was not only an expert on languages and photo interpretation, but also a qualified sniper. I looked in her direction again and thought, *You remind me of a black widow, deadly. You have the looks and body to entice any man alive and the knowledge, along with skill, to kill. I don't want anything to do with you. It ain't normal for a woman to train to be a sniper.* I thought a bit more on the subject and finally realized times had changed, but I hadn't. I was still thinking of a wife in the kitchen getting supper ready for her husband when he came home from work, but those days were long gone. Every living thing alive was now a killer or soon died.

I finally reached the conclusion the reason I wanted so badly to dislike Kate was simple; I was attracted to her. I also realized that since Sandra and I had not been alone in close to a year, most of my attraction toward Kate was pure physical need. I loved Sandra with all my heart, but I'm a man and every woman knows most men do their thinking from below the belt. I'd seen Kate's body and I have to admit, it impressed me, only now I'd get to see how her mind worked, and that was what really mattered in the field. When bullets started flying and people dying, the size and shape of a woman's breasts suddenly lost any importance.

Tom, who was on point, held his left fist in the air and we went to ground. A fist in the air was an old army command to stop and seek cover. Well over twenty minutes passed before he moved to us and whispered something to Willy. Willy stood, pointed at me and then down the trail we'd just walked. I moved at a slow walk, knowing he wanted me on point as we backtracked a ways. Dolly walked beside me as if she was on a stroll on a country road. She hadn't growled, so that meant there was no one in front of use when we stopped or the wind was such she didn't smell anyone.

Once in a while I'd glance back to see when Willy wanted me to stop or move in a different direction. Finally, when I glanced back after about a half mile he point to the woods on the right side. I moved about fifty yards into the trees and then squatted as I waited.

A few minutes later the group joined me and then Willy asked, "Now, what was that about a tank?"

Tom looked as serious as death as he said, "I saw a tank by the river. I'm no tank expert, but it looked like a T-90S to me. I know the damned thing had two machine guns on top."

"Chill a little. I didn't hear a tank."

"The crew was working on the tracks when I saw it. They had a long link of track in front on the left side. It looked like the track had come loose and continued rolling until they stopped."

"They're not a real threat right now, but might have some things Colonel Parker would want to get his hands on."

"Willy, that thing has a huge gun, and I saw two machine guns."

"The gun is a 125mm smooth-bore gun and the guns on top were a 7.62mm machine gun and a 12.7mm air defense gun. The crew is made up of three men, a commander, gunner and driver."

"Had at least ten men there and I know they weren't all crew."

"Most likely the others were left for security as the crew repairs the tank." Willy replied.

"What now? Do we take the tank or go around?" I asked, really hoping he'd not say what I expected.

"We take the tank, but only on our terms."

CHAPTER 21

Willy handed a grenade to me and one to Tom. I felt my heart beating hard in my chest and wondered if the others could hear it pounding. I had a Claymore in my pack, but it'd be like throwing rocks against a tank, or so I thought. Kate was positioned on a slight hill behind us where she could snipe, if need be, and the others were lined up in the grasses as close to the tank as we dared go as a group. I looked at my watch, and it was 0500, time to start the show. I looked at Dolly and commanded, "Stay." I knew she'd be there when I returned, if I returned.

We lowered ourselves to the ground and slowly started crawling forward. About half way to the huge vehicle, I spotted a guard leaned against the rear of the tank, and touched Tom on the arm. He nodded, so I knew he'd seen the man. Earlier in the day, just before dusk, we'd watched the Russians eat and then the crew went inside the tank, while the rest moved to holes they'd dug in a rough circle around the tank. I'd spotted a machine gun pit along with an assistant gunner or ammo carrier, but all the other holes had just one man. I'd seen a few sandbags thrown around, but I don't think any of them seriously thought they'd be attacked.

My shotgun was in my left hand, and in my right I carried an old United States Marine Corp Ka-Bar knife that I'd had for twenty years. My father had owned it before me and used it in Vietnam. Suddenly Tom stopped moving, touched me and pointed off to his left. I knew he wanted me to kill the man in the hole to our left, while he moved forward.

I moved with caution toward the lone occupant, except a few minutes later I heard his soft snores and relaxed a little. I quit moving less than two feet from his hole and waited. As soon as the clouds moved a bit more and blocked the moon, I'd strike hard. I saw the faint outline of his head and shoulders and noticed his head was hanging to the side as he slept.

As the clouds moved, I waited with every nerve on edge, because the slightest noise or smell, and I could very well die within the next few minutes. Then, just as the moon slid behind the clouds, I sprang forward and placed my left hand over the Russian's mouth and slid the sharp blade of my knife over his throat as I held his head back. His body twisted and turned, but I held him firmly in place as blood spurted into the air. I heard a few muffled Russian words behind my hand, but then it changed to choking, until his body went limp a few minutes later. I felt blood running down my left arm and a coppery smell filled the night air.

As I turned to move toward the tank once more, I saw the silhouette of Tom moving for the guard at the rear of the big vehicle. Then, as I watched, the shadows mixed and became one. Crawling to the tracks of the tank, I waited, praying Tom had taken his man out. *Okay,* I thought as I saw the outline of Tom's boonie hat against the sky, *let's get this over with. This thing sure has a strong odor of diesel. Hell, they might have a fuel leak too.*

When he neared me, he smiled to let me know he was okay. Motioning with his thumb, he let me know he was ready to deliver our eggs. We both climbed on top of the tank and I was happy to find the hatches open, because if they'd been closed we'd made a wasted trip. Willy assured me that most tankers didn't button up at night if they could help it and wanted the fresh air. He claimed with the smells of oils, fuels and men passing gas, a closed up tank turned foul pretty quickly. I suspected with men circling them, they had a false sense of security.

Tom glanced at me as I pulled my grenade from my shirt pocket and pulled the pin, holding the handle tightly. He held up three fingers and I knew when the last one dropped, so did my grenade. Like me, he'd already pulled the pin on his grenade, holding the handle closed in his left hand. We wanted to deliver our surprises at the same time. He lowered the first finger, then the second and finally the third, I simply let the grenade fall from my hand into the tank.

It landed with a loud *clunk,* followed a second later by a second almost identical sound. I heard one of the crew ask a question and then heard a loud command of some sort. The drivers hatch opened and a man started out when the explosion occurred, throwing the screaming man into the air. We both jumped from the tank, just as flames shot from the open hatches and screams sounded. I prayed the men in the foxholes had no idea who we were and thought we were members of the tanks crew running to escape the flames.

As soon as the explosion filled the darkness with light, I heard one, two, then a third controlled shot from the hill Kate was positioned on. I kept running toward the trees and heard the sounds of Willy and the others firing. Large clumps of dirt jumped from the grass in front of me and it took me a second to realize it was from the machine gun. I began to run in a zig-zag pattern to avoid bullets.

I reached the trees in safety and Tom was hot on my heels. We move to the right and approached Willy and the rest of the crew. The Russians no longer returned our fire and I watched for movement, but saw nothing. Willy gave us a thumb up when we neared.

The tank blew at that moment, throwing the turret high into the air as the ammo and fuel exploded. The light from the explosion was so bright, I could see the individual trees across the field, well over two hundred yards away. I saw a head pop up and look around, heard Kate fire, saw the man partially raise up and then fall back half out of his hole. The light was intense, as was the heat from the fire, so we waited.

"Skinner, run back to Kate and ask her if she's any trapped down there or how many she thinks still live. Be sure to ask her about the damned machine gun!" Willy ordered.

Skinner took off and returned a few minutes later out of breath. Once his breathing was under control he said, "She thinks the crew on the machine gun crew are dead and the only one yet alive is on the other side of the tank, on the far side."

Willy looked at his watch, then glanced at the sky and said, "It'll be daylight in about ten minutes. We'll approach the tank and kill any survivors. Then, go over all the clothing and take everything you can from the pockets. Take any maps, papers, or personal letters you find, take it all. Pick up the weapons, ammo, and anything else we can use. Any questions?"

There were none, so we waited.

Just as the sun peeked over the tree behind us, Willy said, "Let's get this done and then continue our mission." We moved forward as a group.

I heard Sandra's shotgun fire once, followed by a penetrating scream and then the Russian machine gun opened up! I saw Vickie go down and Skinner's head explode as I dove for the ground. I fired at the gun, pumped in a fresh shell and fired again. Suddenly it grew quiet.

"Cover me," Willy yelled, and ran at the machine gun. Once at the hole, he fired four rounds from his sawed-off shotgun into the Russians. I stood on unsteady legs and looked around. Sandra was moving toward Vickie and Tom was checking Skinner. Me, I joined Willy and we made our rounds, shooting into men at each of the holes we found.

When we returned, Sandra met my eyes and said, "Vickie has a sucking chest wound and it doesn't look good. Skinner is as dead as he'll ever get and half his head is missing."

"Well, this idea was pretty damned stupid, huh? I get two people killed, blow a tank to hell and back when I didn't want to do that. I wanted the communications in this tank, because we need it! I don't understand how this happened. Sonofabitch, I lost two people and gained not a damned thing!"

Tom lowered his head and said, "I poked holes in the bottom of the gas cans at the rear and sides of the tank before we threw the grenades inside. I did the job right after I killed my guard. I never thought of anything other than the fire that would—"

"Enough. The fuel used on these tanks is diesel and it's not as dangerous as gasoline, but when you poked the cans, the fuel had time to run into every nick and corner of the tank. I wondered what had caused all the fire, and now I know. Now, everyone start searching the bodies and gathering up weapons."

Tom lowered his head and said, "Willy, I'm—"

"Let it go, buddy. I should have warned you, but didn't. You've been trained to destroy and by God, we've done that! It don't mean nothin', as my daddy used to say."

A half an hour later we gathered by Vickie as Sandra said, "She's tough and is still hanging on. Only I think she's all torn up inside, because the bullet tumbled after hitting bone. The exit wound was near her hip."

Willy pulled his pistol and said, "We can't be held back by someone we don't expect to survive. If I thought this woman had one chance in hell of living, I'd carry her every single step of the way back in my arms. But, I can't risk our lives." He pointed the gun at Vickie's head and squeezed the trigger. Her body jerked once, quivered a few seconds and then stopped moving.

Willy crossed himself and walked toward the woods. As he moved he said, "Let's go, we're going back to the see the colonel." I watched him pick up four AK's and slip the slings over his neck.

Just before I entered the woods, I looked back at the tank. Black oily colored smoke rose high into the sky and the dead littered the field. The smoking turret was fifty yards away, laying on it's side and flames were still coming from the hatches. My attention was distracted as Dolly made her way to me with her tail wagging. I took one more backward glance and looked into Vickie's unseeing but open eyes.

Shortly after entering the woods, Willy took a compass heading and we moved in a new direction. *He's wanting to throw anyone who may try to follow us off our real route,* I thought. Tom brought up the rear and Willy was on point, so I kept Dolly on a leash beside me as we moved. Sandra and I often took turns with the dog, but I'd had an uneasy feeling about the attack on the tank and felt revenge would be swift. While Dolly would do whatever Sandra told her to do, her response time to me was much shorter.

It was then I saw Willy drop to one knee and bring his fist into the air. He cupped his left hand behind his ear. I listened, but didn't hear anything, but then picked up a high pitched whine and it seemed to be overhead.

"Down, now!" Willy screamed.

I had no idea what in the hell was going on, but I fell to the ground and rolled up next to log. I heard an aircraft pass over us at a high rate of speed and caught a slight glimpse of the silver body. I then heard an explosion and looking behind us, I caught sight of a huge ball of flames rising to the sky—napalm! Thank God, we were too far away to feel the heat, but some people had just been burned to death.

Willy moved back to us, pulled out his map, and whispered, "There is a small town on the other side of where we attacked the tank. I suspect the Russians think that's where the attack originated."

Another jet screamed overhead and once it passed us, Tom asked, "No one lives there, do they?"

"I suspect not, but if they did—"

The sound of another explosion was heard and, a fireball roared into the sky near the first one.

"If they did, they're dead now. Let's move people, and do the damned job quickly."

We took to the trail once more at a jog, which I hated since I was carrying about sixty pounds of gear and equipment from the Russians. I glanced down at Dolly and she met my eyes and grinned. She was enjoying the run.

Every hour we stopped for ten minutes, until finally, when darkness was about an hour away, Willy moved us back into some stunted cedars surrounded by tall oaks.

Kate, sweating profusely and breathing hard, threw her pack on the ground and bent over trying to get her breath. I flopped to the ground and pulled Dolly close, scratching her ears as I tried to breathe. Sandra sat beside me, winked and then gave me a big smile. *I have one hell of a wife. She just jogged about ten miles after attacking a Russian tank, and she smiles,* I thought as I smiled back at her.

Whispering Willy said, "Our original mission was to meet a guide in the village the Russians hit with napalm earlier. I doubt our guide stuck around after our fight with the tank, but if he did,

Colonel Parker is now short one guide. With no guide, we'll return to camp."

"Do you think the Russians are on our back trail?" Tom asked.

Willy shrugged and replied, "Hard to say, really, because they don't think like we do. I'd say they suspected the attack came from the village and they burned the shit out of it already. No, I think our backside is clear."

Kate reached into her pack, pulled out a set of straight shank climbers, and started attaching them to her legs and boots.

Sandra gave me a questioning look so I said, "Climbers, just like a lineman uses to climb poles."

Sandra nodded as Kate said, "I'm going to climb to the top of the highest oak I can find. I'll take my rifle and see if anyone is following us. My scope means I won't need to take binoculars with me."

"Tom, you go with her to provide security as she scopes the area."

A few minutes later they were gone.

I took all our canteens to a small stream, filled each, and returned to camp. I leaned with my back against a tree watching Sandra eating her MRE, which reminded me I was hungry. I'd just pulled my meal out of my pack when I heard a single shot. I started to go to ground when Willy said, "That was a 30.06, and it sounds like Kate found a target."

I then heard two more shots with less than three seconds between them. I opened my meal and began to eat. As I reached for my pack, so I could put the plastic from my meal in it, I heard another shot.

We waited, but Willy seemed cool about it, so I relaxed. I knew he had complete confidence in Kate and while I wanted to trust her, the only ones I really trusted were Tom, Sandra and Dolly. I wasn't sure about Willy yet and while he had his shit together, he sometimes made some strange decisions or forgot to tell us important things, like our attack on the tank and the gas cans. Now I realize a leader can't remember everything, but most of us lacked the training he had and none of us had been a Green Beret or Special Operations. Granted Tom had been a Ranger, but some folks with us had no training at all.

A little after dark, Kate and Tom returned.

"How many were on our back trail?" Willy asked.

"How many shots did you hear?" Kate replied.

"Four."

"I don't miss."

Tom said, "We visited the kill site, and they had a Russian and 3 locals in the group. I brought back the weapons, grenades and foods."

Willy was quiet for a minute, then asked, "Clean kills, Tom?"

"Each was a head shot."

"Eat, and we'll be sleeping back to back tonight."

Morning dawned chilly compared to most mornings and as we loaded up to move, I saw Kate holding an AK47 in her hands. Her sniper rifle was on a sling around her neck. I moved to the trees to relieve myself. I'd just started to pee when I heard a twig snap. *Oh, this is just great! Here I stand with my stuff in my hands taking a leak and folks are attempting to sneak up on us,* I thought and tried to cut the flow of my urine, but that takes time. A few seconds later I buttoned my jeans and made my way back to camp.

I neared the group and whispered, "Danger."

Everyone went to ground before I did, so I felt a bit pissed as I fell to the ground and crawled up beside Sandra. I heard and saw nothing, only I knew that meant little. Dolly was beside us, so why no warning growl?

I looked over then, and spotted movement. However, I watched, hoping to see the movement develop into a man. That didn't happen, but it continued to move parallel to our position, and finally I got a good view. A huge 12 point buck walked into a narrow clearing. I reached behind me, removed the compound bow I'd been packing for months, and made an arrow ready. When the buck lowered his head to eat, I raise to my knees, pulled the bowstring back, and released the arrow.

The arrow struck the buck right behind the foreleg and I knew it was a killing shot. Usually a deer will run a few yards before falling, but this one collapsed. Willy appeared beside me and whispered, "What?"

"Big deer."

"Killed?"

I nodded and pointed, "Check your 12 O'clock position."

"I see it. Quarter the meat, we need to leave."

CHAPTER 22

When we returned to Colonel Parker, he was happy to get the meat, and even happier we'd destroyed the tank.

"By God, they'll think the only group strong enough to have attacked them was the ones with the Chinese backing. I hope, and I'm likely correct, they'll retaliate against the other group."

Top, looking better, but still a bit weak said, "Our dead can't be identified by any markings, so they'll naturally assume it was their biggest enemy."

Willy was standing near the table, and had just shown Parker where the tank had been and the small town we'd seen burned. "One of our dead was a mercy killing."

"No one life is worth the risk of others and we all know that." Parker said bluntly.

"I think your guide got his ass out fast, once he heard the fight." Top said, and then continued, "The town has been empty for years, so I doubt the Russians did much, except burn some places."

"Yep," Parker said, "he's a smart man and an excellent guide. Prior to the fall he was a wildlife management officer for the state and knows every damned rock and stream in the whole state."

"'Possum patrol, or so we called them before the fall," I said, and then laughed.

"What now?"

"We're gearing up to attack." Parker said, and then smiled.

"Attack? Hell, there ain't but a handful of us, so who could we attack?" Tom asked with a confused look.

Parker smiled again, which worried me more than just a little, and said, "The big base your team sketched and visited a while back."

Willy's jaw dropped and he said, "Not me. I don't have a death wish."

"Relax," Top said, "and it won't just be us. How does close to three thousand of us sound?"

Parker ran his hand over his stubble covered chin and said, "Not a month ago we joined forces with another large group and combined under one central commander. Our total strength is close to four thousand, but none of them are gathered in any large groups. We're scattered all over the state, but in the morning, we'll all start moving toward one location. I will not tell anyone this location until we are moving and then only those with a need to know. Once together, we'll form up and attack the base. Keep in mind, we'll take no prisoners and can't because when we leave we'll leave quickly."

Top, obviously unaware of all of this, asked, "Am I to accompany this group on the attack?"

"Top, you can go, mainly because I'm tired of listening to you bitch and moan everyday about how you hate G2. Additionally, when the actual attack takes place you're to remain with me, the commander. Do you understand the order?"

Top snapped to rigid attention and replied, "Loud and clear, sir! Airborne!"

Tom, Willy, and I gave a loud "Hooaahh! Airborne!"

While Sandra smiled, Parker looked shocked, but finally he said, "Damned airborne troops, get the hell out and let me get back to work. Willy!'

"Sir?"

"Feed your folks good tonight. I've asked the cook to give each member, including Kate, a steak from the deer you brought back. Prepare to march in the morning, let's say an hour before daylight. Now, get out of here. Dismissed!"

As we left, we were all in a good mood and there was the usual grab-ass and jokes as we made our way to the door of the barn. Dolly moved to my side, so I asked, "Willy, does Dolly get a steak, too?"

He'd just put his beret on and it hung at a cocky angle on his head as he replied, "Of course she does. The colonel said every member gets a steak and she is a member of our team."

I scratched the top of her head and said, "We'll eat good tonight, girl."

Morning came with a misty rain that I hoped wasn't an omen of what was to come. I wondered what we'd do if Russian Aircraft showed, because we had nothing that would down a plane or chopper. While I'd not seen any Russian choppers, if they had airplanes it seemed to me they'd have to have them around, too. I put my makeup on, jumped up and down to listen for noise, then checked my weapons. I'd oiled my shotgun and it was hanging on my shoulder, near the bow on my pack, but I now carried an AK47, which I respected a great deal.

Willy walked to me and said, "You and I will be point for the group. Our heading is 120 degrees and here's the map. Remember our magnetic declination is zero degrees for Mississippi. I'll count the paces when we're relieved, until then Tom will do the job."

I gave him a smartass look and said, "Let me guess, he has his ranger beads out, right? He carries those things like some do a rosary."

Willy gave me a big grin and said, "Now you know he does. Tom's a Ranger all the way. I was wondering, too, why you never tried to be a Ranger or Green Beret."

"I thought about it, but my first wife got pregnant at about that time and I decided to get out of the army. I loved the army and I'm as patriotic as the next guy, but I didn't want to get my ass killed and leave a wife with a child to raise on her own."

"Well, you have what it takes to be either, and I don't say that lightly. Did your child survive the fall?"

I lowered my eyes and said, "No, the fall killed my two kids and my wife. My wife's death is a long story, but my kids were killed when things turned to shit, and the have-nots came looking for those that had. My boys were grown by then, but both were killed defending their families like real men. Unfortunately they didn't save them in the long run. I lost both boys and four grandchildren that day. Not to mention both daughters-in-law as well."

Willy cleared his throat and said, "I lost all of my immediate family and none of my brothers or sisters survived either. My father, who was ill, killed my mother, who was even sicker, because they couldn't find any food or medicine. He then turned the gun on himself. Listen, we could stand here all day and talk about this shit, but we need to get moving and do it now." He gave me a quick pat on the shoulder and I knew most of us carried heavy losses.

The barn was a real animal house as folks ran around trying to locate gear, ammo, or their lost heads. Most had no idea what we faced, and I heard a couple say they were looking forward for their first combat mission. I knew they'd return, if they survived, different folks then they were now. No one can see the elephant and not change inside, no one.

Colonel Parker entered and folks grew quiet. He wore his camouflage makeup, had an M16 in his right hand, and an old steel helmet on his head. He said, "We are about to start the first of many efforts to regain the control of our country, the United States of America. Look around at the faces on either side of you. Some of you will not be returning. Many of you will die in this effort, but your death will not be in vain. I promise you, once we have our nation back, we will always honor those who fall this day. Now, Chaplain James, please lead us in prayer."

A short black man with little hair walked from the group with a Bible in his hand. He look at us as if searching each soul. Finally, he said, "Let us kneel. Oh heavenly Father, we are about to embark a dangerous mission, and death for many of us is a real possibility. We do not fear death, Father, because we know once we throw away our human bodies, we are born again in your kingdom. Father, we do not kill because we are murderers, but to regain our nation and to bring glory to your name. Once you assisted our forefathers in carving a nation out of the wilderness and we thank You for that, only now we need help again. Return our nation to us and we will glorify the name of God for evermore. This I ask in the name of Jesus Christ, our Lord and Savior. Amen."

Parker stood, put his hands on his hips and yelled, "Let's go kick some Russian ass, Hooaahh!"

The barn echoed our loud war cries and I heard at least four people scream, "Airborne."

Well, they're loud enough, but it remains to be seen if they can fight worth a shit, I thought as I moved for the door. *Yellin' doesn't win wars, guts do that.*

"I hope to hell they make less noise than this once we get in the field." Tom said as he walked to my side. "If not, we might as well stay home."

"Tom, these folks aren't soldiers or fighters, but keep in mind, they'll learn quickly or die. In the past our citizen soldiers have saved our country many times, and I suspect if these people get pissed enough, they'll fight."

"I don't think they'll have much of a choice in the matter once we hit the base. Every swinging dick on that base has experience, so our folks better be fast learners. You know, I never in my wildest dreams, *ever* imagined our country would go hell like it did, and so fast, too."

Parker shouted, "Okay, form into your groups in a few minutes and from this point on no talking at all, and I mean not one damned word. If one of you compromises this mission due to noise, I'll personally shoot your ass when we get back. Let's move people, we have a mission to complete."

Folks began to move around, some obviously lost, but the colonel came over to us and said, "Willy, you're the point man for this goat roping affair, so keep your group a good hundred meters in front of us. Avoid contact, if you can, at all costs. Once we meet the others, we'll decide then how to best attack the place. I'm afraid this group, while their spirits are high, really couldn't overrun an empty shithouse."

I chuckled and then Parker continued, "John, I want you and Willy to run a recon on the base once we meet the others. It's imperative that you not be seen or even suspected of being in the area before we attack. Do you think you two can do the job?"

Willy grinned and said, "Yep, as long as you keep these folks far enough away that they can't be heard. Keep in mind, the Russian and Chinese have aircraft in the area so when you get to the staging area, get these folks under cover and quickly."

Parker looked at his watch and said, "Let's move, we've an appointment that I don't want to miss."

The misting had stopped, but fog filled the valleys and low spots as we moved into the woods. It felt cooler, so there was a cold front moving in, but the fog would help us in reaching our destination. My concern was if any of the aircraft the Chinese or Russians had could see through the clouds using thermal imagining or infrared technology. I'm a grunt, not a fly boy, but I know both methods work, only I was unsure how the weather might come into play.

Someone had located or brought in two old RT-10 survival radios and they were the pits, unless you were kids. The range was line of sight, or less, depending on hills and other obstacles that might block the radios. Top, who walked with us had one radio and the colonel had the other. We had two spare batteries, but when I looked at them earlier, the batteries had expiration dates of five years ago. My only hope was that we didn't have to depend on them to save our asses, because I had absolutely no trust in them.

"Echo One, go Golf One."

There was a minute or so of silence, then Top said, "Roger, copy five by five."

Top stored the radio in his old Air Force survival vest and gave me a grin. I liked the man and wished I'd had served with him on active duty. He was at least twenty years older than me, only I suspected he could walk me into the ground, and I saw how he reacted when injured at the cave. See, some folks grow scared after being injured in combat, and I think it's a perfectly normal reaction. I had an old first sergeant named Wilcox who said, "The best thing for a troop after being injured and they are released from the hospital, is to go on another mission." I know I'd been injured twice, neither were life threatening, but both scared the hell out of me. I jumped after every loud noise or sudden movement for a long while. Finally, Wilcox, who must have seen my jitters, sent me on a recon. It didn't cure me, but it did relax me a bit, and then after a few more missions I calmed down some. I've always remained vigilant, but I'm not as jumpy.

Hours passed and I was surprised that I heard nothing from the group behind us. Then, Tom stuck his fist into the air and we went to ground. He pointed to himself, then his eyes and raised two fingers, and then pointed straight ahead. This clearly meant, he saw two men. Then, he'd indicated he was going to check them out.

I flipped the safety on my shotgun off. I heard Top break squelch on his radio, which meant to the colonel to hold up a few minutes.

Minutes passed slowly before Tom returned and moved to my side. He cupped his hands around my ear and whispered, "Two men guarding an intersection of two dirt roads. I need you to take 'em out with your bow. Can you do that?"

I nodded and then slipped the safety back on and handed my shotgun to Willy. I removed my pack and pulled the bow from the D rings. I made one arrow ready, met Tom's eyes and nodded.

Willy, realizing what we were about to attempt, shook his head as if we were crazy and then grinned. I think he liked the idea, which scared me, because Willy was dangerous at times. Before I could move forward, Kate appeared and pointed at her rifle.

She'd made some sort of silencer for her sniper rifle and I chuckled when I saw it. Using an old plastic soft drink bottle, she'd attached it to the muzzle of her gun. The bottle was held in place by a radiator hose clamp. I'd seen them before, in various military classes I'd attended on unconventional warfare, but had never seen one actually used.

Willy gave a huge broken tooth grin and nodded in an excited manner, so I cupped my hands over her ear and said, "Let me try to take them both, if something goes wrong and it likely will, you take 'em out."

She nodded in understanding and we moved forward very slowly. As we moved I thought, *Kate is a confusing and complex woman. She's beautiful, intelligent, a sexual tease, and cold when it's time to kill. She is a perfect woman for the conditions we live in now. While I love Sandra and deeply, Kate is a real woman in many ways. I respect the hell out of her.*

Tom stopped and pointed to his 10 O'clock position. I saw three men, not two, and they were sitting on a sandbagged position, obviously guarding the crossroads. All three were wearing a mixture of old military and civilian clothing. Kate moved to the left and Tom right, so I gave them a few minutes to get into position. After about five minutes, one of the guards moved straight toward me, unbuttoning his pants as he neared. I'd already stuck two arrows in the soil beside me, so they'd be handy. I pulled the bowstring back as far as it would go. He'd just pulled his penis out when I released the arrow and saw it take him in the middle of his chest. He staggered, looked down at the blood on his shirt, and then fell to the ground without saying a word. I noticed, just before he fell, the arrow had gone completely through his body.

"LeRoy! What's the matter with ya? LeRoy?" A huge figure of a man called from the sandbags. He was well over two hundred pounds, six feet and then some, and wore a camouflage cowboy hat. The hats had been popular a few years back, so I wasn't surprised. I watched as he slipped the safety off his open sights 30.06 deer rifle. He turned and said something to the other guard, which I couldn't hear, who promptly moved behind the sandbagged position.

The big man was experienced and as he moved toward the downed man, his head scanned his surrounding and his weapon was held at the ready.

I'd picked up another arrow as soon as my first had struck LeRoy, so I was ready for the man. I pulled the string back and thought, *Just a few more feet and I'll put this right in your breadbasket.*

He stopped beside the downed man and just as I released the arrow, he squatted. I saw my arrow take him high, in the shoulder, so I picked up another arrow, but before I got it to my bowstring, he was up and charging right at me. While he'd dropped his rifle when the arrow struck, I saw a huge Bowie knife in his right hand.

He struck me hard and knocked me ass over teakettle. The big bull of a man was on me in a flash, so I raised my hand to block his falling blade. My hand met his and I knew he was stronger than me, injured or not. I pulled my Ka-Bar knife and heard him grunt as I pushed it into his soft belly. My blade hadn't gone in far, when he suddenly rolled from me and then rose instantly to his feet. Blood was pouring from his gut and shoulder, but he still looked as mean as hell to me. I knew his injuries had weakened him some, but he was still much stronger than I was, and as pissed as a grizzly bear with a toothache.

He suddenly charged and I sidestepped, extending my left leg hoping to trip him, but he simply jumped over my leg and then turned and rushed me once more. At the last second I fell to my back and using my legs, I caught him in the chest and propelled him over me. He landed on his belly, so I rushed to where he lay and pushed my blade to the hilt into his back near his kidneys twice.

He raised his head to scream, and I grabbed his hair and cut his throat. He moaned and then began to choke. A few minutes later he died clawing at the dirt.

I heard a soft pop and when I glanced at the last man, he was down, the upper half of his body draped over the sandbags. Blood from his fatal injury flowed slowly down the sandbags to the dirt below.

I turned back to the man I'd killed. I stripped him of a grenade, Bowie knife, pistol, and all of his ammo. I retrieved his rifle and cowboy hat. The hat fit, so I tossed my old hat away and donned his. Tom suddenly appeared and whispered, "Cover me."

I flipped the safety off the 30.06 and watched as he approached the man I'd killed with the arrow. Tom squatted, and his knife flashed once as he cut the man's throat and then he stood. He then moved to the man on the sandbags and when he neared, he sheathed his knife. Picking up gear and supplies, he returned a few minutes later.

Kate returned as well, wearing a big grin.

Tom looked at Kate and said, "Head shot at the sandbagged position and your silencer worked well. Now, Kate, I need you to return to the colonel and bring him forward."

"I could use the radio." Top offered. He and the rest had moved to our position once they spotted us walking fully erect.

"No, no radio. Let's not use it unless we need it. I want to keep the noise level down as much as possible." I realized Tom didn't trust the radios either.

Top nodded and Kate disappeared down our back trail.

CHAPTER 23

"Parker looked at the dead men and said, "This was a remote outpost to check any vehicles or people moving on the roads. Pull the bodies into the woods, remove the sandbags, and make it look as if no one was ever here. Now, I know we can't cover every trace and a well trained eye will even spot our attempt to cover the killings, but the average person will see nothing. Continue your mission, Willy."

We moved forward once again and I was holding Dolly by her leash when she suddenly growled and I thought, *Hell at the rate we're moving, it'll be next year before we get to our target.* I looked, but saw nothing. I raised my fist into the air knowing everyone behind me would freeze.

Minutes passed and finally I spotted a large buck step into a clearing. I gave a loud sigh of relief and moved forward. The buck saw my movements and in two jumps was back in the woods. I chuckled inside, because Dolly hadn't been much of a deer hunter in the old days.

Four hours later we'd seen no one and neared the rally point of our other forces. Once again I was on point with Dolly, when a man wearing bib-overalls and ball cap stepped from the woods. He pointed an old double barreled shotgun at me and said, "That's fur 'nough. Who are ya, and what're ya doin' heah?"

"I'm takin' my dog for a walk."

He laughed, spat a glob of chewing tobacco from his mouth and replied, "Bullshit. Yer wearin' all that green crap on yer face. I'm smarter than I look."

You have to be, I thought, but said, "I'm the point man for a larger group and we're to meet some friends near here."

"Well, I ain't hear'd tell of no point man, so I ain't sure what in the hell ya be, but I reckon we mighten be that group of friends yer looking fer." He gave the call of an owl, which made me almost laugh, since it was still daylight and owls only come out at night. I was surprised to hear an owl answer him.

"What now?" I asked.

"Sit yer ass in the dirt and keep that dawg of your'n on a short leash. Now, we wait."

A few minutes later a man walked from the woods, smiled and said, "Good job, Bubba Lee. Who are you, sir?" Before I answered, I looked the man over. He wore a Green Beret at a cocky angle, his shirt was an old BDU, and his pants were jeans. In his hands he carried an AK47, and beyond a doubt, he knew how to use it. I hoped he was one of us, if not, I could kiss my ass good-bye.

I explained that I was here to meet some friends and we were all going to attend a party.

I heard movement behind me and when I turned, Willy stood in the clearing. Smiling, he said, "Jacobs? Frank Jacobs?"

"Willy, you old sonofabitch! How ya been, buddy?"

"I'm fine. Listen we're part of the group you're expecting and John here, with his dog, is our point man."

Frank motioned for me to stand, moved forward and shook my hand. He had a solid grip and I like that in a man. He said, "Sorry about Bubba Lee, but he did what was expected of him. He don't look like much, but he's a real bad ass in a fight. Dumb as a box of horseshit, but loyal to America and those he calls friend."

Willy waved the rest of our folks forward as Top pulled the radio and alerted the colonel.

During the next few days, men and women arrived from all over the state and gathered in the woods around us. I prayed the Russians didn't send any choppers up or we were toast. Many of the people were motivated and dedicated to the dead American dream, but few knew how to fight. I wondered how many of them would be alive next week. The commanders and leaders of the various groups spent a great deal of time making their people camp under the trees and not out in the open.

Finally, I heard Colonel Parker say, "We'll strike at first light tomorrow. Willy, I want you and your group to take out the towers and guards on the inside of the double fences. Once that is completed, hang back and wait for us to breech the fences. Once we're inside, I need you to support the hotspots."

Willy said, "We'll do our best, sir."

"Since we will strike early, I want your people in position just after midnight tonight. Move in close and at 0500 start taking out the targets on the this side of the base. I'm depending on you to silence the night guards."

Good God, it sounds like we take out the guards, then they attack as one huge pissed off mob, I thought. *It might work, but I'm glad as hell I'm not in the first few ranks of the mob, because most of them will die come morning.*

"This side will be silenced first, then we'll go completely around the base and take out as many as we can. We'll do our jobs."

"I'm sure you will, Willy, and good luck."

It's a little after midnight, and I'm watching a couple of men in a tower sleep. The guards that walked the fence line were not seen and hadn't been since I'd arrived. *Perhaps they've grown confident and lazy since they've Russian support,* I thought and glanced at Willy. He grinned and then winked.

Over the next almost five hours, I watched the base but saw nothing moving and that worried me. Were the guards in the towers really asleep or just pretending? Could this be a plan to massacre our attacking forces? I didn't think so, but it concerned me.

Finally, at 0500, Willy touched my shoulder and I moved to Kate's side. I spotted for her as her sniper rifle with the home-made silencer sent two low thuds into the night air. When I looked at the tower, both men were gone. It was then I saw the guard with his dog walking the fence line.

I touched her shoulder and pointed.

Her first shot killed the dog instantly, because I saw it's head explode as the bullet struck. Her second shot hit the dog handler in the center of the chest and he fell without making a sound. We moved to the next tower.

The next four towers were easy kills for Kate and I must admit, she's one deadly shot. Unlike the military, we didn't document her kills, but she was good. As we neared the final tower she slipped and fell and her rifle struck a tree trunk. She retrieved it, glanced at me, and said, "My scope has been knocked out of alignment, so you'll have to use the bow on this one." She then shrugged.

This tower looked no different the others, except the guards were now awake with the rising of the sun. I watched as one opened a thermos and poured something hot into the plastic cup. I notched an arrow and then pulled the string back. Lining my arrow up on the guards back, I released and saw the arrow take him in the middle of the shoulders. He didn't scream, but I watched him turn in my direction and then look down at the arrowhead. His hand came up to feel it and at that point he collapsed. The other guard turned and scanned the area, his weapon at the ready, so I grinned when my arrow hit him in the center of his chest. However, he gave a loud scream just before he fell from the tower, and landed not ten feet from me.

I heard a loud explosion, followed a few seconds later by a second, and then hundreds of loud screams. I suspected the fences had blown up. The attack was happening. A machine gun began to spit death, but I had no idea who owned the gun. We were on the opposite side of the camp and instead of going around the fence, Willy placed a grenade on the first fence. Once it blew we did the same with the second. We were inside the base within seconds. It would have taken too long to run around the fence to help the others.

I took Dolly's leash from Sandra as we began to move forward at a run. A man ran from the open space between what looked to be aircraft hangers. My AK47 spat flame, and he fell screaming. Willy ran to the first hanger, looked inside and smiled, just before he pulled a grenade from his vest and pulled the pin. Tossing it, he screamed, "Fire in the hole!"

The grenade exploded, followed by a much larger blast, and two figures ran from a side door engulfed in flames.

"Move!" Willy yelled as he ran toward the second hanger. Just like the first, he tossed in a grenade, yelled for us to move on and two explosion were heard. However, the first hanger suddenly blew to bits, with parts of aircraft, the structure and people flying high into the air. A loud *'boom'* filled the morning air. Knocked to my ass by the concussion and landing beside Willy, I screamed to be heard, "What in the hell was in there?"

As we gained our feet, Willy replied, "Fuel truck!"

Flames rolled into themselves high in the sky, and black smoke poured from the building as we moved forward to continue our battle and to escape the heat of our destruction. A squad of men ran from a small white building and we opened up on them. AK47's fired, along with M16's, and I heard a few loud *booms* from shotguns. The squad was torn to rag dolls as our bullets and buckshot struck them. Screams were heard as the men fell.

A bullet zipped by my ear, missing my head by less than an inch, but I suspected it was a stray round. I heard a scream behind me and knew someone had been hit, only I couldn't stop to find out. We had to keep moving. Willy moved toward the small white house and as a group we followed him. When I moved to his side, he yelled, "Throw in a grenade! I'll kick the door open!"

I removed a grenade from my BDU shirt cargo pocket, removed the tape over the pin, and held it firmly. Glancing at Willy, he nodded. I pulled the pin, watched the handle fly into the air, and heard the *hiss*. Knowing I held a live grenade, Willy kicked the door, but it didn't move an inch. There were four small panes of glass at the top of the door, so using the butt of his rifle, Willy knocked them out.

I tossed the grenade into the room and fell to the ground. I heard screams and confusion inside the building, only not for long. The grenade exploded, knocking the door from its hinges and our people rushed inside. The firefight lasted just a few seconds and then it grew quiet.

Willy, who'd been one of the first to enter, exited with two men with their hands over their heads. Both were Russians.

"Kate and Sandra! Keep an eye on our friends and watch them closely. Both are clean, but we need to move forward. Stay here and if they move, kill 'em." He then spoke to the Russians, who nodded in understanding, and said to me, "High ranking officers, a colonel and general."

"What now?" I asked. I suddenly heard a series of loud blasts and when I turned, five huge fireballs were climbing to the sky. *Damn, looks like the colonel got himself a few aircraft of some kind,* I thought.

"Link up with the colonel!" Willy shouted, and we moved toward the crazy mass approaching us. Before we'd attacked, each of us had placed a two inch strip of yellow or orange material around our left arms. This was to aid us in identifying each other in the heat of battle. Our uniforms, or our lack of uniforms, made it difficult to tell us from the bad guys. The only enemy I was sure of wore a Russian uniform. Another hint was we all wore camouflage face paint.

We weren't halfway to them when I saw fingers of red and green tracers cut through the group. Screams of pain and dying filled me with shock, but Willy was already moving toward one of the sources. To our left the loud *tat-tat-tat* of a machine gun was heard. One of the bad guys lay near me with a Rocket Propelled Grenade and I picked it up and fired. The machine gun flew high into the air with the explosion, and smoke and dust was all that remained.

The other gun would be harder to silence and we were out of grenades.

"Flank the thing! Go around and come in from the back!" Willy yelled at me. I tapped Tom on the shoulder and off we ran. We'd not gotten far when a large group of Russians ran toward us and we knelt as we fired in a controlled manner, one well placed shot at a time. Finally, I realized they were going to overrun us, so I fired on fully automatic as Tom did at almost the same time. Bullets struck the concrete in front of me, sending bullets in all directions. Tom gave a loud grunt and when I glanced in his direction, he was down. I didn't have time to check him, or I'd soon join him, so I kept firing. Dolly growled and barked, but stayed by my side. My gun snapped on empty, so I change magazines and slowed my shots down. I reached down and released Dolly's leash from her collar. Perhaps she'd survive, because it didn't look good for Tom or me. I cursed loudly, because I didn't have enough ammo to keep my weapon on fully automatic for long.

Most of the surviving Russians went to ground, but two ran right for me. The one in front I sent to hell with a bullet in his head. I lined up my sights on the last man, took a deep breath and as I released it, I squeezed the trigger—nothing! I heard Dolly give a series of loud warning barks!

Shit! I thought and then saw the bayonet on the end of his Russian SKS rifle. I prepared to meet the man head to head, when I heard a shot and down the Russian went. Glancing at Tom, he smiled.

I started to move toward Tom when someone struck me from behind, knocking us both to the ground. As my luck would have it, I was on the bottom and the wounded Russian had a pistol in his right hand. I grabbed his wrist and held tightly, because to let go would mean my death. Blood spattered on me from the man's chest wound, but he was still as strong as an ox. I watched the pistol turn toward me—then heard a loud shot.

I felt no pain and felt the man fall to the left. I opened my eyes, which I'd closed to avoid powder burns, and saw Tom standing over me, still grinning. He held his rifle in both hands. Dolly was tearing at the Russians throat and I called her to my side. Her teeth and mouth dripped warm blood.

"Come on, we still have a machine gun to blow up!"

"How bad are you hit?"

"Bullet grazed my right arm and knocked me on my ass! Let's move, folks are dying."

Putting Dolly back on her leash, I ran after Tom. Tracers filled the air and bullets bit deeply into the concrete as we ran, throwing fragments high into the air. We neared the machine gun, and I saw a man covering their rear, rifle at the ready. I fired once, and saw him fall against the gunner, who turned and looked behind him. From less than fifty feet, I saw his eyes grow huge as he realized he'd been flanked.

Please, Lord, don't allow any of Parker's people to shoot this way, or it'll get rough! I prayed as I ejected my clip and inserted a fresh one.

The gunner attempted to turn the gun, but he and I knew he didn't have the time. His ammo man, who'd been the last to see us, pulled his pistol and fired. Bullets zipped by the side of my head, but none struck home. The gunner, now frightened, ran from his sandbagged position, so I released Dolly from her leash.

Tom fired once and the ammo man fell, but he raised from the sandbags a second later with a grenade in hand. I instantly flipped my weapon to automatic and stitched him the length of his body with lead thread, starting at his crotch. He fell back, as Tom and I went to ground. A hollow boom sounded and when I glanced up, smoke fill the air over the position.

A deathly silence filled the early morning air. Not a sound, except the moans of the wounded and cries of the dying were heard. I heard no gunshots, no explosions, and it surprised me.

It was then that Tom nudged me and pointed behind us, as he said, "Damn!" A group of maybe a thousand people were running toward us and all were armed.

CHAPTER 24

Shaking my head and hoping Sandra knew I loved her, I prepared mentally to take as many with me as possible when I died. Just as I was about to release a stream of lead into the crowd, I saw armbands on them, and I realized they were our troops! Dolly suddenly appeared by my side and I heard her low warning growl. I reached down and scratched her bloody head.

I looked behind us, and Colonel Parker and what remained of his group were moving forward. I wasn't sure of the cost of this place in lives, but the surrounding area had many down and most were not moving.

Parker reached us first, congratulated us on wiping out the machine gun and then said, "This group nearing us is from up north, around the Tennessee line. Good people."

Suddenly the two groups blended into one, and folks were laughing and shouting to the point I grew concerned about the noise. I was about to turn away and start helping the injured, when Parker approached with another man and said, "John and Tom, meet Colonel Frank Hanks. He's the commander of this group."

Hanks smiled and said, "Sorry about our holdup, but we ran into two tanks and it took some work to take 'em out. They were just inside the fence line, behind the hangers."

"Top!" Parker yelled.

"Sir!"

"Form details and search for our wounded. Have other details remove everything from this place we can use, and I mean anything."

"What of the enemy wounded, sir?

"These assholes left no wounded of ours when they started this mess, so no prisoners."

"I'm sorry sir, but that doesn't answer my question."

"Kill 'em! By God, is that plain enough, Top Sergeant?"

"Yes sir, as you ordered."

"Sir, do you have other need of Tom or myself?" I asked, worried about our group at the small white house. During the battle we'd separated and I was concerned about Sandra. While I'd left them with the Russian POW's, that didn't reduce my fear level by much.

"No, that'll be all. Gather your group and move back to our base camp. Make sure it's secure, and then have one of the men I left there return to let me know."

"Yes, sir." I replied, and then began to look for my wife.

The battlefield was cluttered with dropped weapons, bodies of both sides, blood, and damage to almost everything standing. I neared the small white building, or what remained of it, and found the two women sitting on the ground. The two officers were still there, but the General had a new bullet hole in his left arm. Willy, who I lost somehow in all the confusion, was squatted beside the Russian colonel and talking with him.

Sandra ran to me and threw her arms around my neck. She kissed my dirty cheek and said, "So much noise and confusion, I thought you'd been killed."

"Close a couple of times, but I'm safe. When you get a chance look Tom over, he got burned by a bullet."

"I love you." She said, and then moved toward Tom.

Dolly, who was sitting beside me gave a warning growl and when I looked at the prisoners, the general was removing something from his pocket.

"Stop!" I yelled, and his hand froze in place. My shotgun was ready to fire.

"Willy, tell him to remove his hand slowly and when I see it, it'd better be empty or he's a dead sonofabitch!"

An exchange of words took place and then Willy said, "He was getting a cigarette and lighter. He will remove his hand when you nod."

"I want his hand empty, understand?"

"I told him that much. He knows the rules."

I nodded and he removed his hand—empty.

"Willy, Colonel Parker said no prisoners." Tom said as he moved toward me.

"He'll want to keep these two, I promise. The general is in charge of all Russian troops in the United States and the other is his executive officer, or so he claims. Personally, I think the colonel is the base commander here."

Tom grinned and said, "Well, it's your ass, but don't be surprised if Parker shoots 'em both when you take 'em to the base camp."

Pulling some plastic ties from his pocket, Willy tossed them to Tom and said, "Secure their hands behind their backs."

"Parker also ordered us to return to the base camp and send one of his men back if all was secure," I said.

"Saddle up, we've a walk to take. Tom, you stay with the prisoners and Kate, you pull drag. John, I want you walking point. Sandra, if one of these Russians makes a break for it, use your shotgun and blow 'em in two. See, I suspect they both speak English, but neither will admit they can."

I saw both Russians blink rapidly, and knew they understood Willy's orders.

As Kate walked by me, she smiled and then winked. Only this time, I simply grinned back. I was happy to be alive, my wife had survived and my last dog was still healthy. I was on top of the world.

The walk back was uneventful, the birds were singing and the weather was perfect. I was in no rush and carefully scanned the countryside, but it remained safe. As we neared our base camp, a female voice ordered, "Stop!"

I raised my left fist and we stopped.

"Who are you?

"We're a group returning from Colonel Parker and we have two Russian prisoners. My commander is Captain Willy Williams."

A thin woman of middle-age stepped from the woods with a shotgun in her hands and said, "Follow me."

I saw no one until we neared the barn and then a man, also way past his prime, walked from the open door. He was unarmed.

"Hey, Thomas!" Willy yelled, and the serious look on the old man's face quick vanished.

"Willy! How'd the attack go?"

"We won, but the cost was high. I have no idea of the number of wounded and dead, but more than we needed. Look, I have two prisoners, can I turn them over to you?"

Thomas pulled a long pig-sticker with a wide blade and said, "Sure, I'll take care of 'em."

Willy chuckled and said, "Keep these two alive. I know for a fact, Colonel Parker will want to talk with both of 'em. Now, if they try to escape, kill 'em. Best way to do that would be to turn the dogs loose after 'em. Hell, them dogs ain't killed nobody in over a week. I know they're hungry and a little Russian food would do 'em good."

When I met Willy's eyes, he winked, but I saw the general give an involuntary quiver and he glanced at the colonel.

Colonel Parker and the rest didn't get in until early the next morning. They'd spent the night in the woods and from listening to the survivors talk, they'd just saved the world. Little did they know our war to regain our nation hadn't even started yet, and that it would soon turn bloody.

They'd returned with ten horses and all the warriors loaded down with something. They'd taken what they could and destroyed the rest. We now had cases of ammo, grenades, mines, flares, and a mountain of food. Unlike our MRE's, the camp had been eating fresh food, and I looked forward to a nice thick steak this night. And, it would be beef and not venison.

Our team gathered in the colonel's office as he said, "Our casualties were light, considering we were attacking a base camp, and ten percent is acceptable. I'd feared well over forty-five percent, only your group made the difference. That machine gun you took out killed most of our folks, but thank God you did what needed done. As a result of your actions, Willy, you're now a lieutenant colonel and the others of your team are promoted two ranks. All your medical personnel with college degrees are lieutenants as well."

I turned, found Sandra and grinned, because I'd now be sleeping with an officer and me a newly promoted E-7. I was proud of her, but realized no money came with our promotions, just more responsibilities.

Turning to Kate, Parker said, "Kate, according to our newest lieutenant colonel, you did an outstanding job, so consider yourself the commander of our sniper unit, lieutenant."

Kate gave a loud unladylike horselaugh and then said, "Sir, we have no sniper unit."

"No, we don't, but you'll see we will soon have one, right? We'll talk more about this in the coming days."

"Sir," Top said, "I hope you realize the Russians will stop at nothing to find their general."

"I thought of that already." Parker said, and then added as he shook his head, "There will likely be killings or hostage taking in an effort to have us return him."

"What'll we do if they start shooting folks as reprisals?" I asked, knowing full well they would do it.

"We kill 'em back. For every American they kill or take hostage, we will kill ten of them. See, that's the main reason Kate is starting a sniper group. I intend to keep them fully employed."

"Lawdy, sir." Willy said and continued with, "How are the American people, what's left of us anyway, going to react?"

"Colonel, it doesn't matter. Once our people get mad enough, they'll join us by the thousands. Like you, I don't want anyone to die, but it can't be helped. There ain't no way in hell I'm returning a Russian General and Base Commander, not alive any-way. As a colonel, Willy, start looking at the big picture and not the small shit."

Willy thought for a moment and then asked, "As a colonel, does that mean I can't lead my team in the field?"

Parker grinned and replied, "Of course you can still lead your team. However, once and if, we regain control of our country again, you'll be a real colonel with back pay coming."

"Hell, by then I might be a general!"

We all laughed, except Parker. He gave us a serious look and said, "By God, you very well might be. This is going to be the roughest war in the history of our nation. Most of us will likely not be alive when we gain our freedom, but you can be damned sure of one thing."

"What's that, sir?" Tom asked.

"We *will* win this war, no matter how many of us die or are captured. We will drive the enemy from our soil! We are Americans!"

The roomed echoed with cries of Airborne, Hooaahh, and Rangers lead the way!

A week later the atrocities started. We were out on patrol and edging through the woods, when I heard a loud voice scream an order, only it wasn't in English. Willy stopped and cocked his head the right to hear better.

He motioned for us to move forward with him to the brush that lined the road. I counted forty Russians moving around on the road and a five American men standing on the back of a flatbed truck. I kept Dolly at my side and as I waited, I scratched her ears.

As I watched, ropes were thrown over a huge oak limb right above the bed of the truck. Nooses were quickly tied and placed over five necks. The long end of the ropes were secured to the tree trunk.

A Russian officer pulled a sheet of paper from his pocket and in heavily accented English read that these five were the first of thousands who would die until their POW's were returned. Finished, he folded the paper, stuck it in his coat pocket and said, "You have 2 minutes to pray to your God."

Heads bowed, but the oldest of the condemned men looked to the sky and began to sing. He was quickly joined by the others.

> "Oh, say! can you see, by the dawn's early light,
> What so proudly we hailed at the twilight's last gleaming; Whose broad stripes and bright stars, through the perilous fight,
> O'er the ramparts we watched were so gallantly streaming? And the rocket's red glare, the bombs bursting in air,
> Gave proof through the night that our flag was still there;
> Oh, say! does that—"

The officer looked pissed as he nodded, and a sergeant banged hard on the truck door. The driver goosed the truck and the singing stopped instantly as all four hit the end of the ropes. I heard their necks snap from where I was. The bodies twisted and turned as the ropes unwound.

Willy had not been watching and when the Russians neared our dead to joke and look, he elbowed me and handed the clackers of two Claymore mines to me. I nodded, still shocked by the deaths and patriotism I'd just witnessed.

I exploded both mines and when I looked up at the road, all the Russians were on the ground and a few were screaming. "Attack! Take no prisoners!" Willy yelled as he moved forward.

I came off the ground, spotted the driver of the truck sneaking toward the woods and placed a solid hit in the middle of his back. Moving forward, I shot into anyone I suspected was still alive.

Sandra discovered one young man hiding under a truck, but Tom squatted, smiled, and said in English, "Son, this just ain't your day." He pointed his rifle at the Russian.

Dolly had moved to Tom's side and was giving a low threatening growl.

The Russian was still smiling when the bullet from Tom's gun struck him just a little above the left eye, blowing the back of his head away and spattering the underside of the truck with blood and gore. The dead man was still smiling, his unseeing eyes open, as I turned and walked toward Willy.

"We need to move, and now," I stated.

"Let's move, people! Before you leave, take all weapons, ammo or anything we might need." Then, taking out a deck of cards he'd always carried, he placed the ace of spades into the blood-filled mouth of the dead Russian officer.

Seeing me looking at him, he said, "My dad was with a unit in Vietnam that did this to those they killed, so the enemy would know which unit did the nasty deed."

"I guess we have a new business card, huh?"

"Yep, and when we get back, let's all start drawing them on cardboard. Each ambush we complete, we'll leave a card in the mouth of the senior member. They'll soon start to fear us."

Colonel Parker sent us back out almost immediately and what we discovered was not good. Tom had been walking point when he froze and raise a fist. I knelt on the trail, knowing the sides of trails were often booby trapped. I looked forward, but all I could see was the smoking remains of some large building that had recently burned to the ground. Suddenly the smell of burned human flesh filled my nose and I noticed a thin cloud of smoke overhead.

Willy passed me as he quickly moved forward to see what Tom had found.

I noticed Willy and Tom talking, but heard nothing. A few minutes later, Willy returned and said, "The Russians must have burned a few folks alive in a building, because it's still smoking. They are putting up signs warning others that more deaths will happen, unless the general and colonel are returned immediately. The signs say more Americans will burn unless their demands are met. I make out five Russians, so lock and load."

Minutes past and then a truck neared, obviously to pick up the men still nailing signs to oak trees.

Willy whispered, "Now!"

We ran forward as a group and Russians began to fall with our first shots. The driver slipped his vehicle in gear and gunned the gas pedal, but before he'd gone five feet his windshield exploded into thousands of small pieces of flying glass and his head fell limply forward, resting on the steering wheel. The back glass of the truck was spattered with blood and brains. In minutes it was over, but Tom had taken one man alive, and the man was terrified. The prisoner was as ugly as sin, with a huge nose and a round face. His hair was cropped to his scalp and he looked like a half-wit to me.

The Russian was on his knees with the barrel of Tom's M16 against his neck, as Willy neared.

Willy slapped the Russian hard on the right side of his face and began speaking to him in his native tongue. The man mumbled something a few seconds later and lowered his head.

Willy said, "This piece of shit, a senior sergeant, had the idea to burn the forty prisoners in an old barn. He wanted to save ammo. He was under orders to kill these folks, but no one told him how to do the job."

"Good God!" Sandra said.

The smell of burnt flesh was rough on me, and I fought a strong urge to gag or puke. I heard someone behind me puking, but didn't turn. I can usually take the smell of a burned bodies, but forty is a bit much even for my stomach.

"I speak little the English." The Russian said.

"Do you believe in God? Do you pray?" Willy asked.

"Да, Русская Православная Церковь, I Christian, yes."

"You have one minute to pray and then right after that, you'll be standing in front of God and can continue your prayer in person." Then, turning to Tom, Willy said, "Get me a gas can from the truck."

Tom hesitated and asked, "Are you going to do what I think you are?"

"Tom, I gave you an order, now get the damned gas can and do it now!"

"Willy, think! Do you want to live with this act the rest of your life? Good God, you can't do this!"

"Get the damned gas can or I'll get the sonofabitch myself!"

Cursing, Tom made his way to the truck, removed a can of gas and returned.

While Tom was fetching the can, Willy had secured the prisoners hands and feet using plastic ties. Taking the can from Tom, Willy poured gas on the prisoner and said, "Everyone move back."

"No! Please! No fire! Нет! Пожалуйста! Нет огонь! " The Russian NCO screamed.

Sandra moved toward him and softly said, "Willy, don't do this, it's inhumane. You'll not be able to live with yourself if you do this."

Willy responded brusquely, "Get the hell away from me, and move back like I told you to do! This bastard just burned a group of American people alive, American people! Payback is a sumbitch."

When Willy removed a pack of matches from his pocket the Russian's eyes grew huge, and he screamed and continued to beg in Russian. Willy, his heart made cold by the smell of burnt American bodies, struck a match and dropped it on the prisoner. Instantly, a loud *woof* was heard and the man was engulf in a ball of almost invisible flame.

Screams came instantly as the man twisted and jerked to escape his blanket of flames, but to no avail. After a few minutes, I saw the plastic ties separate and the man's body began to twitch violently as his central nervous system shutdown. The sweet scent of burnt flesh grew stronger, and I leaned to the right and puked. I think it was more from the drawn up black body than from the smell.

Willy had not watched the mans grotesque death, instead he'd gathered gear from the dead and the truck, placing it all near the woods. Then, he'd gone to each body, poured gas on the remains and ignited them. One must have been playing possum, because a piercing scream was heard for a few minutes, but I didn't dare turn to watch. I fell to my knees and gagged. Moving to the truck, Willy poured the remainder of the gas on the driver and the seat. He then threw a match inside, moved to the first man he'd burned, and placed an ace of spades in the mouth of the still smoking hot corpse.

"Brute force is all Russian troops understand. From now on, we'll treat them as they treat us. Now, gather up the gear near the trail and let's return to the base camp. John, you're on point and Tom, you're got drag. These Russian sonsofbitches want to play rough, well by God two can play that game."

CHAPTER 25

Weeks turned into months and each day we were out looking for Russians or their allies, and killing small groups of men. During the same time, we found thousands of dead Americans and while most were shot or hanged, a few died horrible deaths. We left no Russian alive, not a single one, and each leader we killed had the ace of spades in his mouth.

Finally, one afternoon, Colonel Parker called us into his office and said, "The Russians have agreed to release thirty Americans in exchange for the general and colonel. I have agreed, but they'll be super pissed when they get them back. Under no circumstances are our prisoners to be released before the Russians release our people. We will release them at the same time, or the deal is off." He then sat on the corner of his desk.

"Who will handle this exchange?" Willy asked.

"I'll go with your group and we'll handle the exchange. Additionally, Kate is bringing five of her snipers to keep the Russians honest. See, I don't trust them, and in war they are cruel and vicious as a people. You can be sure, if they try to screw us over, Mother Russia will be short a few soldiers come morning."

I'd been thinking about the colonel's comment about the Russians being pissed to get their people back, so I asked, "I don't understand how getting the general and colonel will piss off the Russians."

"John, I'm not a cruel man by nature, and actually I considered myself a liberal until the fall of this great nation. However, I lost everything within a year of the fall, including most of my family. I turned mean. I turned junkyard dog mean and I give as good as I get."

"Colonel, no disrespect, only you're not making much sense to me."

Parker gave a dry laugh and said, "No, I guess I'm not. See, each time the Russians killed a large group of Americans, a body part was removed from the general. When the general ran out of parts, I move to the colonel."

"And, sir, what kind of shape are the two men in now?"

"Sergeant Leeds, bring the prisoners in, please?"

The man who usually guarded our briefings left and returned a few minutes later leading two men by dog leashes attached to ropes around their necks. Both had canvas hoods over their heads.

"Gentlemen and ladies, meet General Sidorov and Colonel Alexandrov of the Russian Army." Parker removed the hoods.

Both men had been horribly mutilated and neither had a nose, ears, lips, or eyes. *Good God, what have we done? The Russians can't allow this to go unpunished!* I thought, and fought off a twist of fear in my gut.

Parker waited a few minutes for the brutality of what he'd ordered to sink in and then said, "In addition to what you see, both men are blind, their eardrums have been ruptured, and their tongues have been torn out. The Russian's will be madder than wet hornets in a mason jar when we return these two men in this condition. In addition, I think the colonel only has two fingers left, the others were all removed. Of course, no anesthesia was used at any point. As Willy said to me, 'We must reduce ourselves to the level of our enemy, and I have. We must become as brutal and vicious as our enemy. Once the prisoner exchange is completed, we'll break up into small groups of perhaps a squad and go into hiding."

Willy, who I'd expected to smile, shook his head and said, "They'll come after us hard now, colonel. They can't allow this to go unpunished."

"They will be looking for a large group, not almost a thousand small groups. We will hide, but we will not stop fighting. Each group will organize random terrorist attacks, as well as hit and run strikes against our enemy. They will be the famous Russian bear alright, except fighting thousands of hunting dogs attacking at the same time. It's a fight they cannot win. Now, get your troops ready. We leave in an hour."

I crouched behind some brush and looked the group of Russians waiting in a large field over closely. I saw no armored vehicles, but a group of about fifty men standing and one was obviously in charge, by the yelling he was doing. I don't speak Russian, but an ass chewing is the same in any mans army. The formation came to attention and then lined up properly. A group of about thirty poorly dressed people were sitting in dirt in front of the soldiers with their hands on their heads. A machine gun had the group covered. Dolly didn't make a sound, but watched the group closely, her ears standing up.

Tom and Sandra had moved off to our right to cover the meeting with an old 50-caliber machine gun we'd taken from the earlier attack on the base. Tom would be the gunner, as Sandra provided assistance with ammo. Kate and her crew had scattered to the winds as soon as we'd arrived, each wanting to work alone. I had Parker on my left and Willy to my right, the prisoners behind us and on a leash held by the colonel.

At exactly 1300, Parker whispered, "Okay, I'll move forward with the prisoners, but once the Russians see me, I'll stop. At all costs, we must free those Americans."

Parker stood, pulled the leash, then walked into the clearing. The Russian's became quiet and the colonel stopped.

Long minutes passed until I heard a voice call out in good American English, "Bring the two forward. We will meet you half way. Once we meet, the exchange will take place. I have told your people to walk to the woods, so tell ours the same."

"I don't speak Russian, so you tell 'em yourself, you sono-fabitch!"

I heard the Russian laugh and then he yelled in his native tongue. I knew he was wasting his breath, because neither the general or colonel heard a word. "Now, Yankee, bring your men to me."

"I ain't a Yankee, I'm a Southerner. We're a bit different, or don't ya know?" The colonel was speaking as he moved toward the center of the field.

"All Americans are Yankees."

"Not true, Ivan, not true at all. See, we fought a war years ago and the Yankees won that one, but they ain't even here for this one—yet! Right now you're fighting the best of the South and we're a mean bunch. Hell, one redneck could beat the shit out of any five of your men."

Our group of civilians were on their feet moving toward us, and I noticed a single Russian Officer bringing up the rear. He was making small talk with Parker as they walked toward each other.

The Russian shrugged and replied, "Who cares who is who in America? This is our land now!"

Parker laughed and then said, "You are here, but you do not control the land! You do not control the people! But, take a good look at our land, Ivan, because we'll bury you here."

"Your people are like sheep, we gather them to butcher."

"The Ace of Spades has butchered a few Russians too, haven't we comrade?"

"Oh, so you are leading that group of animals? I am surprised, because you remind me of a school teacher I had in the second grade. He was full of shit too."

They were less than ten feet apart, and I could plainly see deep anger in the Russian's eyes.

"Most Russians are full of shit, so I guess you mean the two of you. See, we Americans kick the shit out of folks, *and* we do what we say we will do, always. Now, here is your general and colonel." He handed the leash to the Russian.

The Russian smiled and said something to the general, but he received no answer. He then turned and addressed the colonel, again no reply.

He'd just began to untie the rope around the general's neck when Colonel Parker yelled, "Run folks, make for the trees!" Then, he either did the dumbest or bravest thing I've ever seen, he remained standing within ten feet of the three Russians, unarmed.

Pulling the bag from the general's head, the Russian gave a loud gasp, his eyes grew large and he yelled something. The machine gun opened up on our group, but most were safely in the woods.

"Lay down, get down low!" I screamed.

I heard two shots and the machine gunner, as well as his assistant, were kicked back and down, where they remained unmoving. The man in the middle of the field, who had pulled the bag from the general's head, threw it to the ground and them pulled a pistol from the small of his back. Three of our snipers fired a single round each and all three Russians fell dead or dying. I'd actually seen the general's head explode as he was struck.

I heard Tom open up with his machine gun and the *'tat-tat-tat'* sound demonstrated good fire discipline. His bursts were short, but deadly on the enemy.

"Run, Colonel!" Willy yelled.

As the man ran toward us, I could see he was laughing as if it had all been one big joke.

However, at that exact moment, two Russian Ka-52 helicopters slipped up from the trees and made a run toward us. I saw rockets fired toward Sandra and Tom as well as a pair sent toward us. The first rocket fired at us exploded well behind us, while the second hit right behind the colonel. I grinned when I realized they'd missed Tom as well, because I could still hear him firing. I glanced back at the field, and Colonel Parker was gone; all that remained was a smoking boot—and an ace of spades was moving over the ground like a wind-blown leaf in the fall.

"Pull back, disperse and regroup back at camp!" Willy screamed to be heard as the choppers passed overhead. He then blew a whistle three times, our signal to withdraw.

As I turned to leave, I saw a rocket hit almost exactly where Tom and Sandra were positioned, but there was nothing I could do, except pray they both lived. Each of us took a few surviving civilians under our wing to lead back, but Willy shot those too badly injured to travel. He was crossing himself and crying as he pulled the trigger, again and again.

I had three women, one child near ten, and four men in my group. I said, "We move fast and you do exactly as I say. I'm not a babysitter, so if you cannot keep up, I'll leave you. Understand?"

"Do you have any weapons you can share?" one of the men asked.

I handed him the colonel's rifle, one of my pistols, and said, "Give the pistol to another man. Now, let's move, people. We'll not stop until we reach safety."

I'd moved the group forward about a hundred yards, when Dolly growled and I saw Kate nearing from my right. She gave me her usual warm smile, I grinned in return, and she said, "I'll join you for the walk back. All of the snipers have joined different groups. I have Anita bringing up our rear and I'll take point."

"Move us fast and continuous. The bad guys are livid right now and looking for blood. Did you see if Tom or Sandra survived the rockets?"

She lowered her head and replied, "John, I don't really know, but from where I was in the trees it didn't look good. I saw the gun fly in the air, but that in itself means little."

"Please God, keep my Sandra alive for me. I love her, and she's all I have left of my old life. This I ask in the name of Jesus Christ, our Lord and Savior, Amen," I muttered under my breath, as I felt tears running down my cheeks.

"What's that?" Kate asked.

"A prayer, Kate, just a prayer."

Coming Soon in paperback,

THE FALL OF AMERICA

Book 2
Fatal Encounters

Also available for the Kindle

The Fall of America: Book 1

The Fall of America: Book 2

The Fall of America: Book 3

The Fall of America: Book 4

The Fall of America: Book 5

And Books 1-3
as Audiobook editions

ABOUT THE AUTHOR

W.R Benton, a pen name, is a retired U.S. military senior Non-commissioned Officer with over twenty-six years of active duty service. He grew up in the Missouri Ozark Mtns., where hunting, trapping, camping, and other outdoor activities were the norm. Additionally, he spent more than twelve years teaching survival and parachuting procedures to U.S. Air Force per-sonnel as a Life Support instructor. Mister Benton has an Associate's Degree in Search and Rescue, Survival Operations, a Bachelors Degree in Occ-upational Safety and Health, and a Masters Degree in Psychology near completion.

Mister Benton is a member of the America Authors Association (AAA). You can visit W.R. Benton online http://www.wrbenton.net or his War Paint Site at http://www.warpaint.info.

Visit him on Facebook at
www.facebook.com/wrbenton01

"**Simple Survival -** A Family Outdoors Guide" is more than a book—it is an outdoor resource bible that every family should have a copy of. This is one of those books that you should have in your camping bag along with the tent and other equipment. However, reading it at home before you go off on some outdoor adventure would be a great help when potential situations happen.

Available at Amazon and other online bookstores

This helpful and comprehensive book covers most major disasters and how to stay safe if you decide to evacuate or stay. It has a section on prolonged survival, which will assist keeping you alive after the natural disaster has done its damage. Many people die following natural disasters, from one mishap or another, but you can learn to survive.

Learn to deal with Tornadoes, ice storms, hurricane, flooding, blackouts, riots, and much more. Contains easy to understand information, and critical gear/equipment lists you will need.

Available at Amazon and other online bookstores

On a trip to the Lake Clark area of the Alaskan bush, a sudden arctic weather system forces down the small plane of Dr. Jim Wade, and his son David. Both have survived the crash, but not unscathed. Food, fire and shelter are all a priority. Following the death of his father, now it is up to David to figure out what to do next, and how to survive, on a remote Alaskan mountain—in winter!

This is a fictional story of survival, resilience and of the spirit to live. It is both authentic and accurate, having been written by a former Air Force life support survival instructor. For ages 10 and up

Both are available at Amazon and other online bookstores

Set adrift, a family of three are cast out to sea in a rubber raft, where they must find a way to conquer one terrifying tragedy after another or die in the process.

In this gripping story of survival everyone will be tested to their limits. Christian faith and hope are hallmarks of this tale that will touch your heart..

www.ingramcontent.com/pod-product-compliance
Lightning Source LLC
Chambersburg PA
CBHW070924190726
48292CB00004B/1096